Vintage Ladybug Farm

Center Point
Large Print

Also by Donna Ball and available from
Center Point Large Print:

Love Letters from Ladybug Farm
Keys to the Castle

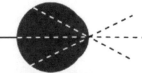

**This Large Print Book carries the
Seal of Approval of N.A.V.H.**

Vintage Ladybug Farm

— ❦ —

Donna Ball

CENTER POINT LARGE PRINT
THORNDIKE, MAINE

This Center Point Large Print edition
is published in the year 2013 by arrangement with
Donna Ball, Inc.

The text of this Large Print edition is unabridged.
In other aspects, this book may vary
from the original edition.
Printed in the United States of America
on permanent paper.
Set in 16-point Times New Roman type.

ISBN: 978-1-61173-644-1

Library of Congress Cataloging-in-Publication Data

Ball, Donna.
  Vintage Ladybug Farm / Donna Ball. — Center Point Large Print
edition.
    pages cm
  ISBN 978-1-61173-644-1 (library binding : alk. paper)
  1. Female friendship—Fiction. 2. Farmhouses—Fiction.
    3. Life change events—Fiction.
    4. Shenandoah River Valley (Va. and W. Va.)—Fiction.
    5. Domestic fiction. 6. Large type books. I. Title.
PS3552.A4545V56 2013
813'.54—dc23
                                                    2012041321

ONE

Dreams and Schemes

Chapter One

Resolutions

On the last night of the old year, the house stood as it had for a hundred and twenty years, nestled in the shadow of the mountains of the Shenandoah Valley, smoke drifting from its chimney tops, golden light spilling from its windows. A steady rain washed the faded brick clean, glistening on the clay tiles of its mansard roof and gurgling in the copper gutters. The stately wrap-around porch with its white columns and wide front steps was as welcoming on this wet December night as it had been in the full bloom of a blowsy summer day when fern baskets swayed from the eaves and a pitcher of lemonade sweated on the white wicker table that sat between the rocking chairs.

Only yesterday the windows had been decorated with lighted Christmas wreaths and the columns draped with garland, but as everyone knew—at least, according to Ida Mae Simpson, who had kept the old house and all of its occupants in order for close to fifty years—it was bad luck to have the Christmas tree up on the first day of the New Year. So, in a frenzy of activity that had been repeated every New Year's Eve since they lived there and yet still never failed to take the current occupants

7

by surprise, every member of the household spent the afternoon skimming ornaments off the tree, whipping down red bows and gold angels, lugging boxes back up to the attic, and dragging crispy greenery through the rain out to the compost pile.

Of course, that was before they realized they were giving a New Year's Eve party.

This had come as very little surprise to Ida Mae, who just gave a contemptuous sniff and shuffled back to the kitchen, where she proceeded to put together a batch of her prize-winning homemade cheese straws, as though she didn't have enough to do. It seemed to her that those city women (as she still called them in her mind, even though she'd grown quite tolerable of them over the past few years) never were much for planning ahead. If they had thought about it for even a minute, for example, they never would have walked away from their fancy Baltimore houses and sunk their life savings into this old place—which had surely been a beauty in her time, but it was clear to anybody with half a brain they'd bitten off more than they could chew when they decided to give up their city ways and turn the place into what they now called "Ladybug Farm." What did they know about sheep? Or grapes, for that matter? Or tending sixteen acres of fruit trees, vegetable gardens, flower gardens, outbuildings, berry bushes, and even chickens and goats?

On the other hand, Ida Mae had to admit they'd

earned her respect over time. Cici—that was the smart one—could handle a hammer and saw as well as any man, and the redhead, Lindsay, sure had a green thumb, and that was no lie. Bridget, who Ida Mae liked to call "Miss Priss" because she could be a tad on the bossy side, was a pretty fair cook if you liked fancy food, and though they'd had a tiff or two in the course of things, they'd finally come to an uneasy agreement as to who was in charge of the house (it was Ida Mae, of course).

If the truth were told—and Ida Mae, being a good Christian woman, liked to tell the truth whenever possible—those women hadn't done a half-bad job, all things considered, when they moved in and started to put the shine back on the place. The old house had really started to feel young again when Cici's college-aged daughter, Lori, had moved back home from California. And when Lindsay, the redhead, had gone crazy and decided to adopt the county vagrant Noah, even though he was fifteen years old and practically a grown man, Ida Mae locked herself in the pantry and cried for twenty minutes, and that was the God's honest truth. Because she still knew some things those women didn't. And she still prayed for Noah, morning and night, every day of her life.

The thing she didn't understand and could never quite reconcile in her mind was what had ever taken hold of them in the first place and persuaded them to move way out here in God's country to live together in the first place. They weren't even related, for heaven's sake. Three women, and not a husband among them, taking on a big old house and trying to turn it into a working farm. What were they thinking?

Of course, trying to figure that out was one of the things that kept Ida Mae around.

The call had come at three-thirty in the afternoon, just as the final box was shoved into the attic—tangled lights to be sorted out next year—and the last Christmas candle had been wrapped in newspaper and put away in the cellar. Cici came into the parlor, where Bridget was running a dust cloth over the mantel and Lindsay was sweeping up the last of the pine needles into the dustpan that Noah held. Ida Mae polished the staircase just outside the room.

"That was Paul," Cici said, looking puzzled. "He and Derrick are on their way down. They're bringing champagne."

Bridget said, "As in, party?"

Cici shrugged. "Paul said we should see the New Year in together."

Lindsay stopped sweeping. "But they just left. I mean, we had the big Christmas party. I thought we'd have a quiet New Year's Eve."

"I've got that church thing tonight," Noah

spoke up quickly. He knew from experience how out of hand the ladies' parties could get.

Cici looked skeptical. "What church thing?"

"You know," Bridget volunteered, "that lock-down thing."

"Lock out," Lindsay corrected.

"Lock *in,*" Noah said patiently. "And I promised Amy I'd help with the little kids."

A look passed between the three women that said without saying, *Amy?*

Lindsay said, "I'll give Paul and Derrick your regrets."

Noah looked cautiously hopeful. "Does that mean I can borrow your car?"

"As soon as you sweep the porch."

"'The laborer is worthy of his reward,'" he declared cheerfully as he grabbed the broom from Lindsay. "First Timothy 5:18." He made a quick job of sweeping the last of the pine needles into the dustpan and rushed to the porch.

Bridget stared after him. "Since when does Noah quote scripture?"

Lindsay shrugged. "Since some church contest about memorizing a verse a day. I think there's a pony at the end."

"Rodeo tickets," Cici corrected. "Two tickets to the Sherriff's rodeo in May to the boy or girl who can quote the most verses at the end of thirty days."

"Wow. Noah must really like the rodeo."

"He really likes Amy," Lindsay said.

Cici raised an eyebrow. "So it's Amy now?"

Lindsay shrugged. "Apparently they got to know each other painting scenery for the Christmas pageant."

"At least she's the pastor's daughter," Bridget offered.

Cici said, "The pastor's going to be there, right?"

"Right." Lindsay hesitated. "I think." She frowned a little. "Guess I'd better make a call."

While Lindsay moved toward the kitchen and the nearest phone, Bridget said, "I suppose we could make crepes."

Cici lifted a skeptical eyebrow. "Oh, that sounds easy."

"Well, it is New Year's Eve, and we have all that shrimp and lobster left from the Christmas party and . . . oh!" Bridget's eyes lit up. "Ida Mae can make cheese straws. I just need to make sure we have enough cheddar."

She thrust the dust cloth into Cici's hand and moved quickly toward the kitchen, passing Lindsay, who was on her way out.

"Totally supervised, plenty of chaperones," Lindsay said, looking relieved. "Just like I thought. They're having a midnight bonfire with s'mores," she added a little wistfully. "Do you remember doing things like that when you were a girl?"

"No," Cici said. "How are they going to have a bonfire with all this rain?"

Lindsay drew a breath to reply, realized she didn't know the answer, and started back toward the telephone. Cici stopped her with a wave of her hand. "They'll figure it out."

She cast a critical eye around the suddenly barren-looking parlor. The elegant mantel, the floor-to-ceiling windows, the carved plaster moldings all looked suddenly bleak without their Christmas finery. "What do you suppose Derrick and Paul want to come all the way back out here for on New Year's Eve? It's not like they don't have plenty of options in D.C." And now it was Cici's turn to look wistful. "Remember when we used to get all dressed up and go into Washington for New Year's Eve? We'd get a room at the Washington Plaza and party all night."

"Candles," Lindsay said abruptly, staring at the mantel. "What did we do with all the white candles?" She rushed to the front door and opened it. "Noah! Run out back and cut me some cedar boughs, will you?"

Cici heard him protest, "It's raining!"

"No, it's not. That's just the sound of your New Year's Eve date with Amy slowly dripping away."

"But we just spent all day throwing out green stuff!"

"And don't track mud on the porch."

"Yes, ma'am."

Lindsay closed the door just as Bridget was

coming back from the kitchen. "Ida Mae already started the cheese straws," Bridget reported happily. "We've got plenty of ham for breakfast and there's enough smoked salmon and roasted red peppers left over from Christmas to make hors d'oeuvres."

"If I can find the box with the silver and gold rope beads in it I can put them in champagne glasses and really sparkle up the mantel," Lindsay said. "We can spray-paint some cedar boughs gold and make a fabulous centerpiece for the coffee table."

"The white candles are in the cellar," Cici said, "in a box marked 'white candles.'"

An excited spark came into Lindsay's eyes. "Do we have any silver spray paint left? If we paint the tapers silver and use the hall mirror as a runner on the dining room table with gold and silver Christmas balls, it will look fabulous!"

"We just packed up all the gold and silver Christmas balls," Cici reminded her.

"It'll only take me a minute to find them." Lindsay rushed toward the stairs and then turned back. "What do you suppose Paul and Derrick want to come all the way back out here for on New Year's Eve?"

Bridget looked at Cici; Cici looked at Lindsay. As one, the three women shrugged.

"Oh well," Bridget said happily. "Who cares? It's New Year's Eve, right? Let's party!"

And so, with only four hours' notice, they pulled together an intimate but elegant New Year's Eve celebration for five: evergreen boughs and white candles on the mantel, champagne glasses filled with miniature gold and silver balls and draped with rope beading on the coffee table; greenery in the windowsills; and fires dancing in all five of the house's wood-burning fireplaces. On the menu were Ida Mae's homemade cheese straws served with Bridget's smoked salmon and roasted pepper spread, an artichoke-parmesan soup made with the canned artichoke someone had sent them in a gourmet gift basket for Christmas, seafood crepes in a sherry sauce baked with a gouda topping, and—because it was a holiday— Ida Mae's black chocolate cake served with a warm chocolate ganache and whipped cream.

Parties, even of the impromptu kind, were one thing the ladies did very, very well.

Lindsay had pulled back her auburn hair and donned a satin shirt and black velvet slacks, but her shoes, which had begun to hurt her feet approximately five minutes after she put them on, were discarded in favor of bedroom slippers. Cici, a tall, freckle-faced honey-blonde, honored the occasion with a deep blue velour track suit trimmed in gold piping that made Paul, who wrote a syndicated style column for the *Washington Post*, roll his eyes in dismay.

"Darling," he said as he kissed her, "let me know when visiting hours start at the assisted living home." To which Cici responded by bopping him on the head with her rolled-up copy of the *Post*, just before accepting the platter of lobster puffs he brought for the party. Bridget, a petite platinum-blonde who loved dressing up more than her two younger friends combined, had pulled together a silver *lamé* turtleneck and a long peacock-blue skirt with slouch boots and a chunky beach glass necklace that was to die for and which caused Paul, when he saw it, to kiss his fingers to the air and declare, "I am unworthy!"

Paul and Derrick were their oldest friends from the days of Huntington Lane, when they all had been neighbors in the suburbs of Baltimore. Though the couple had initially been as skeptical as everyone else when the three women decided to pool their resources and buy a neglected old mansion on sixteen acres in the Shenandoah Valley—complete with overgrown gardens, crumbling outbuildings, and, as it turned out, livestock—they'd quickly come to love Ladybug Farm almost as much as Cici, Bridget, and Lindsay did. Paul was always on hand with the perfect drapery swatch or an online source for vintage reproduction wallpaper patterns. Derrick owned an upscale Georgetown art gallery and had effortlessly taken Noah, who was himself a budding artist, under his wing, even shepherding him through an internship in the gallery over the past summer. When they had all lived within walking distance of each other on Huntington Lane, they spent every holiday together, celebrated birthdays together, took the train to New York for dinner and a show together. Now that they lived almost three hours apart, it sometimes seemed they saw Paul and Derrick even more often than when they lived next door. Though neither of them claimed to be the bucolic type, Paul was wild about Ida Mae's cooking, and Derrick never tired of admiring the details of the old house's architecture. Ladybug Farm had become like a second home for Paul and Derrick, but it did not explain why their good friends would have made it a point to drive down from the city twice in the space of two weeks for a holiday visit.

They gathered in the parlor before the fireplace with a little over half an hour to spare before midnight. White candles glowed on the mantelpiece; silver candles sparkled among the beads and champagne glasses on the coffee table. Rain drummed on the roof and logs crackled in the fireplace. Paul made the circuit, topping off everyone's glasses, and Derrick, settling down into the sofa with his arm stretched along the back, said, "So, Noah is doing the church thing—which I must say I'd find very odd if there weren't a girl involved—but where's our princess? Not back at school already?"

Cici held up her glass to be topped off. "Lori and Mark had dinner reservations at some fancy restaurant in Charlottesville. She said they'd try to drop in tonight, but . . ." She glanced worriedly toward the window. "I'm not crazy about the idea of them driving in this rain."

As Paul filled Lindsay's glass with bubbles, an eyebrow lifted. "We like Mark?"

"We adore Mark," Bridget assured him, holding out her glass. "Even though he did break Lori's leg."

"Oh, *that* Mark," said Derrick, rolling his eyes.

"It was an accident," Lindsay said, "and he was so sweet afterward that of course she fell in love with him."

"His mother's a surgeon," added Cici, "and his father was in the House of Representatives."

"State or national?" asked Derrick.

"State."

"Republican or Democrat?"

"Republican."

Paul thought about that for a moment, then shrugged. "Well, at least they're rich."

"They have a house in Maui," Cici said.

"Some of the greatest romances in history started with a broken leg," Derrick agreed benignly.

Paul shot him a look. "Name one."

Derrick drew a breath and Cici supplied firmly, "Mark and Lori."

"What happened to that fellow in Italy?" Paul wanted to know.

Cici shrugged and sipped her champagne. "He's in Italy." She smiled and lifted her glass. "Lori is not."

The other four raised their glasses in unison, grinning. "Hear, hear."

"So seriously, you guys," Cici said, when toasts were drunk and Paul settled down on the sofa beside Derrick, "it's not that we're not honored, but what made you decide New Year's Eve wouldn't be complete unless you drove three hours in the rain to spend it with us?"

"Ida Mae," declared Paul, lifting his glass again. He looked around. "Where is she, anyway?"

"Asleep," said Lindsay, licking bubbles off the side of her glass. "She's a hundred and twenty, for heaven's sake."

"But really," Bridget said, sipping her champagne. "It's not that we don't love you, but you couldn't get better dates for New Year's Eve?"

Paul and Derrick exchanged a look and a half-grin, and Paul said, "Really? You don't know?"

Cici, Bridget, and Lindsay looked at each other, each hesitant to admit that yes, in fact, they did not know what Paul and Derrick were referring to. This gave Derrick a chance to go to the hall tree and retrieve a gold-wrapped package from his coat pocket.

"Four years ago," Paul announced, rising as

Derrick returned to the room, "you signed the papers on Ladybug Farm. Happy anniversary, darlings."

As he spoke, Derrick presented the package with a flourish. For a moment the women just stared at it, motionless. "It's for all of you," Derrick prompted, and Bridget snatched the present with a squeal of delight.

"You guys!" she cried, ripping off the paper. "I can't believe you remembered!"

"I didn't even remember," admitted Cici, crowding in to see what Bridget uncovered.

"Four years?" said Lindsay. "Has it been four years?"

"Oh, my goodness," Bridget breathed. From the gold foil wrapping, she withdrew a slim book with tattered edges and a title stamped in faded gold: *A History of Blackwell Farms*. Blackwell Farms had been the name of their property before they bought it.

"Are you kidding me?" Cici exclaimed, diving for the book.

"Really?" Lindsay echoed, scrambling for a look. "Our house? Really? Where did you find it?"

Paul and Derrick beamed at each other. "We wanted to give it to you for Christmas," Paul admitted, "but it didn't come in time. We had to order it from a book collector in England."

"England?" Cici stared at him. "What was it doing there?"

"Who knows?" Both men watched, their smiles uncontained, as the women crowded together, turning the pages.

"Look, it's our house!"

"Oh my goodness, that's the original vineyard."

"Is that Judge Blackwell? Hey, he was good looking."

"How did you find this?" Bridget demanded, her face glowing as she clutched the book to her chest.

"Fortunately, someone in the Blackwell family thought they were important enough to rate a book," Derrick said. "It was a limited printing—hardly surprising—and most of them went to family members. We tracked this one down on the Internet."

Cici pried the book from Bridget's hands. "Look at this." Her tone was reverent. "Photographs from the twenties. Look at that staircase."

Bridget pointed to the opposite page. "Lindsay, look—it's the folly, when it was first built. It looks like a little fairy castle in the glen with all that gingerbread trim."

Lindsay leaned in and turned a page. "Oh my God, did you guys see this? There's a whole section on the Blackwell Farms Winery." She pulled the book from Cici.

Paul and Derrick sipped their champagne, looking enormously pleased with themselves. "Glad you like it."

The women flung themselves upon the men,

hugging them, spilling champagne, declaring their thanks, and laughing with delight. When they all settled down again, Cici had the book and Lindsay said, "I can't believe you came all the way down here just to give us this."

Paul said, "Well, actually . . ." But Derrick poked him hard in the ribs.

"Ten minutes 'til countdown," he said, glancing at the big clock on the mantel. "What are our resolutions?"

Cici looked up suddenly from the book, her head cocked. "What is that?"

"Resolutions," Paul explained patiently. "It's a foolish undertaking performed by people worldwide on New Year's Eve—"

"Seriously, don't you hear it?" Cici's brows drew together in a frown. "It sounds like something splattering."

They all were silent for a moment, listening.

"It's the fire," suggested Derrick.

"Or the gutters need cleaning again," said Bridget.

"I'll get Noah on it tomorrow," Lindsay said.

"Resolutions," Derrick reminded them. "What is everyone going to accomplish this year?"

"Personally," said Paul, topping off his glass, "I'm hoping to gain ten pounds and drink twice as much. Anyone else?"

The ladies were thoughtful. "Well," Bridget offered after a moment, "we have two graduations coming up. Lori from college and Noah from high school. And we've got to get Noah on those college applications, and—"

Derrick waved his glass dismissingly. "That's for them, not for you. What are *you* going to do this year?"

Lindsay said, "Wow, that's funny. Every year since we moved in here we've had a list a mile long of New Year's goals. Getting the gardens back in shape, restoring the ponds, turning the old dairy into an art studio . . ."

"Repairing the barn, getting all the old furniture out of the attic, restoring the tile in the sunroom, refinishing the floors . . ."

"Now Lindsay has her art studio," Bridget said, "and it even has a real bathroom. The sheep and the goat and the chickens all have nice houses, and so do we."

"And don't forget I sold a painting last year," Lindsay reminded her, blowing a kiss to Derrick, whose gallery had managed the sale.

"My Ladybug Farm gift baskets are doing great," Bridget went on. "My children and grandchildren are happy and well . . . I can't think of a single thing I want." She thought about it for a moment. "I know. Maybe I'll learn to make goat's milk soap this year."

"I think I'll grow heritage tomatoes from seed," Lindsay decided with a nod.

Cici held up the book with a grin. "And I'm

going to read this book. For the first time in recent memory, I actually may have time to read a whole book all the way through. How about you guys?"

Paul looked at Derrick. Derrick looked at Paul. They shared a grin. "We," declared Derrick with a flourish, "are building a house."

"We sold the gallery," Paul added, "and we meet with the architect tomorrow to site our house on the property we bought from Richard last year. We're going to be neighbors!"

The room erupted in a chorus of squeals and the ladies descended on them again. "You did it, you really did!"

"That's why you drove all the way out here in the rain."

"Congratulations! What a way to start to the New Year."

"It's an adventure, all right," Derrick said. "I don't know how a couple of city mice are going to like living in the country, but it's always been a dream of ours. And when Richard decided to sell his property last year, it seemed too portentous to pass up. All that rolling acreage, fenced and cross-fenced for horses—all that's missing is the manor house."

Cici's ex-husband, Richard, had had a brief and ultimately misguided notion that he would retire from his high-profile life as a Hollywood entertainment lawyer and build a house in the Virginia countryside, which would have been far too close to Ladybug Farm for Cici's comfort. Fortunately, he'd seen the error of his ways before it was too late and offered the property for sale. Paul and Derrick snatched it up.

"Best of all," Paul said, "we're only fifteen minutes away. Think of the parties we'll be having this time next year."

"I can't believe it," Cici said, beaming. "Now I really couldn't ask for anything more. How did life get so perfect?"

In the hallway, the big clock began to chime the countdown to midnight.

"Wait, does everyone have champagne?"

They raised their glasses, counting out loud. "Five, four, three, two . . ."

They turned to the sound of the front door opening with a gush of rain and giddy laughter. "Mom!" Lori cried. And in another moment, she was at the parlor door, dripping wet, pulling an equally soaked and delighted-looking Mark with her.

"Lori! Mark, what on earth—"

"I'm sorry, Mom. I know you said not to drive down in the rain, but we couldn't wait to tell you." Lori held out her hand where the sparkle of something brilliant on her finger was unmistakable. "We're engaged!"

Even before a breath of surprise could be drawn, Ida Mae appeared at the doorway beside the two dripping young people. Her grey hair was in curlers and she wore an overcoat over her flannel pajamas and work boots. She looked around sourly. "Y'all gonna do anything about that leak?" she demanded.

Cici moved her stunned gaze from her daughter to Ida Mae, the champagne forgotten in her hand. "Ummm . . . What leak?"

And that was when the roof fell in.

Chapter Two

Resolutions Revised

For a moment no one moved. The section of plaster in the foyer that had crashed to the floor was only about one foot square, but it brought with it a gush of water that splashed the toes of Lori's already-soaked sequined shoes and the hem of Mark's pants and caused Ida Mae to take a startled step backwards. The water marked the baseboards and the wallpaper before dissipating across the glossy wood floor like a small river freed of its banks.

Cici watched it all as if in slow motion, staring without seeing. She didn't see the decorative plaster rosette slowly pull away from its molding, swing damply by a thread of melting joint compound for a moment, then plop to the floor. She didn't see the raindrops rippling in the shallow pond that had become their floor. She

26

didn't see the handsome young man in the water-splotched tuxedo, the young woman in the glittering little black dress with her coppery curls pulled back in a cascade down her back and raindrops sparkling on her eyelashes. What she saw, in a single, astonishing flash, was a fair-haired baby in a pink-and-yellow striped blanket, a freckle-faced preschooler in calico Garanimals playing with a fluffy gray kitten, a ballerina at her first recital, a teenager in a prom dress. And could it have been only four years ago that they'd said good-bye to the house on Huntington Lane where Lori had grown up? Moving through the elegantly decorated rooms at their last Christmas party there, twinkling lights and Christmas greenery in every room, laughter and music and beautifully dressed people everywhere, saying good-bye to all their friends, leaving behind the only life they'd ever known for new adventures—Lori off to college and Cici to a broken-down old mansion in the middle of the Shenandoah Valley with her two best friends. She could practically smell the Sterno from the buffet table, hear the murmuring voices, taste Bridget's chocolate truffles with peppermint cream. It seemed like only yesterday. Lori had been a child, teetering on the verge of womanhood, and now . . .

And then everyone moved at once.

"The floors!" cried Bridget, then ran for towels. On her way past, she threw Lori a kiss and added, "Congratulations, sweetheart! Be right back."

"Is anyone hurt?" Lindsay demanded, rushing forward. "Ida Mae, are you all right? Lori, Mark—so happy for you! Don't go anywhere."

"I'll get a bucket," Paul said quickly, and Derrick called after him, "Bring a mop!"

Paul grabbed Lori and gave her a quick kiss on the cheek as he went by, and Derrick added to Mark, "Get used to it—something is always falling out of the sky in this place. Best wishes, by the way." He hurried toward the broom closet, calling back, "You're getting a treasure!"

Ida Mae said, "You're gonna need more than a mop," and pushed past them all with heavy, clipped strides.

Lori was still gazing at the ceiling, wide-eyed. "What happened?"

Mark agreed, a little awed, "I never expected that kind of reaction."

Cici didn't move. She stood in the center of the room, champagne glass still in hand, and stared at the two young people. "You're getting married?" she said.

Lori turned her attention from the remnants of disaster overhead back to her mother, and a slow grin lit her face. "We're getting married," she confirmed.

Cici looked from Mark to Lori in slow disbelief. "But," she said, "you're just a baby."

Lori burst into laughter and ran to embrace her mother. "Mom, I'm twenty-four years old and I'm engaged. Be happy for me."

And when Lori, with her naturally irresistible enthusiasm, opened her arms to invite Mark into the embrace, he came forward and kissed Cici's cheek, grinning. "Come on, Ms. B, you know you like me."

And because she did like him and she loved her daughter, Cici laughed and hugged them both. "Congratulations," she said. "I'm happy for you. Really."

It was almost true.

In Ida Mae's Kitchen

Ida Mae was awakened at five a.m. the following morning, when that young sprite came clattering down the back stairs with her beau in tow—fiancé, it was supposed to be now, although how that was supposed to give her the right to go living in sin right under her own mother's nose was beyond Ida Mae's ken. Sometimes, she had decided after many a year of prayerful thought, it was best to leave the judging up to God, because it could just about wear a body out, the way the world was these days. So the best she could do was put on a pot of coffee and shoo them both

29

out of the way while she warmed up a plate of muffins from yesterday, because they were so anxious to get on the road they couldn't take time for a proper breakfast. Kids these days, bound for tarnation on an empty stomach.

About the time they were ready to start rolling out the door, each with a muffin in one hand and a thermos cup of coffee in the other, Cici came down and there was a lot of hugging and chatting and promises to call and checking to make sure they had everything, and even more hugging, right there in the middle of her kitchen while Ida Mae was trying to mix up biscuit dough. Finally, they were out the door and Cici, looking droopy-faced, went off somewhere else to mope.

No sooner had Ida Mae gotten the biscuit dough stirred up and set on the back of the stove to rest, and was thinking about sitting and sipping a cup herself, than Miss Priss came bustling in, fussing over the French toast she had put in the fridge to soak last night and going on and on about making sure to use the heart-healthy chicken sausage and not to put any yolks in the scrambled eggs. Ida Mae just held her tongue and let her go on. She'd figured out a long time ago that the fastest way to get rid of Bridget was not to argue with her.

So the biscuits were rolled out, the French toast in the oven, the fake sausage sliced and sitting in a cold pan, waiting to be cooked, and the egg yolks sitting in the refrigerator while the tasteless whites were coming to room temperature on the counter. She figured the yolks would make a right nice custard for supper, and the dog would appreciate the whites when nobody else ate them. She finally had a minute to sit at the table with a cup of coffee, flipping through that book about the old days somebody had left lying around. She'd never been much of one for book reading, but Judge Blackwell would have liked this; he surely would have. And Miss Emily, who had always been the symbol of Blackwell Farms in Ida Mae's mind, and in the mind of just about everyone else around here, as far as that went— she wouldn't have let on, but inside she would have been bursting her buttons with pride. The thought made Ida Mae smile, just a little, as she turned the page.

"Good morning, Ida Mae. How is my favorite person this morning?"

Ida Mae closed the book with a thud and looked up at Paul sourly as she pushed up from the table. "Don't nobody sleep in anymore?"

"This is the most exciting day of our lives," Derrick said, rubbing his hands together in anticipation as he came down the stairs behind Paul. "We don't want to miss a minute of it."

"And what is that delectable aroma coming from the oven?" Paul opened the door to peek and Ida Mae scowled at him.

"If Miss Priss comes in to find her soufflé-top falling, you'll be the one explaining, not me."

Paul quickly and carefully closed the oven. "I'll just run out and get some wood for the fire," he said.

When he was gone, Derrick poured two cups of coffee, adding cream for Paul and two drops of Stevia from a container that he carried in his pocket for himself. "Ida Mae," he said thoughtfully, "do you think we're doing the right thing, moving out here?"

She took the biscuit cutter out of the drawer, dipped it in a bowl of flour, and started cutting out perfect circles from the rectangle of dough on the cutting board. "Now how in His holy name would I know that?"

He glanced toward the back door, where Paul's silhouette could be seen through the window, selecting sticks of wood for the fireplace. "You know," he said, "we always talked about retiring to the country. I just never thought retirement would come so soon."

"So what do you think you're going to do with yourself once you get out here?" She expertly flipped the biscuit circles onto a dark, greased baking pan and brushed each with melted butter.

"That's just it; I don't know. What do people generally do?"

She picked up the baking pan and elbowed him out of the way as she moved to the stove. "Stand

32

around cluttering up my kitchen, as far as I can tell," she muttered.

He hurried to open the door of the second oven for her, and when she had the biscuits in the oven and the temperature adjusted, he seemed to finally get around to saying what he wanted to say, which was, "Do you think people will like us here?"

Ida Mae started sweeping flour off the counter with a dishtowel, collecting it on the cutting board. "Well, I imagine that depends," she allowed.

"On what?"

She shuffled over to the sink and dumped the excess flour into the disposal. "What folks think of you usually depends on what you think of them," she said. "You treat folks right, they're generally going to do the same to you. Leastwise, that's pretty much been my experience." She dusted off her hands on her flour-streaked apron and turned to look at him. "What about you?"

Derrick met her frank, unbiased gaze, and the ghost of a smile traced his lips. "Yes, ma'am," he said. "Pretty much."

Ida Mae gave a curt nod. "Surprises me you lived to be this old without knowing that," she observed, and that made Derrick grin.

Paul started banging on the door with his shoulder, his arms full of firewood, and Derrick went to let him in. They stirred up the fire and set the table while the aromas of home filled the kitchen. By the time the ladies came in for breakfast, everything was perfect.

Cici stood in the foyer in her pajamas and robe, her hand wrapped around a mug of coffee, gazing blearily up at the dripping hole in the ceiling. The sodden plaster had been swept up and a clear plastic tarp was spread over the floor; the gallon bucket that had been placed under the drip was now half full. The occasional thud of footsteps and the slam of a hammer blow from above testified to the emergency patches that were already being made. She could see wet beams and sagging rafters, but thankfully, no daylight. Perhaps the situation wasn't beyond repair, after all.

Lindsay came downstairs in thermal sleep tights and a mismatched Disney character sleep shirt, the belt of her fleece robe dragging on the steps behind her. Her auburn braid was frayed, her eyes puffy. She rubbed a hand over her face a couple of times to establish circulation, then stood in silence beside Cici for a moment before speaking.

"You haven't been here all night, have you?"

"Nuh-uh." Cici lifted her coffee cup and took a gulp. "Just since dawn."

"Jeez. We were up until two. Where are the kids?"

"Left at dawn. They were driving to Richmond to tell Mark's parents."

"Good God. I need coffee. Is that Farley on the roof?"

Bridget, wearing the sateen quilted rose-patterned robe her son had given her and the leopard-print scuffs her grandchildren had given her for Christmas, came in from the kitchen, bearing two mugs of coffee. She handed one to Lindsay. "Ida Mae called him," she said. She glanced worriedly up at the hole in the ceiling. "I hope he's being careful up there. It's awfully slippery."

Cici sighed. "Better him than me."

Farley was their next-door neighbor—next door being three miles down the highway—and all around handyman. From replacing broken windows to disposing of vermin, if it needed doing, Farley was the one to do it. The fact that he often over-estimated his own competence was a small conciliation to make, considering that he never charged them more than ten dollars for anything.

"Bite your tongue." Lindsay elbowed Cici sharply in the ribs. "We'd be up a deep creek without Farley and you know it."

Cici said irritably, "Ow!" She glared at Lindsay. "What's with you anyway? I'm black and blue from you kicking my ankle and poking me in the arm last night every time I opened my mouth."

"Well, what was I supposed to do, let you spoil

35

the happiest night of Lori's life? It's not as though anything you could have said would have changed her mind."

"At least we talked her out of a beach wedding on Maui," offered Bridget. "She'll come down this very staircase, just like you pictured when we moved in."

"Well, there is that." Cici turned to gaze at the wide, gracefully curving staircase with its polished mahogany treads and gleaming banister, marginally cheered. She, Lindsay, and Bridget had refinished every one of the twenty-two stairs by hand the first year they moved in, sometimes using tools as small as a toothbrush. And all the time she'd been picturing this moment. Then she sighed. "I just didn't think it would be this soon."

"And you won on the June bride thing," Lindsay reminded her.

"It's way too hot here in June."

"September is much better."

"The chrysanthemums will be in bloom, and we can have the reception in the rose garden," Bridget said with a nod of satisfaction. "The climbing roses will just be making their second showing, and the black-eyed Susans and asters will be at their peak. It will be just gorgeous."

Lindsay grinned at her. "We do give fabulous weddings."

"And September is the absolute best month for planning a menu," Bridget went on happily.

"Everything is fresh and easy to get. We'll have a giant prime rib and purple potatoes right from the garden and—oh! Mark's parents aren't Jewish or vegetarian or anything, are they?"

Cici frowned into her coffee. "No. They're Republican."

"Because it isn't easy to do a vegetarian wedding, even in September, and I don't think Ida Mae has the first idea how to keep a kosher kitchen."

Cici said, "Lori's too young to get married."

Bridget said, "She's twenty-five."

"Twenty-four. And she's known Mark less than a year."

"Cici," Lindsay pointed out patiently, "you were a lot older than Lori when you got married, and you'd known Richard for years. You see how well that worked out."

Cici and Richard had been divorced most of Lori's life. She scowled and took another sip of coffee.

"I married my high school sweetheart," Lindsay added, "and couldn't even live with him for three years."

"Jim and I had only known each other eight months," Bridget said, "and we were married for thirty years. He was the love of my life." She smiled. "And I was the love of his."

Cici sighed broadly. "I know all that. What I can't understand is why couldn't they just move in together like everyone else?"

Lindsay and Bridget exchanged a look. "You're kidding, right?" Lindsay spoke up. "You cannot be the only one in this room who doesn't know Lori moved in with Mark last semester."

Cici's frown only deepened. "You know what I mean. Why can't they just keep it that way?"

"They explained that. Job offer, long-distance relationship . . ."

And Lindsay added, "Come on, he's perfect for her! At least that's what you said last year, when you thought she was going to run off to Italy to see that boy she was always emailing back and forth."

"Mark," Cici pointed out deliberately, "has a job in San Francisco. Three thousand miles away."

"But it's not Italy."

"And you don't just walk away from a job offer from Google," Bridget said. "Do you have any idea how many people apply for every job opening there? Six hundred! Per job!"

Cici looked at her skeptically. "Who told you that?"

Bridget shrugged. "I Googled it."

"Anyway, the point is," Lindsay went on quickly, "he'll be making more money his first year than I did in practically my whole working life, so why should they wait to get married, if that's what they want to do?"

Cici sighed. "It's nothing against Mark; you know that. It's just that . . . this wasn't the plan.

Lori was going to go to Cornell, get her degree in enology, come back here and open a winery. That was the plan. Not San Francisco."

"San Francisco is in the heart of wine country," Bridget pointed out gently. "And the University of California has a program that's every bit as good as Cornell's."

"Anyway," added Lindsay, "it could be worse. Mark's job doesn't start until after the wedding, so at least they'll be here all summer. Can you imagine trying to plan your daughter's wedding long distance?"

"Which is exactly why she's not getting married in Maui."

Lindsay slipped her arm through Cici's in a brief hug. "I know how you feel. After all, she's our baby, too. I taught her third grade and gave her her first pair of high heels."

"And I taught her how to whistle and how to make brownies," Bridget added. "So if you think you're the only one who's going to be crying at that wedding, you're very much mistaken."

Cici smiled, wanly but gratefully. "Do you know how old I feel right now?"

Lindsay gave her arm a bracing squeeze. "It couldn't possibly be as old as you look." And when Cici stared at her, she defended, "Hey, you know as well as I do women our age can't get by on three hours of sleep. Come on, let's get some breakfast."

Perfectly on cue, there was a knock on the door. Bridget went to open it, and Farley stood on the porch, wearing his perennial camo cap and a stained tan waterproof jacket, his ginger beard streaked with tobacco juice. "Ladies," he said, touching his cap.

"Farley, thank you so much for coming over," Cici said, coming forward. Bridget went to get her purse. "How bad is it?"

"Well." He chewed on it for a minute, then spat tobacco juice into the soda can he carried in his hand. "You got yourself a leak, all right. I got a tarp nailed on her. Should hold you for a while. But looks to me like you got some rotten beams up there." He rubbed his beard thoughtfully. "That's a little more than I like to involve myself in, truth be told. But I can get you a roofer out here, first thing in the morning."

With every word he spoke, Cici felt her heart sink. "Beams," she repeated. "That doesn't sound good."

"No, ma'am," he agreed. "It ain't. But could be worse."

The three of them stared at him expectantly.

"Could be the foundation," he volunteered.

Bridget mustered a weak smile. "Right," she said. "Thanks, Farley." She handed him a ten-dollar bill. "Won't you stay for breakfast? Ida Mae is making biscuits and ham, and I've got baked French toast in the oven."

"I thank you kindly, ma'am." He touched his cap again and dug his billfold out of his back pocket, carefully tucking the bill inside before adding, "But I got me a pot full of greens and jowls simmering on the stove, and you know what they say about having your greens on New Year's."

"Good luck, right?" said Lindsay.

"And money," he replied seriously. "Every leaf a hundred dollar bill."

Bridget's eyes went wide. "Wow. I'm going to speak to Ida Mae about lunch."

Cici said, "Thanks, Farley. If you've got a roofer, tell him to call us."

"Yes ma'am." Once again, he touched his hat and spat into the can. "Y'all have a happy New Year, you hear?"

"You too, Farley. Happy New Year."

They closed the door behind Farley and looked at each other for a moment.

"Well," said Bridget, uncertainly.

"Could be worse," agreed Lindsay.

And Cici said glumly, "Not the plan."

"Look on the bright side," Bridget said after another moment. "We're having French toast for breakfast, and I smell sausage."

"Which is only the bright side if you hadn't planned to start a diet today," Lindsay pointed out.

That made Cici smile, and she finished off her coffee. "Come on," she said. "Let's eat. And . . ."
She paused to give Lindsay's braid a playful tug

41

as she passed. "Thanks for kicking my ankle last night."

Lindsay smiled. "What are friends for?" She slipped her arm around Cici's waist and they walked together to the kitchen.

Chapter Three

A Grand Adventure

Ida Mae didn't like to serve company in the kitchen, and she complained about it every chance she got. She was complaining about it to Paul as the three women entered, and he was responding, as he always did, "But, dear heart, you know we're not company; we're family."

And Derrick added, "Nonetheless, when you get tired of cooking here and decide to come live with us, we'll let you serve every meal in the dining room. Tea, too."

Ida Mae made a grumpy sound and scooped up sizzling sausage patties with a spatula, draining them on a wooden board lined with butcher paper before transferring them to a platter.

"Fine friends you are," Lindsay said. "First, you invite yourselves to our party, and then, you try to steal Ida Mae away the minute our backs are turned."

"Good morning, gorgeous ones," replied Paul cheerfully. He placed a clear glass bowl filled with pinecones, cinnamon sticks, dried oranges, and lemons on a spray of evergreen in the center of the rubbed hickory table and stepped back to critique his work. "And you know perfectly well we'd never try to steal Ida Mae behind your back. We've been trying to do it in full view of God and everybody since we met her."

"You're all of you a bunch of fools," returned Ida Mae, pulling a casserole dish from the oven. Derrick quickly grabbed a couple of potholders and took the dish from her. She scowled at him. "And there's too many damn cooks in this kitchen."

"Cranberries," said Derrick as he set the dish on the table, and Paul snapped his fingers in agreement, then hurried to the refrigerator to secure a handful.

"And don't you go wasting my good cranberries on your fancifulness, either!" warned Ida Mae, although it was with an inevitable sense of approval, even indulgence, that she watched Paul sprinkle a handful of the ruby jewels across the centerpiece.

Though the formal dining room, with its leaded glass windows and crystal chandelier, was a grand and beautiful room, it was easy to see why everyone preferred eating in the kitchen. Before Cici, Bridget, and Lindsay moved in, the house had been owned by the most prominent family in the county, and the kitchen had been designed to accommodate someone who did a lot of entertaining. It was easy to imagine an entire crew of chefs moving back and forth between the two ovens and the oversized refrigerator on busy party nights, arranging trays of hors d'oeuvres on the miles of countertop and simmering sauces on each of the six burners on the range. The big room had a polished brick floor and delft tile backsplash, a huge soapstone farmer's sink, and a well-used butcher-block workstation in the center. But perhaps its most attractive feature was a raised fireplace with an arched stone surround that was centered on the far wall. A cozy hickory table with cane-bottomed chairs was drawn up before it, and in the winter, that was where the ladies preferred to have all their meals.

A fire snapped and crackled in the fireplace, and herbs from Bridget's kitchen garden hung in bunches from a drying rack overhead, giving off a curious mixture of warm fragrances that was part sun-drenched summer and part holiday feast. Paul had set the table with red Fiesta ware and lime-green napkins, crystal stemware, and the good silver. Each napkin was tied with a string of red jingle bells, and every place setting accented by one of the sprayed gold or silver pinecones left over from last night's celebration. Paul claimed that the best thing about staying overnight at Ladybug Farm was browsing the butler's pantry for table settings the next morning.

Derrick poured pink grapefruit juice into the glasses, and Bridget took a crystal bowl of fruit salad from the refrigerator. Ida Mae plucked golden brown biscuits from a baking sheet that was black with age and dropped them into a basket lined with a linen napkin. Lindsay set a heavy dish of white farmer's butter on the table, along with a cut-glass relish dish filled with a selection of Bridget's jams—cherry wine, rosemary-blackberry, and herbed apple. Cici poured coffee. "Now this," she admitted as Ida Mae set a bowl of fluffy scrambled eggs seasoned with red and yellow peppers and another bowl of pale grits on the table, "was worth getting up for."

"Did someone have a teensy bit too much of the bubbly last night?" Derrick teased her.

"Don't mind her," Lindsay said, bringing a platter of ham to the table. "She's just depressed because Lori's getting married."

"Depressed? What is there to be depressed about? I love weddings!"

"The best time I ever had was planning my Katie's wedding," Bridget said.

"And it was gorgeous," Lindsay said. "All those yellow roses."

"Katie didn't get married right out of college," Cici reminded her.

"That wasn't the plan," Lindsay confided to Derrick.

"Ah," said Derrick, pretending to understand.

Ida Mae set a platter of whole-wheat pancakes drizzled with honey close to Derrick's place setting and wiped her hands on her apron, looking at him sternly. "Them sausages is chicken," she told him. "You can have two, but keep your hands off the ham. And there ain't no yolk in the eggs. No butter or salt in the grits, either. Everybody else add your own."

Derrick rubbed his hands together in anticipation. "Ida Mae, you make a heart healthy diet almost worth having a heart attack for." Derrick's heart condition was something they rarely talked about, but everyone knew it had been a precipitating factor in his and Paul's decision to give up the stress of Washington D.C. and build a home in the country.

Ida Mae cast a sour look at Bridget. "It's all Miss Priss's doing. I believe in eating food the way God made it, and that means not trying to turn a chicken into a pig or milk into water. And if you can choke down them grits without butter or salt, you just let me know how you do it."

Cici suppressed a grin and Paul quickly pulled out a chair for Ida Mae. "All right, everyone, let's eat before it gets cold."

Ida Mae sniffed and started to turn away. "Like I got nothing better to do than sit around jawing the morning away with the bunch of you." Then she hesitated, eyeing the feast that was spread

46

out before them, and conceded, "Well, maybe I will have just a bite of ham biscuit."

She sat, and there was a happy confusion of scraping chairs and snapping napkins and exclamations of appreciation as dishes were passed and plates were filled. "So how did you guys ever get an architect to come all the way out here on New Year's Day?" Bridget inquired, gamely spooning grits without butter or salt onto her plate.

"He's a friend," Derrick replied, discreetly passing the bowl of grits to Paul without taking any. "He understands about feng shui."

Paul passed the grits on to Cici. "Also, we paid extra."

Cici passed the grits to Lindsay without even glancing at them, then helped herself to the French toast. "What feng shui?"

"You know." Lindsay hid the bowl of grits between the fruit salad and the chicken sausage, reaching for the ham platter. "Whatever you start on New Year's Day always ends well. It's good luck."

"Like Farley and his greens," suggested Bridget.

"That ain't it." Ida Mae slathered her ham biscuit with butter. "Everybody knows that whatever you're doing on New Year's Day is what you're gonna spend the rest of the year doing."

Paul looked uncertainly at Derrick. "I really don't want to spend a whole year on this house."

"Don't worry," Derrick assured him. "A good builder can build a 3500 square foot home in a hundred and twenty days."

"Add two months to that," advised Cici.

Paul did some quick calculating. "Still, that's only six months. That's not bad. We can move in by June." His eyes brightened with excitement. "We can give Lori an engagement party by the pool!"

"Pool?" Lindsay said.

"It's going to be gorgeous," Derrick said. "Flagstone lined, two waterfalls, a fern grotto, and swim up bar. Salt water, of course."

"And solar heated," added Paul.

"Wow." Lindsay put the biscuit she was about to eat back on her plate. "If I'm going to fit into a swimsuit by June, I'd better start now."

"Feng shui," Cici felt compelled to point out politely, "doesn't really have anything to do with New Year's Day."

"For us it does," Paul assured her, cutting into his French toast. "We met on New Year's Day, we moved in together on New Year's Day, and we're going to site our house so that the front door is in exact alignment with the rising sun on New Year's Day."

"That way we're always looking toward the future," Derrick added.

Bridget beamed at them. "That's beautiful."

Cici leaned her chin on her hand, smiling at

them. "You both look ten years younger. I'm so glad this is working out for you."

"That's what having an adventure will do for you," Lindsay agreed. "We were the same way when we moved in here, remember?"

Ida Mae harrumphed and got up from the table, taking her plate with her. "I never heard the like of foolishness. That swimming pool is gonna freeze."

"We'll drain it," Derrick assured her.

"Waste of water."

"Spring fed."

She scowled at him. "You gonna eat them grits?"

"Yes, ma'am." Dutifully, he took the bowl and plopped a spoonful on his plate.

Bridget casually hid her portion of grits under a half a biscuit and some unfinished egg whites, and served herself another half-piece of French toast. "The best time of my life was when we moved in here," she said reminiscently. "Well, except for when my children were born, of course."

"And you still look ten years younger," Paul declared and raised his juice glass in a toast. "To old friends," he said, "and new beginnings."

"To your grand adventure," added Cici as she raised her glass.

Glasses clinked and then Paul noticed the time. He and Derrick finished their breakfasts

49

hurriedly and hugged both cooks before they left, promising to return in plenty of time for the traditional New Year's feast of black-eyed peas and roast pork loin. The ladies sat at the table for a while after they were gone, nibbling at leftovers and sipping coffee, talking about how much fun it was going to be to have their friends around more often and debating just how easily the sophisticated gentlemen from Baltimore would adjust to life in rural Virginia.

Then Cici said, "You know something? I envy them."

"Me, too," said Lindsay with a sigh. "That house sounds gorgeous."

"Our house is gorgeous," Bridget objected.

"Except for the roof," Lindsay said.

"We'll fix the roof. We always fix things."

"It's not that," Cici said thoughtfully, sipping her coffee. "I mean, look at them. Look at Lori. Look what they have planned for the year. Lori's getting married. Paul and Derrick are building a house. And what are we doing?"

"Fixing the roof?" suggested Lindsay.

Cici gave her an impatient look. "Growing tomatoes. Reading a book. Making soap."

"Those are good things," Bridget said defensively. "Those are the kinds of things we moved here to do."

Lindsay glanced at Bridget with a wry smile. "But she's right. Not very adventurous."

"Well, what do you want to do? Raft the Amazon?"

"I just don't want to sit around and watch other people starting brand new lives while I'm looking back on mine," Cici said. "That's *not* why we moved here." She drew in a determined breath and pushed back from the table with both hands. "This year," she declared, "I want to do something important, too. Something big. Something ambitious."

A slow consternation crept into the faces of her two friends. "Like what?" asked Lindsay cautiously.

Bridget added, "I was only kidding about the Amazon, you know."

Cici frowned with a sharp mixture of impatience and uncertainty as she gathered up the dishes nearest her and took them to the sink. "I don't know. Something."

Bridget said, "Making soap is something."

"Something significant."

Ida Mae took the dishes from Cici and plopped them into a sink full of soapy water. They had a dishwasher, but Ida Mae refused to use it. "Y'all need to tend to your roof," she advised, "and leave the adventuring to the young folks."

"Paul and Derrick are the same age we are," Cici pointed out. "Adventures come in all shapes and sizes."

Lindsay took the bowl of leftover fruit salad to

the work island, where she transferred it to a plastic storage container. "Maybe we could take a trip," she suggested.

Bridget carried the rest of the dishes to the sink. "Who would take care of the animals?"

"We don't need a trip," Cici said. "We need a plan."

"We've got a wedding to plan," Bridget pointed out. "And two graduations, and a roof to repair, and a kid to get off to college. Not to mention a garden to plant and fruit trees to prune and berry bushes to net and a flock of sheep, a goat, a dog, a deer, and chickens to take care of. Isn't that enough? And," she added, almost under her breath, "I'm still going to learn how to make goat's milk soap."

The book Paul and Derrick had given them lay on the counter where Cici left it when she brought the last of the champagne glasses to the dishwasher the night before. She ran her hand over the cover absently, then thumbed a few pages.

"It's not as though we don't have anything to do," Lindsay agreed with Bridget. But her gaze was fixed thoughtfully on the vista through the kitchen window: the muddy lawn, the bare branches, the stark winter orchard and abandoned vineyard that marched in sad, straggling rows behind the barn. "It's just that it's all kind of routine by now. We need something new."

"I don't," Bridget protested. "I've done enough

new things in the past four years to last a lifetime."

"You know," Lindsay said slowly, turning from the window. "Maybe it doesn't have to be something completely new."

A light dawned in Cici's eyes as she looked up from the book. "Maybe," she said, "it could be something we didn't finish."

"The winery," they both said at once.

Alarm flashed briefly in Bridget's eyes. "But—our vines are dead. The hailstorm killed them."

Lindsay turned to her excitedly. "Not all of them. Only the new ones. Dominic said there was a good chance some of the old ones would come back this spring. And don't forget, he took all those cuttings just in case."

"And the old vines are all we need," Cici said. "If we're going to restore this place, we should *restore* it—back to the way it was." She held up the book like a Bible. "House, gardens, winery, tasting room, everything!"

"Now that's what I call a project," declared Lindsay with satisfaction.

"That's what I call an adventure." Cici returned, grinning.

Ida Mae stared at them. "You all don't have the kind of money it takes to run a winery."

"We've got a barn filled with equipment," Lindsay said, "and that's the most expensive part."

"Come on, Ida Mae," Cici said. "Wouldn't you like to see Blackwell Farms the way it used to be? Complete with Blackwell Farms wine?"

"It ain't never gonna be the way it used to be," she declared flatly and turned back to washing dishes. "And you can't make Blackwell Farms wine."

Lindsay and Cici grinned at each other. "But it sure would be fun to try," Cici said.

"It takes more than a few old vines to make wine," Bridget said. "Ida Mae is right. I don't think you should get your hopes up."

"Well," conceded Lindsay, "we'll have to get Dominic out here, of course, and see what he says."

Cici and Bridget shared a quick glance and a suppressed smile. Dominic had been the county extension agent until he elected to take an early retirement a few months back, and he was an expert vintner. More importantly, it had been his father who established the original Blackwell Farms Winery in the sixties, and Dominic had served as his apprentice. He'd grown up on Ladybug Farm. When the ladies had their brief flirtation with the idea of restoring the vineyard the previous year, he'd been almost as excited as they were—and almost as disappointed when a freak hailstorm destroyed their efforts overnight.

It was no secret that Dominic had a huge crush on Lindsay. What was slightly less well known—

and what had, in fact, been the source of much teasing and speculation over the past year—was how Lindsay felt about him.

"Well," Bridget conceded, now that the hint of romance was in the air, "I suppose it wouldn't hurt to talk to him."

"Of course," agreed Cici, straight-faced. "We have to talk to him."

Lindsay looked sternly from one to the other, and just as Cici and Bridget were about to burst into giggles, the back door opened and Noah came in.

He was a tall, broad-shouldered eighteen-year-old, whose latest effort at self-expression was a Mohawk haircut and a pierced ear with a silver skull earring. There was nothing to be done about the earring, but apparently he'd already grown tired of the haircut, as evidenced by the bristly growth around his neck and temples. He entered the room in the way of most teenage boys: like a storm wind, dropping his backpack on the floor, shucking out of his leather jacket, letting the door slam behind him.

He rubbed the cold from his hands as he strode toward the breakfast table. "Man, was that a bust. Two little kids wet their beds, and one of them threw up all over the preacher's wife. Then this other one got a bloody nose, and two of them got lost playing hide-and-seek. We didn't find them till midnight. 'The wrath of the Lord is visited upon evil-doers,' I told them first thing, and that straightened them out, you'd better believe it. Man, this looks good." He stuffed two biscuits with ham and scraped the last of the French toast and the eggs onto his plate. "All they had for breakfast was donuts. Stale."

He took an enormous bite of the ham biscuit, dug into the eggs, and chewed for a moment before asking, "So what's the tarp doing on the roof?" He looked around alertly. "I thought the guys were coming down. What's been going on?"

They hardly knew where to begin.

Evenings on Ladybug Farm were special times. As soon as the temperature rose above forty— sometimes even sooner—the three friends would gather on the front porch with a glass of wine to watch the sunset, discuss the day, and count their blessings . . . or complain about them. But there was a magic to winter evenings, too, when an early dinner was done and the kitchen was cleaned, Ida Mae had retired to her basement suite and Noah to his room to do homework or, more likely, to chat on the phone with his latest girlfriend or play video games on the computer. There was always a fire in the main parlor's walk-in fireplace, with its fan-brick surround and intricately carved mahogany mantel. When they closed the double doors, it provided enough heat to keep the room shirtsleeve cozy. Two Tiffany lamps turned down low spread a subtle golden glow across the polished heart pine floors and left the high trey ceiling with its carved plaster moldings in shadow. Cici's two wing chairs and Lindsay's surprisingly comfortable tapestry demi-sofa were drawn up in a semi-circle around Bridget's tufted velvet ottoman in front of the fireplace. It was there the women gathered on winter evenings with cocoa or cabernet, their slippered feet resting on the community ottoman, a tray of brownies or oatmeal cookies not far from reach.

On the first evening of the New Year, they gathered around the fire and let the sturdy silence of the old house embrace them. They had said good-bye to Paul and Derrick after lunch and, still pleasantly stuffed from the midday repast of curried pork loin, black-eyed peas, hot buttered cornbread, and turnip greens fresh from their own garden, they toasted each other with hot chocolate and nibbled on the last of the fruitcake cookies. The rain had stopped, Ida Mae had gone to bed, and Noah was upstairs, presumably working on the essay portion of his college application.

"I don't know why he put it off 'til the last minute," Lindsay said, frowning as she bit into a cookie. "Those applications should've been out last month."

"Getting the application in early doesn't improve your chances for admission," Bridget pointed out, absently flipping through the *History of Blackwell Farms* book. "He's got twenty days."

"Yeah, but it *does* affect your chances of getting financial aid or a scholarship," Lindsay pointed out, "which we are in desperate need of." She frowned a little and corrected herself, "Of which we are in desperate need."

Cici reminded her, "He already got two scholarship offers."

Lindsay couldn't prevent a small flush of pride as she admitted, "Well, that's true."

She had a right to be proud. When Noah had first come to Ladybug Farm as a virtually homeless waif, his education was sporadic and his attitude sullen and suspicious. Lindsay, a school-teacher for twenty-five years and a secret artist herself, had uncovered a surprising talent for art in the young man and had bargained art lessons for his attention in math, science, and English. After a year of home schooling, he'd not only caught up with his classmates, but surpassed them and was even awarded a prestigious scholarship to a private school in his junior year. If Lindsay was ambitious for him, it was with justification.

"But," she said, "the basketball scholarship is practically worthless—it's only partial tuition for one year and you know what happens to those kids the first time they tear an ACL—and, well, as much as I'd like to see him at SCAD, Savannah is so far away, and besides, their program is limited. We could get a full financial aid package to UVA, or maybe even William and Mary, if he'd just try. Now *that's* an education."

"I definitely vote for UVA," Bridget said. "He could be home weekends."

Cici's smile was wistful. "Just like Lori."

Bridget tasted her chocolate, then paused. "Do you know what would be great in this? Some of that Kahlua Kevin sent us from Mexico."

Bridget's son, Kevin, was a D.C. attorney who had chosen to spend his Christmas holidays on the sunny beaches of Mexico. The elaborate gifts he sent had more than made up for his absence at the Christmas table, and in fact, had inspired the ladies to suggest that he vacation in Paris next year.

Everyone agreed that a touch of Kahlua would be just the thing, although Cici felt compelled to point out, "This is how people gain fifteen pounds over the holidays."

Bridget brought the Kahlua from the corner cabinet that sat beneath a stained-glass window, which depicted a field of lilies against a blue sky. "Actually," she said, pouring a generous dollop into each upheld cup, "a new study says that the average person only gains two pounds over Christmas."

"Ha," said Lindsay, swirling the liquor into the chocolate with the tip of her index finger. "Whoever did that study has never spent Christmas at Ladybug Farm."

"Well, this is the last of it," declared Cici, raising her cup in a toast. "Eat, drink, and be merry, for tomorrow we diet."

"Famous last words," muttered Lindsay, but she clinked her mug against the others and then made a muffled sound of pleasure as she tasted the hot chocolate.

They settled back for a moment of chocolate-Kahlua bliss, listening to the crackle of the fire and the occasional overhead squeak of a floorboard that told them Noah was still up and about. Bridget's feet, clad in snug slipper socks with fuzzy sheep woven into the knit design, stretched toward the radiant heat of the fireplace, and she murmured, "Do you know what I like best about this house in the winter? The smell. It's like opening up an old trunk and the whole past comes flooding out."

"Hmm." Cici sipped her chocolate. "I can't believe it's been four years since we first saw this place."

Lindsay smiled at her. "I can't believe we're going to have a wedding."

"Me, either," Cici admitted.

"Will she wear your wedding gown?"

Cici gave a snort of amusement. "Hardly. I burned that baby the minute the divorce was final."

Bridget said, "Well, look at this." Her eyes

were on the book again, although now with renewed interest. "It says here that during the sixties, people came from as far away as Europe —Europe!—to attend the dinner pairings at the Blackwell Farms tasting room. Can you imagine? They built entire meals around their wines."

"How about that?" Lindsay said. "Ida Mae must have done the cooking for them. We should ask her about it."

"The sixties," said Cici, smiling reminiscently. "Do you remember the sixties?"

"Of course not," replied Lindsay archly, sipping her cocoa. "I was an infant."

Cici kicked her ankle.

"It says here they entertained politicians, movie stars, and heads of state. Right here on Ladybug Farm."

"Do you realize," said Cici, "that if I still had any of that cheap-o furniture I bought when I first married, it would be legitimately considered antique?"

"Bridget's Fiesta ware is antique," Lindsay pointed out, "worth a fortune. And she got it with Green Stamps."

"Remember Green Stamps?" Again, Cici's smile was wistful.

"Of course not," said Lindsay, sipping her chocolate. "I wasn't even born."

Cici gave her a dry look. "Well, I remember my *mother* using them."

"A lot of wineries have restaurants on the premises," said Bridget speculatively. "Remember, girls, all those great little cafes we visited in Sonoma? They were all attached to wineries."

The other two looked at her.

"Well," said Bridget a little defensively, "if Ida Mae could cook for heads of state, I don't know why I can't."

Lindsay said, "I don't either."

And Cici lifted an eyebrow. "I thought you were happy making goat soap."

Bridget tilted her head. "The Tasting Table," she said thoughtfully. "Cute name for a restaurant, don't you think?"

Cici grinned, and so did Lindsay, and they lifted their mugs in salute to Bridget.

"What a year this is going to be," Lindsay said and settled back in her chair with a small, anticipatory shake of her head.

"And just when I was starting to get comfortable," said Bridget, sighing a little.

"You know where all the comfortable people are," said Cici.

"In the rest home?"

"In the cemetery."

"Oh, that makes me feel so much better."

"Good," said Cici, smiling and leaning back in her chair. "Because I feel better, too."

Chapter Four

The Importance of a Strong Start

The roofer arrived promptly at 8:30 a.m. on January second. And on the third. And on the fourth. Each day he stayed approximately forty-five minutes, during which time he might walk back and forth on the lawn, rubbing his chin thoughtfully and gazing up at the problem, or talk on his cellphone, or string a tape measure from one end of the porch to the other. Then he brought a friend, and the two of them walked back and forth, gazing up at the damage and talking it over. Once, he even climbed a ladder, only to climb back down again, get in his truck, and drive off.

Cici managed to catch him on the third visit.

"Well, you got yourself a complicated situation," he told her, once again rubbing his chin as he pondered the bright blue tarp that still covered the hole in the roof. "A house this old, you can't just go tearing in there without knowing what you're doing."

"I understand that." Cici, who only had time to pull on a sweater before she rushed out into the cold, stood beside him on the lawn and hugged her arms to warm them. She tried to sound patient and reasonable. Long ago she had learned that the laborers in this county had no respect for pushy women. "What I don't understand is why you haven't even taken the tarp off to look at the damage."

"Well, now you don't want to go tearing things off before you're ready to start putting them back on. What if there was to come a storm?"

Patience, Cici reminded herself. *Reason.* "Couldn't you at least give us an estimate?"

"Yes, ma'am," he agreed, equally as reasonably. "Just as soon as I can get up there and have a look around."

She managed to keep her expression pleasant, her tone level. "And when do you think that might be?"

"Well . . ." He gazed upward, considering the situation. "First, I'm going to have to tear off the tiles, see how bad the decking looks all around there. My guess, you've got more than one weak spot. Then I'll have to check how far back the damage to the beams goes . . ."

"Wait." Cici flung up a hand. "Just wait." She took a breath. "Do you mean to tell me you're going to have to tear off our roof before you can even give us an estimate?"

"Well . . . Yes, ma'am. I reckon that's about right."

Now it was Cici's turn to consider the roof, gazing long and hard at the blue tarp as it glistened in the morning sun. "Any idea when you might get started on that?"

He joined her in gazing at the roof. "Well, like I said, you don't want to go tearing things off—"

"Before you're ready to start putting them back on," agreed Cici. "Maybe tomorrow?"

"Nope. Can't do it tomorrow. I'll tell you what I'll do, though. I'll get a couple of fellas out here Saturday with a piece of plywood to patch up the hole. We'll put down some felt to keep it weather tight. How's that sound?"

Cici smiled weakly. "Wonderful. Thank you."

She went up the steps and into the house, closing the door firmly behind her. "We need a new roofer," she announced to the house at large.

But, of course, no one answered. The phone, however, was ringing. Again.

Paul and Derrick rode the elevator to the offices of Daniel Bradstreet, Architectural Design, for the fourth time in two days, pushed open the gold-stenciled double glass doors, and gave a dismissive wave to the secretary who rose, with an expression somewhere between surprise and alarm on her face, to greet them. "He's expecting us," said Paul as they breezed by, and Derrick opened the door to the inner office with a peremptory knock.

Daniel Bradstreet, president and CEO of Daniel Bradstreet, Architectural Design, was on the phone when they came in, safely ensconced behind his nine-foot long ebony and chrome desk, but he finished quickly when he saw them. "Seriously, guys," he said, standing, "you don't have to come down here every time we make a change. Like I told you on the phone—"

"No trouble at all," Derrick said. "I'm a visual person. I need to see it on paper."

With a smothered sigh, Daniel moved from behind the desk to the drawing table that was set up in the light-flooded alcove formed by two sets of floor-to-ceiling windows. "I thought you might say that."

"We just want to make sure that we're keeping the integrity of the design," Derrick assured him. "You know, simple country lodge meets Frank Lloyd Wright. Sturdy but elegant."

"I'd say we're still in that ballpark," Daniel assured him. He refrained from mentioning that the house had ceased being simple or lodge-like several revisions ago.

"All I want to know is why we can't have the swimming pool," said Paul. "That was the most important feature of the house."

"I didn't say you couldn't have the swimming pool," Daniel explained patiently. "I said you couldn't have a spring fed *and* solar heated pool. Not where you want it located, anyway."

He spread the blueprints on his desk and used a pointer to demonstrate on paper what he already explained to them over the phone. "There isn't enough sun on the north side of the house, and there's no efficient way to get water from the spring on the south side."

"What about the west?" suggested Paul.

"I'm afraid your budget doesn't allow for removing part of a mountain."

"It might be interesting to have the pool at the front entrance," Derrick said, albeit reluctantly.

"Where would the pergola and koi pond go?"

"Oh. Right."

"Maybe if we rotated the entire house forty-five degrees . . ."

"Then we'd lose the entire feng shui," Derrick pointed out.

"Well, the feng shui is going to be blown anyway if we move the pool. The water has to be on the north side."

"Then you're going to have to find an alternative way of heating it," Daniel said. "And on that subject, spring water might not be the best option for a swimming pool in Virginia. It comes out of the ground at about forty degrees."

"What if we put the koi pond on the north side?" suggested Derrick. "That would keep the feng shui."

"Then we're back to putting the pool in the front entrance. With no heat and no spring."

And so it went for another twenty-two minutes, by Daniel's watch, until they finally agreed to sacrifice the spring water and the feng shui for solar heating, just as he suggested originally.

Meanwhile, Daniel settled back, ordered coffee, and relaxed. To have done otherwise, he learned early on, would have been a waste of time.

"You know, fellows," he observed, just as they began a discussion about whether to move the folding glass doors in the kitchen so they opened up onto the pool terrace rather than the outdoor kitchen, "this is supposed to be the easiest part. You haven't even started building yet and you're already behind. If you keep micromanaging you're never going to get this thing done."

"There's a difference between micromanaging and attending to details," Paul objected, a little pointedly.

"You can't underestimate the importance of a strong start," added Derrick cheerfully. "Now . . ." He helped himself to a cup of coffee and made himself comfortable in the guest chair. Paul did the same. "Let's talk about the meditation garden."

"And the sauna," Paul reminded him. He told Daniel, "We've decided to move it from the master bath to the outdoor cabana near the hot tub."

Resigned, Daniel picked up the telephone. "I'll be a while," he told his secretary. "Hold my calls."

He picked up his pen and pad for note taking, forcing a patient and, he hoped, inviting smile. "Anything else?"

"Well, as a matter of fact," began Derrick, leaning forward.

By the time they departed two hours later, the simple country lodge had transformed itself into an Italian palazzo with touches of French country chic, and the architect was starting his eighth set of plans.

Fortunately, he was being paid by the hour.

Cici almost made it out the door before the phone rang again. She winced and considered not answering. "Ida Mae!" she called hopefully, even though she knew better. "Are you back?"

Ida Mae went into town every Thursday morning to do her "shopping," returning at noon with such essentials as a jar of hand cream or a pair of socks from the dollar store. They took turns driving her, and today, the short straw had fallen to Noah, who was still on the school's winter break. She had not heard the SUV pull around the gravel drive, and it was still an hour short of noon, so, as she expected, nothing but the continued insistent ringing of the telephone answered her voice. She pulled the door closed against the chill and retraced her steps to answer it.

"Hey, Mom," Lori said. "I almost forgot. Be sure to ask Dominic what he thinks about trying the Jurançon region vinifera, especially the manseng. I know we talked about only producing reds, but a lot of Virginia wineries are having good luck with the petit manseng . . ."

"Lori," Cici said, trying hard to sound at least as patient as she had been with the roofer, "I'm not going to be able to tell Dominic anything if you don't stop calling. This is the fifth time this morning. Don't you have a class to go to or something?"

"I'm just trying to help," Lori said, not sounding in the least insulted. "After all, the whole idea for the winery was mine in the first place. The least I can do is make sure you get off to a good start."

"It might have been your idea," replied Cici pleasantly, "but I'm the one who's actually doing it. Besides, you're going to be in San Francisco."

"You don't have to sound so happy about it."

"I'm not happy about it, sweetheart. I'm devastated about it. Fortunately, I have a winery to keep my mind off my broken heart."

"Sweet, Mom, really sweet. And just because I won't actually be here doesn't mean I'm not still interested. Besides, the more involved I can be in helping start Ladybug Farm Winery, the better it's going to look on my resume when I apply for an internship in California. Dominic might even write me a reference."

There were a lot of replies Cici might have made to that, but she chose the least incendiary. "Honey, you do have a wedding to plan."

She blew out a puff of dismissive air. "How hard

can that be? We put together a whole society wedding for perfect strangers last year in three weeks."

Cici thought the "we" part was a bit of an exaggeration, but before she could point that out, Lori added, "Oh, that reminds me. I invited Mark's parents out to meet you this weekend."

"You *what?*" It was almost a screech.

"Not for the whole weekend," Lori assured her. "Just for Sunday. You don't have to change the sheets or anything."

"Here? You invited them *here?*"

She sounded a little defensive. "Well, I didn't think it would seem very hospitable of you to just meet them in a restaurant like a homeless person or something."

"But we have a hole in our roof!"

"Oh, they won't care. I've told them all about the place. They'll think it's cute."

Cici closed her eyes and counted to three.

"Mom?"

"This weekend? Three days from now? And you just remembered to tell me?"

"They're driving all the way down there from Richmond. And then they're flying to Hawaii for a month, so it was now or never, more or less. Of course," she added, "we're stopping in Los Angeles to have dinner with Dad."

Cici blinked. "You're flying to Hawaii?"

"Of course not. They're flying to Hawaii. I'm

flying to Los Angeles next week to introduce everyone. Then I have to be back in class."

"Oh, right," murmured Cici. "That little college thing." She tried to remember a time when she had the kind of energy it took to fly across country for dinner, plan a wedding, finish college, and still have time left over to give advice to her mother. "Honey," she said, "don't you think you might be just a little bit over-scheduled?"

Lori laughed. "Me? You're the one who's planting a vineyard, opening a winery, rebuilding your house, and planning your only daughter's wedding." A note of anxiety crept into her voice as she said, "The roof *will* be fixed by the wedding, won't it?"

Cici ignored the last part. "Actually, I was hoping you and I could start planning the wedding together, this weekend. Alone. A mother-daughter moment, you know."

"Oh, we'll have plenty of time for that," Lori declared airily. "I'll be home all summer while Mark is back and forth getting set up for the new job. So you ask Dominic about the manseng, okay? And we'll see you Sunday. Love you!"

"Love you, too," Cici replied a little absently, but Lori had already hung up.

Chapter Five

Crush

"These days," Dominic explained, "most small wineries use a garage or a metal storage building to age their wine. Not many folks have a set-up like this. You're already way ahead of the game."

Bridget and Lindsay were walking with Dominic through the long-abandoned winery that had been built beneath the original barn in the nineteen twenties and outfitted with modern winemaking equipment in the sixties. While Dominic inspected the equipment, checking fittings and jotting down what needed to be replaced in his notebook, the women grew ever more dismayed as they brushed away cobwebs and used their gloved fingers to rub away forty years of grime in random spots here and there. It was beginning to look as though it would take another forty years just to get the place clean.

"Of course," Dominic went on, copying down a serial number and completely unaware of the ladies' waning enthusiasm, "Judge Blackwell never intended to run a small winery, and he didn't. Blackwell Farms wine shipped all over the world, won all kinds of awards. But I guess you know that."

The last was said with a smile that was directed at both Bridget and Lindsay, but it seemed somehow to linger on Lindsay. Lindsay responded by stuffing her hands deep into the pockets of her jeans to warm them and hunching her shoulders a little inside her short, faux-fur trimmed jacket. "We know. We had a bottle that almost made us rich. But turned out it had the wrong label on it."

"Oh, right," he remembered. "That artist, Mary Ellen—no, Emmy Marie—who stayed here one summer designed that label. We only did half a run with it, and it became a collector's item." A pleasantly reminiscent spark came into his eyes. "I was wild about that girl. Completely broke my heart in the end, of course."

He was a wiry man with sun-darkened skin and work-roughened hands, thick platinum hair that fell to his collar, and shockingly blue eyes. But it was his easy charm, even more than his natural good looks, that most people remembered about him, and that was what made Lindsay laugh now.

"I'm sure you deserved it."

"I'm sure I did, too. I was an incorrigible young upstart." He glanced around. "She painted a mural for the tasting room, too. It was really something—twelve feet tall and fifteen feet wide, with trompe l'oeil columns framing a view of the vineyard. I remember if you looked carefully at the clouds, you could see Pegasus the winged horse there. She was really very talented. I don't know why they painted over that mural."

"She was Noah's grandmother, you know," Lindsay said. "At least according to Ida Mae."

"Is that right?" He seemed mildly surprised. "I always wondered what happened to her."

Bridget said, "Tasting room? There was a tasting room here?" She looked around, peering into the shadows for signs of what might once have been an elegant tasting room. "Where was it?"

He tilted his head toward the ceiling. "Upstairs. What you all were using as a barn was Judge Blackwell's tasting room. Or part of it was, anyway. He used to have big parties and fancy sit-down dinners out here every spring and fall for the blessing of the vines and the burning of the vines."

"Oh, my." Bridget's eyes were beginning to light with the possibilities. "That sounds like fun."

"Blessing?" Lindsay repeated. "Burning? What's that?"

"It's a vineyard tradition," Dominic explained. "Every fall, the vine prunings have to be burned to make sure no diseases carry over to the next year's crop, so in the early days, the farm laborers would gather around the bonfire and bring food and drink the off-cast vintage that the chateau owners would pass down to them. Eventually, the party started to look like so much fun, I guess, that the bosses joined in, and then the owners, and it was passed down through the generations. Same with the blessing of the vines in the spring, to ensure a good crop. Of course, that's a little bit more on the subdued side."

"We definitely have to do that," Bridget said with a nod of her head. "Who knows? Maybe if we'd blessed the vines last year the hail wouldn't have killed them."

Lindsay looked skeptical. "I don't think Baptists bless vines."

Dominic said, "In most modern wineries, the blessing and the burning are events to draw a crowd. They have tastings, food pairings, vineyard tours, even hot air balloon rides and hundred-dollar-a-plate dinners among the vines prepared by top chefs. You know, to raise money and get exposure for your wine."

"And bring people to your restaurant," added Bridget. "It's all a part of the process—everything supports everything else."

"Exactly," agreed Dominic. "Are you ladies going to add a restaurant to the plan?"

"Well, we have to find a place for it first." Bridget, in an ivory corduroy jacket with pink calico trim and matching pink suede Uggs, picked her way carefully across the dusty concrete floor toward a row of chipped porcelain sinks, which she examined with a barely concealed expression of dismay. "I don't think we can have it in the barn. That's where we keep the ewes in lambing season, and Bambi and Rebel sleep there in the winter, and it's awfully close to the chicken coop."

"Not very elegant," agreed Lindsay.

Dominic chuckled a little. "Well, you have plenty of time to think about that. First you make the wine, eh?"

Lindsay smiled at him. "That sounded very French."

His eyes took on a twinkle. "Put a Frenchman within twenty yards of a vine and his accent will return—even if he was born in the US."

The overhead hatch at the far end of the cellar squeaked open and a square of light spilled down the shadowed stairs, followed by the sound of Cici's footsteps. "The first thing we're going to do," she said as she descended, "is put a real door at the top of the stairs. Every time I come down here I feel like I'm a runaway on the Underground Railroad."

She reached the others and announced, "Lori is bringing Mark's parents for Sunday dinner."

"But we have a hole in our roof!"

"Sunday? That's only three days away!"

Cici looked at Dominic. "She said to ask you about something called petite mandrake from the Euro region."

Dominic looked blank for a moment; then his expression cleared. "Of course. That's a good idea. Jurançon varietals do very well here, and some of the petit mansengs have won awards. I

77

think it would be well worthwhile to make them a part of your long-term plan."

"Did the original vineyard have those petit whatevers?" Cici asked.

"No. The original vines were Bordeaux varietals—cabernets, shiraz, merlot."

"Then that's what we're doing," Cici said.

Dominic gave a slight lift of his eyebrow, but didn't argue. "Well, then," he said. "Shall we talk about the plan?"

"I hope it includes replacing these sinks," Bridget said dubiously, twisting a dry faucet open and closed. "They don't look very sanitary."

"Stainless steel would be better," Dominic agreed. "But that's another expense." He glanced around until he found a towel, stiff with age, crumpled near the sinks, and used it to wipe off a tall table in the center of the room. He opened a folder there and invited them to join him. "Basically," he said, passing around papers from the folder, "there are three different approaches to running a winery. The first is the way we talked about last year, by operating your own vineyard. Since you already have established vines, that certainly makes the most sense. But it's also, as you've seen, a risky way to a slow profit."

"And expensive," added Lindsay with a sigh. "All those vines we lost last summer just about wiped out the profit we made from hosting that wedding."

"There's nothing cheap about owning a winery," agreed Dominic. "Or," he added with a wink toward Cici, "having a wedding. Congratulations on your daughter's engagement, by the way."

"Thanks," she replied a little distractedly. She held one of the papers at arm's length in order to better read it, frowning. "What is this—312 cases per acre?"

"That's how much wine your vineyard will produce at maximum capacity," he explained, "if everything goes right."

"Which it never does," Lindsay pointed out.

Bridget, who had the foresight to bring her glasses, finished examining the sheet much more quickly than the other two, and now did some rapid calculating in her head. "It says here 2000 cases the first year, 10,000 cases in five years." She looked up at him over the rims of her readers. "We only have six acres in vines. We can't even make 2000 cases, much less ten."

He nodded. "The difficulty is that any winery with a production of less than 5000 gallons a year has very little chance of success, and you'll come in just under that even if all goes well."

"Wait a minute," said Lindsay, looking up from her paper. "You said that the Blackwells didn't run a small winery, but they had the same amount of acres we do, right? So what did they do?"

He smiled. "You don't make money from a vineyard," he explained. "You make money from wine. Which brings me to the second way to run a winery." He passed out another set of papers. "You buy the grapes from someone else."

Bridget's eyes widened. "We have a whole vineyard, and we're buying grapes?"

Cici's frown only deepened. "Lori's business plan didn't say anything about that."

"Your original business plan was good," he assured them, "as far as it went. But it allowed for slow growth, and, frankly, not much room for error—like the kind of weather disaster we had last year. You wanted me to help you recreate the Blackwell Farms vineyards. Well, in essence, this is what they did. The reason Judge Blackwell brought my father over from France was to make wine, not to grow grapes, so the first thing he did was search out the best varietals in Virginia to mix with the European stock the judge was growing."

"No kidding," said Lindsay, surprised. "That little sneak."

"It's done all the time," Dominic assured her. "In fact, I don't know of a winery in the country that hasn't, at one time or another, supplemented their vintage with grapes from another vineyard."

"Sounds expensive to me." Bridget looked worried.

"And we still wouldn't be able to start selling for . . . ?" Cici looked at Dominic inquiringly.

"A year, at least, from harvest time," Dominic admitted. "Two for some varieties."

The three women looked from one to the other uneasily. "I think I liked Lori's plan better," Cici said. "We still didn't make money for three years, but the up-front investment was a lot smaller."

"And we didn't have to worry about cleaning this place up for three years," added Bridget, wrinkling her nose.

"There is a third way," Dominic said, and passed out another paper. "Custom crush. That's when you buy the actual crush—the wine, if you will—already crushed, pressed and fermented, to be shipped here for storage and bottling under your label."

"But that's cheating!" Bridget exclaimed.

"It wouldn't even be our wine," Lindsay objected, and Cici was shaking her head in agreement.

"It will be as much your wine as you want it to be," Dominic said. "You can create custom blends, decide how to age it and for how long, choose the varietals. You'll bottle, brand, and label it. It will be your wine. And you can start selling this year."

Now they were interested.

"How soon this year?" Cici asked.

"Depending on what you order and what's available . . . late summer."

A flash of excitement went around the group.

"Now we're talking." Cici grinned.

"We could have our tasting room ready for tourist season," Bridget said.

And then Lindsay said, "We could open our first bottle at Lori's wedding!"

A moment of reverential silence fell, held in expectation that didn't quite dare to become hope. Cici's eyes lit up, and she beamed.

Dominic said, "My recommendation, if you're really serious about this, is to use a combination of all three methods. Use custom crush to finance the operation until your first harvest and import grapes to supplement your yield. You can be in business in six months."

As one, the three women held up their hands and slapped palms. "We can do this," said Lindsay. "We really can!"

"Who knew?" agreed Bridget, grinning broadly.

And Cici declared, "Dominic, you are a genius."

Dominic smiled, but he looked torn. He brought out the final set of papers and passed them around. "Here's the bottom line," he said.

The minutes passed as the women studied the spreadsheet, and the ebullience in the room sank like a hot air balloon in cold weather.

"Tractors . . . harvest crew . . ." murmured Cici.

"Label design, operations manager," added Bridget, her eyes glued to the paper.

"Licenses, permits, bottles," said Lindsay. She looked up. "We didn't even think about bottles."

"The good news is that you have all the equipment," Dominic said, almost apologetically. "The presses, the barrels, the bottling apparatus.

Really, you can't imagine how important that is. It puts your chances of success in the highest percentile. But even starting out with custom crush, as you can see, you're looking at a significant investment."

For a moment, no one said anything, and no one dared to raise her eyes from the paper. Bridget swallowed. Cici cleared her throat. Lindsay murmured, "Too bad we can't afford to make wine. I sure could use a drink."

"Come on, we knew this wasn't going to be cheap," Cici said. She drew a breath and looked at Dominic. "So how do people generally go about financing this sort of thing?"

He shrugged. "Various ways. A lot of folks these days are using their retirement funds and cashing in their investment portfolios. A small business loan isn't out of the question. You have all the elements of a solid business plan. You just have to put it together. Of course, it would help if you could get a few investors."

"Investors," Bridget agreed, cheering somewhat. "I like that idea. Where do we get those?"

Dominic's smile seemed a little hesitant, almost shy. "Well," he said, "if you'll permit me . . . I'd like to be the first. Not for money," he added quickly, as he saw an excited mixture of hope and protest form in their eyes. "But if it suits you, I'd like to offer my services as operations manager and vigneron for a percentage of the profit. That will cut your operating costs almost in half, and we'll draw up a contract that you can take to the bank."

Bridget's eyes grew big. "You would do that? For us?"

"I'd do it for me," he corrected, and a noticeable relief relaxed his expression and caused his eyes to crinkle at the corners. "I've got a good pension and I don't need the income, plenty of time, and nothing would give me greater pleasure than to see this winery up and running again."

Cici gave a muffled cry and flung her arms around his neck, hugging him hard, followed by Bridget. Lindsay stepped forward awkwardly, gave him a brief, one-armed embrace, and took a quick step back, looking embarrassed. "Thank you," she said. "This is incredibly generous of you."

He extended his hand to her formally, a spark of amusement in his eyes. "I look forward to a long and prosperous partnership," he said.

Lindsay laughed and shook his hand, relaxing a little. "Really," she said. "How can we thank you? Would you like to come for dinner Sunday? The least we can do is make you a meal."

"As much as it pains me to turn down a chance at your cooking, Miss Bridget," he said, with a nod in Bridget's direction, "it appears you all are going to have your hands full meeting the in-laws on Sunday."

"Oh, that's right," Lindsay said, obviously disappointed.

Cici spoke up quickly. "You don't have to be here for that, Lindsay. Why don't you take Dominic to lunch for all of us?"

Lindsay swung an alarmed look on her, but Bridget chimed in, "What a great idea! There's that darling new B&B out on the highway, and I heard they serve a wonderful Sunday brunch."

"I've been wanting to check that place out," Dominic said.

Lindsay looked back to him. "So have I."

"We'll need a reservation," Dominic said.

"I'll make it," all three women said at once, and when Lindsay once again shot a look at them, Bridget and Cici just smiled sweetly.

"Sounds like it's a date," Dominic said, smiling at Lindsay. "I'll pick you up after church on Sunday." He turned to Bridget and Cici. "Give me a call if you need any help with the business plan. Meanwhile, I'll get the paperwork started for you to take to the bank, just to show you've applied for your licenses and permits. You'll need to incorporate, and when you're just starting up, it's safer to let someone who knows what he's doing serve as agent for the business and handle all the legal documents and finances. I like that lawyer in town, Frank Adams, unless you have somebody else in mind."

"No, he's great. Of course," added Cici, "Bridget

and I are going to be pretty busy the next couple of weeks, but Lindsay can go into town with you to talk to him if you like."

Another look from Lindsay, which they ignored.

"Sounds good. I want to stop by and say hello to Miss Ida Mae before I leave, and then I'd better get on back, but I'll be in touch. Call me if you think of any questions."

"I'll walk you out," Lindsay said, deliberately refusing to look at her two friends.

Bridget and Cici pretended to be absorbed in studying the spreadsheet until the trap door closed behind the couple. Then they looked at each other, grinned, and shared a silent high five.

In Ida Mae's Kitchen

Dominic felt like a school boy again the minute he stepped into that kitchen, and he suspected he looked like one, too: wiping his feet on the mat, shoving his hands into his jacket pockets, just standing there grinning and taking in the smells and sights and tastes of home.

"Miss Ida Mae," he said, "I declare you are looking fine. And this place smells like every dream of my faraway childhood."

She straightened up from removing a tray of cookies from the oven, giving him a glance and a small grunt of dismissal. "You always was full of words, boy."

He came forward and took her face in both his hands, kissing her on each cheek. She not only tolerated the affection, but flushed with it and slapped him playfully on the arm with her dishtowel as she stepped away. "You are your papa's son, and that's a fact."

"Whoever would have guessed that after all these years my path would lead me back here, following in his footsteps, eh?" He unzipped his jacket and sat at the work island, watching her plate the cookies.

"I would," she said flatly. "You staying for lunch?"

He shook his head. "No, ma'am. I just came to talk to the ladies and look over the winery. It looks like we might be making wine as early as this summer."

"Is that a fact?" It was impossible to tell from her tone whether she was skeptical or matter of fact. She set the plate of cookies on the counter before him, the warm moist flavor so fresh from the oven that it practically left rivulets of steam in the air as it drifted toward his face. "You sure it wouldn't be anything else that brings you sniffing around here, are you?"

He fought back a grin with only partial success as he broke off a corner of a cookie and popped it into his mouth. "Some things," he admitted, "are irresistible."

Ida Mae took two onions and three potatoes from the vegetable bin and brought them to the cutting board. Dominic took another cookie, a whole one this time.

"An odd situation, isn't it?" he observed. "Three city women buying a big old house like this out here in the country. But then, I guess they're not ordinary women."

Ida Mae brought the sharp edge of a chef's knife down on the end of an onion, severing it with a clank. She peeled away the skin and began to rock the knife back and forth, producing neat, even slices.

"That young one of Miss Cici's, Lori, is as sharp as a tack. And Lindsay has done a world of wonder with Noah. I'm as proud to work beside him as any man I've ever known, and that's no small thing when you consider where he came from. You have to have a big heart to reach out to an orphan boy like that and make him your own. She's quite a woman."

Ida Mae turned the onion slices over and began a deft chopping motion. Dominic pretended to watch her.

"Not," he added casually, "that they're not all fine women. But . . ." He took his time selecting another cookie. "Supposing a man was to take a particular interest in courting just one of them. I wonder what would happen."

Ida Mae scraped the diced onions to one side of

the board and sliced the head off a second one. "Not a thing in this world," she said sharply, "if that man don't get out of my kitchen and speak up for hisself."

Dominic's grin was slow and abashed. "Ah, well, now no one can say I haven't tried. The truth of the matter is, there's so much estrogen in the air around here I'm not sure any man has a chance to even be noticed through it."

"Is that a fact, Mr. Fancy Words?" She did not look up from her chopping. "I reckon you'd best just go on home, then."

He broke his cookie in half and chewed one half of it thoughtfully. "What they've done here, what they all have together, it's really something special. A fellow would be a fool to try to break it up." He stood up. "It was good visiting with you, Miss Ida Mae."

Ida Mae scraped the onions to the side of the board and began paring a potato with swift, economical movements. "A house full of women is a soft place to land, that's a fact. But it's also got itself some hard edges, and I don't reckon anybody you'd ask would deny that. Now that boy, he's got his own time coming, and he won't be wasting much time brushing the dust of this place off his feet. Seems to me it might be a welcome thing to have a man around to chop the wood and climb the ladders and leave his wet towels on the floor from time to time. Just seems to me."

Dominic paused and looked back at her speculatively. Then he smiled, snagged another cookie, and saluted her with it. "Thanks for the cookies, Miss Ida Mae," he said. "I'll see you later."

Bridget came into the small room off the sun porch that they used as an office and tapped Cici on the shoulder. The little room might once have been what the original owner would have called a morning room, with east-facing windows that flooded the room with early light and just enough space for a breakfast table and a few occasional chairs. They had furnished it with a wrap-around desk, a computer, wooden filing cabinets painted in bright colors, an easy chair, and walls decorated with Lindsay's artwork and enlarged photos of the three of them on various vacations together. Here they paid bills, checked emails, reconciled the household accounts, and, on occasions like this one, labored over special projects such as preparing a business plan for Ladybug Farm Winery.

Cici clicked the mouse and brought up another screen without glancing at Bridget. "The child goes to college for four years to learn how to write a business plan," she muttered, "and where is she when I need her?"

"Quitting time," Bridget said and handed her a glass of rich red cabernet sauvignon.

Cici accepted the glass with both hands. "You are my best friend forever," she declared fervently and took a sip.

Bridget tilted her head meaningfully toward the front of the house. "Bring a coat," she advised.

The two of them took their wine to the front porch, Bridget wrapped in a thick, scratchy Alpaca wool throw, and Cici in a heavy knit cardigan that she had grabbed from the front hall tree. Lindsay was already outside, standing at the front porch rail in her fur-trimmed jacket, wine in hand, gazing out over the most spectacular sunset any of them had ever seen.

A silver-edged, scarlet cloud bisected the deep purple mountain landscape. Beyond it, a slash of clear cerulean-blue faded into pink, bright yellow, and viridian green. Against this breathtaking backdrop, the black fingers of winter trees stood in stark relief.

"Oh my," said Bridget softly, leaning against the rail beside Lindsay.

"Wow," agreed Cici. Her breath frosted on the chill evening air. "Now I remember why we live here."

Across the barren, winter-brown meadow, a black-and-white border collie circled a flock of muddy, lazy sheep. They gave him little argument as he moved them with laser-like efficiency toward the shed where several bales of hay had just been unwrapped. No one ever told the border collie what to do with the sheep; he just did it. It was a mystery.

"I'm not speaking to you," said Lindsay, staring straight ahead. She spared a quick impartial glance toward Bridget. "You either."

"Good," said Cici, enjoying the sunset. "Let's not spoil the moment."

Bridget sipped her wine. "Oaky," she observed. "A touch of blackberry. A little young, I think."

Both women stared at her, and she shrugged. "Just trying to develop my palate. Dominic says that's the minimum requirement for a wine maker."

Cici tasted the wine, tilted her head thoughtfully, and shrugged. "Pretty good for $11.95, if you ask me."

The scarlet cloud turned purple, giving off a radiant glow of orange and pink, and they watched in respectful silence for a moment.

"Dominic," said Lindsay, tossing back a swallow, "doesn't know everything. And it doesn't taste like blackberry. It tastes like thyme."

Bridget took a sip, and so did Cici. Bridget pursed her lips thoughtfully and agreed. "You're right."

Cici took one more sip. "So that's what it is."

A dove-gray shade descended over the mountain, leeching brilliance from the sky. The women moved back into the shadows of the porch and settled into their rocking chairs, watching the last of the light show from a distance. Bridget arranged the throw over her shoulders, and Cici zipped up her cardigan.

Lindsay said, "If I wanted a boyfriend, I could get one for myself."

"Absolutely," agreed Bridget. "You've always had the most interesting sex life of any of us."

Cici's eyebrows shot up in protest. "I beg your pardon."

"Sorry, Cici, but it's true," Bridget said, unperturbed. "Although," she added kindly, "I'm sure you could be a contender if you had more free time."

Cici drew a breath to reply to that but seemed to fall short of words. Instead, looking a little confused, she took another sip of wine.

"I don't need you guys making dates for me." Lindsay maintained her stiff shoulders.

"Well, someone needs to," Cici said. "Dominic has asked you out four times already."

"I went with him for ice cream at the county fair, didn't I?" Lindsay defended.

"With Noah and Ida Mae tagging along."

"And to the Christmas parade," Lindsay pointed out.

"You were dressed as an elf," Bridget replied patiently, "and he was a reindeer. Not exactly what I'd call romantic."

Lindsay frowned uneasily. "I'm too old for romance."

"That's probably true," Cici agreed, and when Lindsay shot her a surprised look, she explained. "Romance is all about hormones, and we hardly have any hormones left."

"Speak for yourself," muttered Lindsay.

"No, I think she's right," Bridget said. "Not necessarily about the hormones part, or even about the romance . . . but women our age are looking for an entirely different set of things in a relationship than someone, say, Lori's age."

"Exactly," agreed Cici. "For example, a man who knows how to give a good foot massage is going to win out over a guy with great pecs every time." She thought about that for a moment. "Well, maybe not every time."

"If anyone were to tell Lori that the most important thing to look for in a man is someone who knows how to listen," Bridget said, "she would laugh."

"Someone who knows what you're thinking before you do," added Cici.

"Who can take care of himself and not be underfoot," added Bridget.

"Who always has something interesting to say," Lindsay suggested, "and knows how to be quiet."

"Someone who makes you laugh."

"Who knows things you don't know and doesn't try to make you like everything he likes."

"Who makes you feel like there is someone who's always on your side."

"The trouble is," said Lindsay, smiling a little into her glass, "I already have somebody like that." She glanced at them in the bluish twilight. "You guys."

"Well," Cici said, "except for the foot massage part."

They all laughed softly and rocked in gentle silence for a while, sipping their wine and enjoying the still breath of winter on their hands and faces as the day slipped away into a pale purple evening. In the distance, Rebel gave forth a series of barks that seemed to have no purpose whatsoever, except to announce his presence to the coming night, and then was silent.

"Anyway," said Lindsay with what sounded suspiciously like a muffled sigh, "it doesn't matter now. If Dominic is going to be our business partner, he can't be my boyfriend."

Bridget stopped with her glass midway to her lips. "Who says?"

Lindsay seemed momentarily confused; then she shrugged. "There are rules."

"They only apply to companies with ten or more employees," Cici assured her earnestly.

"You know what I mean." Lindsay frowned uncomfortably. "We're depending on him. He's taking money from us. It's complicated."

Bridget nodded, pretending to understand.

"Which is why no one ever dates her accountant."

"Or lawyer," added Cici, "or building contractor, or piano teacher."

"Ah," Bridget remembered with a smile, "I had this piano teacher once . . ." And when the other two stared at her, she insisted, "What? I was of age." And then she hid her grin with her upraised glass. "Well, almost."

It took a moment for Lindsay to bring her attention back to the matter at hand. "What I mean is," she said, "what if we have a fight, or he gets tired of me, or I get tired of him . . . ? How happy is he going to be about helping us out then? I don't want that kind of responsibility."

Cici, with one last puzzled glance at Bridget, replied patiently, "Lindsay, you're awfully cute, but I really don't think a grown-up man with a college degree and thirty years of expertise would agree to go into business with three women he barely knows just because he likes you. He's doing it because he wants to and because we're paying him thirty-five percent of our profit for the first five years."

"We are?" Bridget said. Then she turned to Lindsay and added practically, "Besides, grown-up people don't just get mad and walk out when things don't suit them. By the time you get to be this age, you know there's not a whole lot of time left for second chances, so you're a little more careful about what you leave behind."

"But," added Cici, "if it bothers you, you should talk to him about it. After all . . ." She smiled as she sipped her wine. "You've got a date Sunday."

"Yeah," said Lindsay, as though the thought had caught her by surprise. "I guess I do." And then she lifted the glass in a tiny half-salute to herself and sipped.

The last of the day vanished abruptly from the sky, leaving nothing but charcoal smudges across a paler dark background, like a blind man's failed attempt at finger painting. The cool of a night that would soon turn cold crept up damply from the ground, smelling of still, icy streams and deep, dark earth. Yet the warm fragrance of their own wood smoke mingled with comfortable kitchen aromas kept them content, and they stayed and rocked and sipped their wine.

"You know," Bridget said thoughtfully, "the barn really is the perfect place for the tasting room. Right there just steps from the barrels and the bottle storage and close enough to the kitchen that you could cater almost any sized crowd without much trouble at all."

"It's not insulated," Cici pointed out.

"I would love to try to repaint that mural Dominic was talking about," Lindsay said. "Wouldn't that make a fabulous backdrop for the restaurant?"

"There's only one electrical outlet," Cici said.

"But it has a great stone floor," Bridget pointed out.

"Which smells like sheep pee."

"Well, we wouldn't use that part."

"There's no plumbing."

"Oh my goodness." Bridget sat up straight, her eyes dancing. "We could have Lori's reception there!"

Cici looked alarmed. "In a barn? Did you hear the part about no plumbing?"

"Noah could help with the painting," Lindsay said excitedly. "Wouldn't that be something—to help recreate his grandmother's art?"

"I wonder if there's a picture of the tasting room in that book," Bridget said, rising.

"Maybe there's a picture of the mural!" Lindsay followed her inside.

"Wait." Cici twisted around in her chair to call after them. "In a *barn?*"

But the door had already closed behind them, and after a moment of debate, Cici, with a shrug, settled back to finish her wine.

Chapter Six

A Matter of Faith

Cici and Bridget stood on the front porch in their Sunday best, shivering a little in the cold, watching the Lexus make its stately way down their long and mostly barren driveway. Lindsay, in her Sunday brunch best—which involved slightly more décolletage than the other two—lingered stubbornly beside them before departing on what she liked to call her "diplomatic mission" on behalf of Ladybug Farm. Of the three, it was generally agreed that Lindsay was destined to have the most fun . . . if only she could be persuaded to go.

"Okay, they're here," Cici said impatiently, glancing at her watch. "Go, already. We've got this."

"Are you kidding?" Lindsay replied, standing on tiptoes to watch the car round a blind spot in the drive. "Do you think I'm going to let Lori get married before I meet the in-laws?"

"Dominic will think you stood him up," Bridget said worriedly.

"No, he won't. I texted him."

Both women stared at her. "You text?"

"Nice car," observed Lindsay as the sound of the car's tires crunching on the gravel drew closer.

Her two friends turned their attention back to the approaching vehicle.

"I don't know," Bridget said with a small frown. "I kind of expected a limo."

Cici spared her a dismissing look. "It's a Lexus, for heaven's sake."

"But he's a congressman."

"State representative. Former." But Cici rubbed her palms absently along the crease of her jacket, a sure sign of nervousness.

The car pulled up in front of the house and the three women put on their best smiles, lifting their hands in a welcoming wave. Noah had made certain Rebel, the border collie, was locked up in the barn before leaving for his Sunday date with Amy—which would begin with lunch at her parents' house and end with choir practice—but Bridget still glanced around anxiously as the car doors opened. Guests at Ladybug Farm had been known to be assaulted by a goat, chased by a rooster, and startled by the pet deer, in addition to being terrorized by the dog.

The back door opened almost before the car completely stopped moving and Lori got out, long legs clad in dark denim and suede wedge boots, her torso covered by a playful cut-velvet bolero jacket with brightly colored, oversized glass buttons, and her coppery curls gleaming beneath the brim of a tweed fedora hat. She looked around excitedly, waving to the group on the porch, chattering at full-speed to the people who hadn't even left the car yet. Her enthusiasm was contagious, and the women smiled as they watched her.

"You do make pretty babies," Bridget told Cici and slipped her arm through Cici's.

"World class," added Lindsay, wrapping her hand around Cici's other arm.

"That I do," agreed Cici, with an indulgent gaze fixed on Lori, and affectionately bumped each of her friend's shoulders with her own. "Shall we welcome the dignitaries?"

"Hi, Mom! Hi, Aunt Bridget! Hi, Aunt Lindsay!" Lori called as they came down the steps. "Where's Noah? I'm starved! But first, I want to show everyone around, okay? I've been telling them all about the winery. Is Dominic coming for lunch? Because I wanted to talk to him about this place I found in upstate New York that specializes in old vine Burgundies. Their blog said they're releasing two hundred barrels of custom crush this spring, so we'll need to order it now if we're going to get on the list." She gave her mother and then Bridget and then Lindsay a perfunctory hug. "What's for lunch?"

"Sweetheart," Cici said, smiling at the handsome, well-dressed couple that emerged from the front seats. "Manners."

Mark laughed and came forward to kiss Cici on the cheek. "It's okay," he said. "My folks feel like they already know you. But just to make it official, may I present my parents, Jonathon and Diane Clery. Mom and Dad, this is Lori's mother, Cici Burke. Bridget Tyndale, and Lindsay Wright."

Mark's parents had the easy good looks of old money worn casually—his father with the kind of chiseled features that were meant to be captured in oils, and his mother with the delicately polished patina of a real southern belle. They shook hands

101

all around, and both of the newcomers paused to admire the façade of the old house with genuine appreciation.

"Well, Lori's description didn't do it justice," remarked Jonathon. "This is a Jason Anderson design, isn't it? He only did a few private homes in Virginia, but this has to be one of them."

"Why, I think you're right," Bridget said, surprised. "I remember the name from the book," she explained to Cici.

Lindsay shared a quick appreciative look with Cici. "Imagine your knowing that," she said to Jonathon. "You know, the quickest way to impress us is to admire our house."

"I can't imagine you meet very many people who don't," said Diane, with genuine warmth. "How lucky you were to find this place! And just look at this view."

Lindsay turned to Cici and gave her a quick, waist-high two thumbs-up and a grin. She turned back to the Clerys. "I have to excuse myself," she said, once again shaking each one's hand. "I have a previous engagement, but I couldn't leave without meeting you both. I hope I'll see you again soon."

"Lori is a lucky young woman to have such good friends," said Jonathon.

And Diane added, "We'll be seeing a great deal of each other, I'm sure, and I'm looking forward to it."

Once again, Lindsay quickly turned her back on them and mouthed broadly to Cici, *Love! Them!* She briefly hugged Mark and then Lori, whispering in her ear, "Go, girl!" just before she said her final good-byes and hurried to her car.

"Where is Aunt Lindsay going?" Lori said, looking dismayed. "I thought she'd have Dominic here for lunch."

Cici said, with what she hoped was a meaningful look to Lori, "Dominic is taking Lindsay to brunch. You know, private time."

Lori's eyes lit up like a rainbow. "OMG! Aunt Lindsay and Dominic are *dating?*" She wrapped her arm around Mark's and exclaimed to him, "Do you have any idea what this could mean for the winery?"

Cici widened her eyes meaningfully at her daughter. "Don't you dare use that word in front of Lindsay."

She looked confused. "Winery?"

"Dating."

As Lindsay's car sped down the gravel dive, Bridget gestured everyone inside. "We've had a little trouble with the roof," Cici apologized, indicating the tarp.

Diane laughed lightly. "I should imagine that half the fun of owning a place like this is keeping up with the repairs."

"We don't always call it fun," Cici said, liking them both already. She gestured them up the front steps. "We have time for a tour, if you'd like. Come in."

"Mom, Mark and I are going to look at the winery," Lori said. "Don't start lunch without us."

"We haven't had a chance to do much cleaning down there," Bridget cautioned.

And Cici added, "Be careful in those heels."

"Oh dear," worried Bridget, "I didn't know the winery was going to be on the tour. We should have at least knocked down the spider webs."

Jonathon chuckled. "I suspect the two young people just wanted to be alone. A few spider webs won't even be noticed." He turned to survey the view from the porch, dropping his arm lightly around his wife's shoulders. "Look at that view. It's like something out of a pastoral painting, complete with sheep."

"They're usually much cleaner," Bridget volunteered, gazing uneasily at the huddled knot of ragged, muddy sheep, and the Clerys laughed.

"And is that the vineyard?" Jonathon asked.

"What's left of it," Cici said. "We'll be replanting in the spring."

Diane drew a soft breath of delight. "What a perfect backdrop for wedding photos! And that gazebo—it looks big enough for dancing."

Jonathon turned to them with a broad and contented smile. "Ladies, I must confess my envy. You are living our dream."

"Imagine that," murmured Bridget, sotto voce,

as Cici held open the front door and gestured the guests inside. "And they have a house in Maui."

Cici grinned at her and gave her a covert thumbs-up; then the two of them hurried inside.

Diane stopped in front of the tall curving staircase, her gaze moving slowly from the antique drop-crystal chandelier to the stained-glass window on the landing. Jonathon moved around the foyer and gazed into the parlor with leisured appreciation, stopping to caress the hand carved molding around the double doors or to admire the Charleston windows along the front. Cici started to lead the way upstairs, but Diane gripped Cici's hand tightly. Cici felt the cut of a two-carat diamond against her knuckles.

"Thank you," murmured Diane fervently, "for talking Lori out of the beach wedding. This is how I've always pictured my son's wedding. Exactly."

Cici decided then and there that she could definitely grow to like Mark's mother.

And then Diane added, "Now, I know you have everything all planned, so don't let me interfere. My goodness, didn't Lori tell me that you all do weddings professionally?"

"Oh no," exclaimed Bridget and Cici together, and Cici added, "It was just one time, last year. We really don't . . ."

"Oh, wonderful! Then you won't mind my saying that I think a garden wedding in September—with your view of the vineyard—

105

would be to die for! Of course, the weather is always a factor, but I couldn't help notice as we drove up what a beautiful view of the mountains you have from the west, and there's a little hill that would be perfect for the chuppah."

"Actually," Cici said, "that's exactly where . . ." She stopped. "The chuppah?"

"I don't know what you have in mind regarding size, but I want you to rest assured that we will *not* be crowding up the guest list with a lot of stuffy dignitaries. There is absolutely no one in the State House who owes us a favor or to whom we owe one—"

"Couldn't be happier to have all that behind us," added Jonathon.

"So we can easily keep the list down to family and friends. In fact, I just love what Chelsea and Marc did, which seems to me an almost perfect model of an interfaith marriage ceremony, don't you think?"

"Chelsea," repeated Cici, a little blankly. "Clinton? Chelsea Clinton?"

"In fact," Diane went on happily, "I see absolutely no reason why Lori's and our Mark's wedding couldn't be even lovelier. Our rabbi is wonderful about coordinating with other clergy, and we've already spoken with him, of course."

Bridget's eyes were as big as saucers. "Rabbi?"

"Don't worry, he doesn't mind making the trip at all," Diane assured her with a smile. "As long as he doesn't have to travel on the Sabbath. He's very strict about that. In fact, a good many people are, so I was hoping you would consider a Sunday afternoon, or even mid week. Of course we understand it's your wedding," she added, patting Cici's hand confidently, "so we're completely onboard with whatever you want to do about the reception, but I simply can't imagine a more beautiful place than this house. And if you need a caterer, I can recommend several out of Washington who are just fabulous. But what am I saying? I'm sure you must have a whole list."

Cici said, "Umm . . . I don't think Lori mentioned Mark was Jewish."

Diane smiled. "Didn't she? We have a lot to talk about, then."

Bridget said abruptly, "Excuse me. I have to check on something in the kitchen."

Cici tried to disguise a flash of panic as she watched her go. She took a breath and turned back to the couple. "So then," she said brightly, "would you like to see the upstairs?"

Cici left the Clerys in the parlor with a glass of wine and hurried to the kitchen, where she found Bridget frantically trying to pick out pieces of bacon from the beef bourguignon. "I swear I didn't know," she apologized, sounding a little desperate. "How could I not know?"

"You're gonna ruin that stew," said Ida Mae

flatly. "And what am I supposed to do with these vegetables? Everybody knows the only thing that gives winter vegetables their flavor is pork fat."

"The good news is they're reformed, not orthodox," Cici offered. "Maybe that's why Lori didn't mention it. Where is she anyway?" Cici looked around suspiciously, as though expecting her daughter to pop out from one of the cabinets. "I'm going to kill that girl."

"Reformed," repeated Bridget, looking harried. "What does that mean? Do they eat pork?"

"I don't think so," admitted Cici. "I don't know what it means. Maybe you don't have to be kosher."

Bridget told Ida Mae, "Serve the vegetables. Drain off the fat. And don't say a word." She popped the lid back on the casserole and slid it back into the oven.

"What about berry pie?" demanded Ida Mae sourly. "Do they eat pie?"

Cici and Bridget looked at one another, at a loss.

The back door opened and Mark and Lori came in, flushed and bright-eyed from the cold, laughing together.

"You," Cici demanded of Mark without hesitation, "did not tell me you were Jewish!"

"That's because I'm not," replied Mark easily. He took a piece of discarded bacon from the cutting board and popped it into his mouth. "My folks are."

"What does that *mean?*" cried Bridget. "You can't just be un-Jewish!"

Mark stared at her, another piece of bacon poised between thumb and forefinger, and Lori supplied impatiently, "What's the big deal? It's not like I'm going to convert or anything." Then, excitedly, "Listen, Aunt Bridget, I had the best idea. You don't have to have your restaurant in the barn. The dairy is a *much* better place! All those windows, the skylight . . ."

"It's already plumbed and wired," added Mark, "and those walls are solid stone. Easy to add an industrial-looking HVAC system that would fit right in, and you can't beat the ambience."

For a moment, both Cici and Bridget stared at them as though they had suddenly started speaking Greek. Then Bridget said, "The dairy is Lindsay's art studio."

"But she doesn't need that big space, and besides—"

"Wait." Cici threw up her hands as though to physically block the chatter. "The big deal is that this is a *wedding*. There are traditions, and rituals, and—and . . ."

"Ceremonies," supplied Bridget helpfully. "The ceremony is a huge part of a wedding."

"Neither one of us is very traditional," Mark replied easily, finishing off the bacon. "Whatever you guys come up with will be fine."

Lori nodded happily. "Really, Mom, the important

thing is that everyone has a good time, and people *always* have a good time at Ladybug Farm."

Mark added, "There's really not that much to it. My mom will help you out. Some chanting, breaking a glass . . ." He gave one of Lori's curls a playful tug. "A lot of dancing."

She grinned up at him. "Are you going to wear a yarmulke?"

He plucked the fedora off her head and placed it on his own. "How do I look?"

She giggled and snatched at the hat; he ducked and bobbed behind the kitchen island. Cici stepped between them before the game got out of hand, returned Lori's hat firmly to her own head, and thrust a plate of stuffed dates into Mark's hands.

"Go," Cici said sternly, giving both of them a little shove, "and keep our guests company in the parlor."

Lori said, "But aren't you . . ."

"In a minute," Cici said. "Go."

When the swinging door closed behind them, Cici sank back against the counter and released a breath. "Kosher?" she said, indicating the dates.

Bridget replied, "I have absolutely no idea."

Ida Mae nudged Bridget aside as she opened the oven to put a loaf of twice-risen herb bread inside. "You know what the good thing about being the cook is?" she said flatly. She shoved the pan far to the back of the oven and slammed the door shut.

"When people come to your table, they eat what you serve."

Cici looked at Bridget. Bridget lifted her eyebrows and tilted her head. "I hope that includes berry pie," she said, "because that's all I've got."

Cici blew out a breath and tucked her arm through Bridget's. "Come on," she suggested. "Let's go find out."

"Anyway, they were very nice about it," Cici concluded to Lindsay as the late afternoon shadows once again gathered on the porch. "About our ignorance, I mean, not about them being Jewish. I could have wrung Lori's neck. You'd think she might have mentioned a little thing like an interfaith ceremony before she invited the in-laws out to plan the wedding."

"And to think, I almost made a ham." Bridget shuddered.

"Wow," said Lindsay. "Who would have guessed? They seemed so . . . southern."

Bridget gave her a superior look. "There is a huge Jewish community in the South."

"Well, I guess I know that," Lindsay replied defensively. "I was thrown off by the southern accent. I mean, seriously, I almost asked her when she had her cotillion."

Bridget smothered a giggle, and even Cici couldn't repress a rather lopsided grin. "It turns out they're reformed, not orthodox," she explained. "Which basically means Mark was raised Jewish, but he doesn't practice."

"But he still has to be married in the Jewish faith," added Bridget.

"About which I know absolutely nothing," admitted Cici. "Fortunately, none of this seems to bother Lori. And how can you not like someone who spent the whole day talking about how much they envy you? They're already making plans for us all to go on a wine-tasting tour of upstate New York this summer."

The day had turned into one of those bright winter surprises, with temperatures in the fifties and a brassy sun flinging shards of light across a cobalt sky. Bambi, the deer who had followed Lindsay home from a walk one day and stayed for three years, ambled across the lawn, sniffing out shoots of green grass and dried acorns. As the lowering sun formed bleached-white pools of warmth across the porch, the ladies instinctively stretched out their legs toward it, leaning back in their rockers, loosening scarves and unbuttoning jackets.

"So," invited Cici, sliding a glance toward Lindsay, "how was your day?"

The corners of Lindsay's lips twitched in what might have been private memory. "Fine. Nice, actually. The B&B isn't nearly as nice as our house, of course, but they did something really interesting with the front foyer—which is about half the size of this porch—they turned it into a little art gallery. They had some interesting pieces—wildlife, florals, that kind of thing—so naturally I mentioned Noah to the manager, and she wants him to bring in some of his work. Then, Dominic just about embarrassed the life out of me by telling her I was an artist, too, and had actually hung my work in a Washington gallery—without mentioning, of course, that my best friend was the owner and that no one could have been more shocked than he was when someone actually offered him money for my painting—so naturally she had to insist that I bring in something to show her." She shrugged, looking less embarrassed than secretly pleased. "Maybe I will. I mean, my painting of the fox in the berry bushes is twice as good as any of the wildlife she had in there, and of course, Noah's work will make everything else on her walls look like paint by number."

"Well, what do you know about that?" Cici said. "See, aren't you glad you went?"

"Good for you!" Bridget added. "Or I should say, good for Dominic. Sounds like you have a fan."

Lindsay colored faintly. "Well, it was kind of exciting," she admitted. "Of course, nothing will probably come of it, but now that I've lost my gallery . . ." She grinned a little. "It would be nice to think of my work hanging somewhere besides my studio.

"The restaurant was darling," she went on, "but really small, and kind of cutesy-pie. Nothing like yours is going to be, Bridge. Blue willow every-where, lace tablecloths. I had shrimp and grits and Dominic had steak and pommes frites—that's what they called the french fries on the menu. And, oh!—listen to this. They only serve Virginia wines, so naturally, Dominic told them about ours and we already have a customer! So it definitely wasn't a wasted day."

Bridget and Cici exchanged a look. "Well," said Cici, "as long as it wasn't wasted."

Bridget prompted impatiently, "So? What did you talk about?"

"Oh, lots of things. The winery, mostly. How I'd decorate the tasting room. What things were like in the old days."

"And?"

"And what?"

"Didn't you talk about anything personal?"

"Depends on what you mean by personal. He told me some stuff about his life; I told him some stuff about mine. Funny how you can know a person for a long time and not really know much about him at all." She was thoughtful for a moment. "You know, it's really kind of an odd feeling, being around someone who hasn't already known me most of my adult life and who's interested in learning things about me. When I tell them, it makes me see myself, and my life,

114

differently. Have you ever thought about how seldom we get to do that?"

"That's true," agreed Cici. "I guess people our age tend to hold on to the friends they have, and we're not looking to make new ones. But it's fun to see yourself through someone's eyes."

"And so?" Bridget reached across Cici and poked Lindsay with her index finger. "What's the situation? Are you dating or not?"

Lindsay wrinkled her nose. "Dating is one of the few remaining legal forms of torture. You have to color your hair every three weeks instead of every month and shave your legs even in the winter and worry about sucking in your stomach all the time. Who needs it?"

Bridget feigned surprise. "What? You color your hair?"

"You only have to shave your legs," added Cici mildly, "if you plan on taking off your pants. And as for sucking in your stomach, they make shape wear for that."

Lindsay gave her a very dark look. "Shape wear. Another reason dating is not for sissies. Besides, we have more important things to worry about than my social life."

"If you're talking about the wedding," Bridget assured her blithely, "we have it under control. Now that we know what we're working with, that is."

Lindsay gave her a meaningful look. "Famous last words. Remember last year's wedding?"

"That was different," Bridget said, although she looked a little uneasy. "Those people were awful."

"The rooster attacked the bride," Lindsay reminded her. "The goat ate the wedding favors. The pressure cooker exploded . . ."

Cici smothered a grin. "They deserved it."

"And then," concluded Lindsay triumphantly, "there was a tornado! So just don't get so smug. Nothing is ever under control around here. Looks like you'd know that by now. So," she invited, turning to Cici, "tell all. What are her colors? How many guests? How big is the wedding party? Has she picked a maid of honor? What about the dress?"

Cici pulled a strained face. "Oddly enough, her future mother-in-law and I had those very same questions."

"Lori didn't bring her book," Bridget explained.

"Lori doesn't *have* a book," corrected Cici. "Turns out she's—and I quote—not much of a wedding book kind of girl."

Lindsay looked skeptical. "Every bride has a book. She probably just hasn't had time to put it together yet."

"But we did make some progress," Bridget said. "It's definitely going to be a garden wedding . . ."

"Uh-oh," murmured Lindsay. "You're just asking for trouble with that one."

"With the chuppah up on the little hill exactly where we had the canopy last year, only facing the other direction so that the vineyard is in the background instead of the sheep meadow."

"It will snow," predicted Lindsay confidently. "Or maybe the sheep will escape and maraud the wedding party."

"It's going to be an interfaith ceremony," Bridget went on, undeterred, "just like Chelsea Clinton and Marc Mezvinsky's. I just love the Jewish wedding ceremony. Did you know it's one of the oldest wedding ceremonies in the western world? Well," she corrected herself, "the Greek Orthodox ceremony may have elements that are older, but as a whole, the traditional Judaic wedding tradition has been passed down virtually unchanged for over four thousand years. Makes you think, doesn't it?"

Lindsay slid her a skeptical look. "How do you *know* these things?"

Bridget shrugged complacently. "I read it somewhere."

In a moment, Cici said, "I don't think Lori has even noticed that she's marrying out of her faith. And I don't think Mark cares at all one way or another. I think what bothers me is not that she didn't tell me, but that she didn't even think it was important enough to mention. How seriously can she be taking this, anyway?"

"Oh, I wouldn't worry about that," Bridget assured her. "Kids these days are not as concerned about those things as we were."

"Well," said Lindsay, "it's really not surprising. They're exposed to so much more at an early age than any generation before them. The whole world is at their fingertips, and the transition from one culture to another doesn't seem nearly as dramatic. That's not necessarily a bad thing."

"I don't know," said Cici. "I think it's important to be raised in a culture with strong traditions. It helps define who you are."

"Studies have proven that children who are raised with a strong religious background grow up to have better overall mental and physical health as adults than those who aren't," Lindsay said. "It doesn't matter whether they practice that same religion when they're grown up or not. Just the childhood background is what makes the difference."

The other two considered that for a moment, rocking. "Where did you learn that?" Cici asked curiously.

Lindsay shrugged. "Church, I guess."

"Speaking of church . . ." They all turned their heads toward the sound of a vehicle turning into the driveway, the sound they had all been waiting for, without bothering to acknowledge it even to themselves, for the past hour. A black-and-white streak dashed across the lawn and halfway down the drive, barking furiously, then abruptly veered off toward the sheep meadow.

Lindsay looked at her watch. "Really," she said,

"I know he could do a lot worse than Amy, and I should be glad he's spending so much time in a wholesome environment, but we have *got* to get those last college applications finished up tonight."

Cici looked surprised. "You mean they're still not done?"

Lindsay shook her head. "I've never seen him procrastinate like this before. Writing is not his strongest subject," she confided, "and I know he's struggling with the essay. I offered to help him, but . . ." Again, she shook her head. "I'm just not sure he understands how important this is."

"Noah has turned into a very responsible young man," Bridget said firmly as the car, with Noah at the wheel, pulled around the drive toward the garage at the back of the house. "And he has you to thank for that. He always does the right thing in the end."

Lindsay tried to look reassured. "I'm just afraid by the time 'in the end' gets here, the application deadline will have passed."

They heard the car door slam, and in another moment Noah came bounding up the steps. "Afternoon, ladies," he said cheerfully. "Taking in the sunshine, I see. That's good for people your age. Builds strong bones."

"Hey!" objected Bridget with a frown. "How old do you think we are, anyway?"

Noah grinned and lightly tossed the car keys to

Cici. "Thanks for the use of the car. I gassed it up on the way home."

"Thank you, Noah," said Cici. "It was thoughtful of you to save an old woman a trip to the pump. I might have broken a hip swiping my credit card."

She held out her hand and he said, "Right." He dug into his jeans pocket and returned her credit card to her. "Forty-two fifty on the pump," he said.

Cici groaned. "I have *got* to get a car with better mileage."

"Or a smaller gas tank," suggested Noah. He settled one hip on the porch railing, swinging his foot. "Is everyone gone already?"

"Don't worry, you missed them," Cici said.

"You're missing a lot of things lately," Lindsay added pointedly.

He shrugged pleasantly. "I'm a busy guy."

Lindsay opened her mouth to reply, but Bridget spoke over her. "Did you have a good time?"

"Yeah, it was great. They had chicken and dressing for lunch. Not as good as yours, of course," he was quick to add, "but not bad. Then we all went over to the youth center and watched this movie about three kids on drugs who saw an angel and straightened up. Then we went to choir practice. I'm thinking about taking up the guitar. Amy says I have the hands for it." He spread out his fingers and examined them in the light. "What do you think?"

"I think," replied Lindsay, "those hands could be put to very good use finishing up your college essay."

"Almost finished," he assured her.

"I'm not kidding, Noah, this is important. We're already taking a huge chance on not getting financial aid and you can't keep putting this off."

" 'To everything there is a season'," he told her, " 'and a time for every purpose under heaven.' Ecclesiastes 3:1."

He sprang down from the rail and said, "I'm going to change clothes and feed the animals. I hope the company left some pie. I'm starved."

"Don't ruin your supper," Lindsay called after him, turning in her chair. "And we're not finished with this subject."

At the door he paused and looked back. "Um, listen," he said, "I've been thinking and . . . well, I was wondering if I could talk to you about something."

All three women turned. There was an odd look in his eyes that was impossible to miss, as though he wanted to say something and didn't quite know how. Lindsay encouraged, "Sure. What is it?"

He seemed to gather up his courage. "Well, the thing is . . ." Then he hesitated and faltered. His gaze went from one to the other of them, then dropped to his shoes. He cleared his throat and looked back up again. When he spoke next there was no doubt in anyone's mind that it was not what he had originally intended to say. "I've got a chance to pick up a few extra bucks cleaning up after church services, vacuuming and polishing the pews and whatnot. It's only a couple of hours a week, but you know I'm saving for a car and every little bit helps. I was wondering if it would be okay if I took it on until they find somebody permanent."

Lindsay waited for him to say more, and when he didn't, she glanced at Cici and Bridget, then looked back to Noah. "You already have one after-school job," she pointed out, "and I was counting on you to help me with an art project I've been thinking about. But I'll tell you what. When you get your college essay finished, we'll talk about it."

He looked relieved. "Okay, sure. Thanks."

"Noah?" Lindsay stopped him as he started inside. "Was there anything else?"

His expression was perfectly innocent. "Nope, that's it." He tossed her a quick grin and a salute. " 'Who can find a virtuous woman?' " he declared. " 'For her price is far above rubies.' Proverbs 31:10."

They waited until Noah was gone to share another long, puzzled look. Then Cici ventured, "What was all that about?"

"I don't think it was about virtuous women," Bridget said, looking troubled.

"And I can pretty much bet it wasn't about

saving up for a car." Lindsay's tone was grim. "If that girl is pregnant, I will kill them both."

"You won't have to," Cici said. "Her daddy will do it for you. Besides, I don't think it's about Amy." When Lindsay looked at her hopefully, she explained simply, "He wasn't nearly scared enough."

Bridget nodded in agreement and Lindsay cautiously relaxed. "Still . . ." Bridget's expression was thoughtful. "Have you noticed every time you bring up college he changes the subject?"

"Have I ever." Lindsay frowned. "But this can't be about college. We had that conversation last year when we first started getting the applications together. He was excited about it. It was all he could talk about for weeks, remember? The whole thing about getting a car was so that he could have it to get back and forth while he's away at school."

"What if it's not about college," suggested Bridget, "but about the *kind* of college? All this time he spends at church, his sudden interest in memorizing the Bible . . . What if he has a, well, a vocation?"

The other two women stared at her with absolutely blank expressions, not understanding at all, or perhaps choosing not to. Finally, Cici said, "Are you talking about—seminary?"

Bridget nodded. "It would explain a lot. You have your heart set on him going into the arts, but what if that's not his calling?"

Lindsay started to laugh, thought better of it, stared at her friend in disbelief, and then sank, loose-boned, back into her chair. "Noah, a minister. Well, you should pardon the expression, but Jesus take me now, because I've heard everything."

"It's probably just a phase," Cici said, but she looked uncertain.

"What if it's not?" said Bridget.

Lindsay seemed to turn that over in her mind for a moment. "Well, there's only one way to find out," she decided, pushing up from her chair. "I'll ask him."

"I wouldn't do that," Cici said, and Bridget chorused at the same time. "Bad idea."

"Why not?"

"It's not your call to make, for one thing," Cici told her frankly. "He's eighteen. He's worked hard to get this far and he has the right to make his own decision about where he's going to college."

Lindsay said, "Wait a minute. Why does that sound familiar?"

"Because it's the speech you gave to Noah when we all first talked about college last year. I liked it."

"He'll talk to you about it," Bridget assured her, "when he's ready."

Lindsay rubbed her arms against the chill of the dropping sun, looking torn. "Nothing ever turns out the way you expect, does it?"

"What would be the fun in that?" Cici said.

"Ida Mae made fresh bread this morning," offered Bridget, trying to cheer her. "What do you say we warm up the leftover bourguignon and have supper in front of the fire with a great big glass of wine?"

"No, thanks," said Lindsay with a sigh. "I'm on a diet."

Cici lifted an eyebrow. "When did that start?"

Lindsay looked at her watch glumly. "About two hours ago." She opened the door. "The good news is I can have any flavor gelatin I want."

Cici and Bridget hung back as Lindsay went inside, sharing a smile. "She is so dating," Bridget said.

And Cici agreed, "Oh, yeah."

They followed their friend inside and closed the door on the fading day.

Chapter Seven

Wine and Roses

The three friends huddled together in the freezing drizzle, their umbrella tops bumping, while Paul and Derrick posed for the camera a few feet away, a spray-painted gold shovel between them. Their heavy ribbed sweaters were frosted with moisture and their faces chapped with cold, but their determined smiles never wavered as

Lindsay counted down, "Three . . . two . . . one . . . Got it!" She checked the display on her digital camera and held it up to them as both men hurried over.

"I don't know," Derrick worried. "It's kind of dark."

"That's because it's s-s-seven thirty in the morning and raining," Bridget said, trying to keep her teeth from chattering.

"The light's not going to get any better, fellows," Cici agreed. "And those guys on the backhoe are going to go home if it gets much wetter. Do you want to break ground or take pictures?"

"Okay," Paul agreed. "Just one more of us turning over a shovelful of dirt." They hurried back to their spot, and all three women smiled indulgently as he called back, "This is for posterity!"

The property was beautiful, even on a wet, gray winter day. Acres of rolling meadow—currently a well-mown shade of brown—were sectioned with crisp white paddock fencing along a curving hard-packed drive that led from the county road to the small knoll upon which they now stood. A perfect rectangle, approximately 40x30, had been staked out with yellow tape, flanked by two smaller rectangles, 10x20, at diagonal corners. To the east, a tall oak, naked now but no less formidable, stood sentry, and to the west, a blue mountain faded into the sky.

To the north, a yellow backhoe chugged

impatiently, waiting to dig the foundation, while a crew stood around their pickup trucks and smoked cigarettes.

Lindsay snapped the perfect picture of the two of them crouched down to lift a shovelful of dirt while grinning into the camera. "Okay," she called, waving them over. "You're ready for Twitter. Let's go home."

"Don't you want the grand tour?" Paul invited while Derrick busily polished the mud off the shovel with a towel.

The women looked from the square of tape to the impatient heavy machinery operator. "Well . . ."

"It'll just take a minute," Paul insisted, grabbing Cici's arm. When the engine behind him revved up, he turned and shouted, "Who's paying your salary?" To Cici he confided, "You've got to know how to talk to these roughnecks." And she smothered a grin.

"How did you ever get a heavy-equipment operator to come out on a nasty day like this?" Bridget asked, stepping carefully over puddles and holding on to Lindsay's arm as she negotiated the soggy ground in her spike-heeled boots.

"No choice," Derrick answered. "It's Valentine's Day. Can you think of a more auspicious day for breaking ground?"

"One of the luckiest days of the year," Paul added. "Only good things happen on St. Valentine's Day."

"Well, except for St. Valentine himself," Lindsay pointed out. "Wasn't he martyred?"

"And there's that whole St. Valentine's Day massacre," Cici added.

Paul swept them both with a single dismissing look. "St. Valentine is the internationally recognized symbol of hope and love, guaranteed to bring good luck to any project dealing with home and family."

"Where did you hear that?" Bridget asked.

Cici said, "Since when did you guys become so superstitious? First it was feng shui; now it's Valentine's Day luck . . ."

"It's not superstition," Derrick corrected her. "It's caution. This is our dream home, and we don't intend to take any chances."

"So you paid the guys extra to work in the rain?" Cici suggested.

"We told them they'd get a full day's wages for an hour's work if they'd break ground this morning," Paul admitted. "All they have to do is start the foundation and then they can go home."

"Ah," said Lindsay with a sage nod. Bridget glanced nervously over her shoulder as the backhoe engine chugged to life.

"Now here," Paul said, ignoring the sounds of impatience behind them and pointing toward one of the diagonal squares, "is the front lanai, centered around the koi pond with a screened gazebo and wet bar."

"And Moroccan fountain," Derrick called over to him. "Don't forget the fountain."

"Right," Paul said, and something about his expression suggested the fountain was still under discussion.

"Now . . ." He held down the tape for the ladies to step over and made a sweeping gesture with his arm. "Imagine you're standing in a grand foyer, twenty foot ceilings, marble floors, floating staircase to your right . . ."

"And the chandelier," Derrick reminded him. "Ten feet wide, chrome and crystal," he told the ladies.

"Right," Paul murmured again. He led them on. "And here, a cozy library, floor-to-ceiling book-shelves . . . The great room with tri-fold doors opening up onto this view . . ." A gesture took in the white-fenced pasture and distant mountain. "And here, the chef's kitchen. Poured concrete countertops here, big horseshoe island here . . ."

"Brazilian cherry floors throughout," added Derrick.

"Brazilian cherry," agreed Paul, "except for this center section here, which will be a cut out of tumbled stone."

"But *not* limestone," said Derrick, and he turned to Bridget. "Can you imagine? The first time you spilled red wine or bolognaise sauce . . ." He shuddered.

Paul ignored him and took several giant steps

forward, swinging open another set of imaginary doors. "Here . . ." He had to raise his voice to be heard over the sound of the backhoe's approaching engine. "The *pièce de résistance*. The outdoor kitchen, huge fireplace here, pergola covered with grape vines, and three steps down . . . the pool and hot tub grotto."

By now he was almost shouting, and Bridget looked over her shoulder nervously. "I think they really want to get to work."

"Just a minute," Lindsay said, focusing the camera. "I want to get a shot of the pool."

"And you haven't even seen the upstairs yet," said Derrick.

"Or the wine cellar," added Paul.

"Very funny."

"We're going to put in an organic garden over there," Derrick said, indicating a spot to their right, "and plant fruit trees all along the pasture fence."

"That's a lot of work," shouted Cici.

The backhoe began to scrape off a section of one of the diagonal squares.

"And horses," added Paul, gazing serenely over the pasture.

"Do you know how to ride?" asked Lindsay.

He looked at her as though surprised by the irrelevance of the question. "Well, no. But this is horse country. This is a horse pasture. Must have horses."

"Horses are pretty high maintenance," Cici pointed out. She covered her ears against the roaring and grinding of gears behind her.

Derrick spread his hands benevolently. "What else do we have to do?"

"And the best part is," Paul said, "we're only a month behind schedule."

"You're going to be further behind than that," Bridget said, grabbing each of them firmly by the arm, "if you don't get out of the way!"

They hurried across the muddy, uneven ground toward their cars, but just before they reached them, Paul exclaimed, "One more picture!"

In the end, Lindsay charmed one of the construction workers into snapping a photo of the five of them standing in front of the house site, hands raised to frame the backhoe in the background. That was the one that made it to Twitter.

Though Derrick and Paul might have been some-what behind in their project, at Ladybug Farm, matters were moving along with surprising—almost suspicious—ease. January had been unusually mild, and Dominic, with the assistance of Farley's tractor, had trenched the cuttings that would become their new vines in the spring and had hand-tilled the soil for aeration. They had met twice with the lawyer, Frank Adams, and once with the nice young man at the bank who was in charge of small business loans. He seemed very impressed with their business plan, with the fact that a well-known vintner and highly respected county extension agent like Dominic was onboard, and seemed appreciative of the extra pages Lori insisted they add to the business plan, which detailed the amount of projected revenue in terms of seasonal jobs and tourism the winery would bring to the county. They signed documents of incorporation and opened a business bank account with the minimum deposit allowable by law. They applied for licenses. And on warm days, Bridget could be found in the barn, stepping off measurements and making sketches for her new restaurant.

Noah actually completed his college applications and got them in the mail—before, unfortunately, allowing Lindsay to proofread his essay. Though the promise of a second job appeared to be the incentive he needed to complete the essay, he didn't seem too disappointed when the job at the church went to someone else before he could apply for it. When school started again, he got caught up in the basketball schedule and the usual senior class mania, working after school at the hardware store in town, and seeing Amy on the weekends. He didn't win the rodeo tickets—Amy did—but with such an overage of stored-up Bible verses, the scripture quoting did not slow down much. Lindsay admitted to Cici and Bridget privately that, even though she felt guilty for it, she was relieved when weeks went by and Noah didn't mention anything about considering a calling to the ministry. Bridget, apparently, had been wrong.

Dominic had become even more of a fixture around the house than he was before, and sometimes he spent the afternoons with Lindsay in her studio, helping her sketch out what he remembered of the tasting room mural. Other times, Lindsay would walk with him through the vineyard, helping him check the dormant vines. Dominic had a small house and a couple of acres nearby, complete with horses, a dog, and a garden. On weekends he sometimes took Lindsay trail riding, and if the day wasn't too cold, they packed a picnic. He became a regular at Sunday dinner and always brought an interesting wine for them to taste.

Lori decided on a theme for her wedding—vineyard—which came as a surprise to no one, and had set a definite date: Tuesday, September 10 at 2:00 p.m. She still hadn't chosen her attendants, flowers, a color scheme, or invitations. She hadn't registered anywhere. However, she had made plans to come this weekend while Paul was here to look at wedding gown sketches. That was huge.

In fact, everything at Ladybug Farm was going smoothly for the first time since they moved in. Everything except one.

"I see you're making progress on the roof,"

Derrick observed as they returned home from the photo shoot.

The damage to the roof had expanded from a one-tarp job to one requiring three tarps when the roofers began to tear off the clay tiles that were such a decorative part of the old house's appeal and discovered water damage that appeared to have accumulated over a quarter of a century. Weather delays—and the fact that the roofing crew appeared to be unable to work more than two hours a day or two days in a row—had resulted in the bright blue roofing tarp becoming a more or less permanent feature of their front entrance.

"Don't get me started," Cici said.

"Don't get her started," agreed Bridget, carrying in a tray of coffee and cups from the kitchen. Ida Mae followed with a basket of cinnamon rolls that filled the room with the aroma of cinnamon and yeast.

"Ida Mae, you are an angel!" declared Derrick, reaching for the basket.

She twisted away from him, sheltering the basket with her arm and looking at him suspiciously. "I thought you was a on a diet."

"It's worth dying for," he assured her, "if the last thing I taste is this bit of heaven on earth. Besides, cinnamon is great for the cholesterol."

"I could have rebuilt the entire roof by now," Cici said, beginning to fume. "By myself."

"Which is one thing we're really trying to

avoid." Lindsay flipped up the sections of the pie table beside the fireplace in the parlor, and Bridget set the tray on it. Ida Mae, still regarding Derrick suspiciously, followed with the cinnamon rolls.

Paul came into the room carrying a bottle of Montrachet decorated with a red bow and a huge heart-shaped box of chocolates wrapped in pink satin. "Happy Valentine's Day, girls!" he declared, and kissed each of them on the cheek while they exclaimed over the chocolates. "And thanks for your hospitality once again."

"Are you kidding? The worst thing about having you move here is that you won't be staying with us anymore."

"And bringing presents," added Lindsay, eagerly opening the candy. "Are there any red ones?"

"Red whats?" asked Derrick, watching her lift the layer separator to search the bottom chocolates.

"Candies," explained Bridget, pouring coffee. "Today is her red day."

"She's on the color wheel diet," explained Cici. "You can only eat one color of food each day, and every day is a different color."

Paul nodded sagely, accepting the cup of coffee Bridget offered. "Perfectly appropriate for an artist."

"Today is the red day."

"Aha," said Derrick. "Beets, apples, rutabagas . . ."

"And cherries!" exclaimed Lindsay, triumphantly holding up a chocolate-covered cherry.

Cici held out her hand. "I'll take the chocolate. You keep the cherry."

Looking a little disappointed, Lindsay handed over the candy. "At least the wine is red."

The two men watched in fascination as Cici peeled off the chocolate layer and returned the cherry to Lindsay. "So how's it working for you?" Derrick asked.

Lindsay shrugged and popped the cherry into her mouth. "I've gained three pounds." She passed the box of chocolates to Bridget.

"You look like a goddess to me," declared Paul gallantly, and she blew him a kiss.

Bridget selected a chocolate and passed the box to Ida Mae. She took it with a sniff of disapproval. "Eating candy this time of day. You got no more sense than a bunch of young'uns." Nonetheless, she searched the box until she found a candy whose size and shape appealed to her, and while she did, Derrick helped himself to a cinnamon roll.

"Umm," Bridget said, biting into her chocolate. "Amaretto."

"Might've known there'd be booze in it," observed Ida Mae darkly. She bit into a chocolate and handed the box to Cici.

Bridget passed Derrick a cup of coffee. "You should call our builder about your roof," Derrick told Cici, digging a card out of his pocket before he sat down. "He's supposed to be one of the best in the county."

Cici licked the last of the chocolate off her fingers and studied the card. "Hmm." She passed the card to Bridget. "I don't believe I've heard of him. That must be because he's fair, honest, and skilled. We prefer to deal with overpriced liars who don't know what they're doing."

Bridget rolled her eyes. "I told you not to get her started."

"We must have talked to twenty different contractors," Paul told her, "and he was the only one who would even talk about taking on the job. He wasn't stumped by anything, either—the pool, the sauna, the bathtub on the balcony . . ."

Bridget lifted her eyebrows. "You're putting your bathtub on the balcony?"

Paul nodded, reaching for a cinnamon roll. "There's a balcony off the master bath just big enough for a claw foot tub. It's very Fiji-esque."

"Not to mention picturesque," added Derrick. "We're going to glaze it green, with gold-leaf claw feet. Sitting up there amidst all those trees . . . a slice of heaven."

"We got the idea from a picture in *Architectural Digest*."

"Craziest damn fool thing I ever heard of," Ida Mae said. "Y'all are gonna freeze up there in the winter."

Her steel-toed boots clomped their disapproval on the way out—pausing only once to select another chocolate—and Paul and Derrick just grinned at each other.

Bridget slipped the card into one of the drawers of the escritoire that stood beside the door to the parlor. "She's got a point."

"Did you bring the wedding gown sketches?" Cici asked Paul. "Lori said she'd be here by ten." She glanced at the grandfather clock in the corner. "Which of course means she'll be here by lunch."

"I did better," Paul said, wiping his fingers on a napkin as he stood. "I brought samples."

"Why did Lori choose Valentine's Day weekend to look at wedding dress sketches?" Derrick asked as Paul went to the foyer to retrieve the samples. "Don't she and Mark have a romantic evening planned? They're not fighting, are they?"

"She said they had their Valentine's Day early," Cici replied. "Mark gave her a dozen roses and a teddy bear with a diamond necklace around its neck."

"Nice," said Derrick with an appreciative lift of his eyebrow. He reached for another cinnamon roll and Bridget discreetly nudged the basket out of his reach.

"They never fight," she said. "They're far too practical."

"What do they have to fight about?" Derrick observed. "He's giving her diamonds and they're not even out of college yet. What a world we live in."

"Bottom line," Lindsay said, rummaging in the chocolate box for another cherry, "Mark had to study this weekend and Lori's mother has been driving her crazy about getting the wedding plans started, so . . ."

"I have not been driving her crazy."

"Her words, not mine."

"Anyway," Cici said, "I think the real reason she's coming down is to see Dominic about something. Why, I don't know. She talks to him more often than she does to me. Whatever. I'm just glad to have her within lassoing distance. If I have to tie her to a chair . . . Oh, my."

Heads turned in the direction of her gaze and all three women caught their breaths as Paul unzipped the garment bag he carried with a flourish, and a virtual cornucopia of white lace and satin spilled out. Derrick took the opportunity to refill his coffee and help himself to a second cinnamon roll.

"One of the often-overlooked perks of being an award-winning style columnist syndicated in every major newspaper in the country *and* six magazines," Paul admitted modestly as he extracted the bridal gowns, one by glorious one. "I also brought seventeen back issues of *Bride* magazine and a complete guide to color selection from The Knot.com. Wipe your fingers, ladies," he admonished as the three women descended on the gowns with muffled exclamations of delight. "They won't take them back with chocolate stains."

"This one," exclaimed Cici, snatching up a frothy confection of chiffon and ribbons.

"No, this one." Bridget chose a high-necked sheath covered in lace with a thousand fabric buttons down the back. "Very Kate Middleton." She held it up to herself for inspection.

Lindsay selected a strapless, brocaded bodice gown with a dropped-waist A-line skirt that fell into a modest bell train. "This," she said, fitting it around her torso, "is Lori."

Everyone smiled at her. "Try it on," Cici urged.

Lindsay protested, but not very hard. Ten minutes later, they all gathered at the bottom of the stairs as she descended, her hair upswept to show off her bare shoulders, the ivory fabric shaping her long waist and flaring to the perfect train behind her. Bridget applauded, and Cici pressed her clasped hands to her lips, beaming.

"You're a vision!" Derrick declared, while Paul hurried up the stairs to adjust the fall of the train.

"Look how big my boobs are!" she exclaimed, grinning. "Who knew?"

"Exactly what I want for my daughter on her wedding day," replied Cici. "Gigantic boobs spilling out of her dress."

"It's all in the cut of the gown," Paul explained.

"I could only zip it up half way," Lindsay added. "If I turn around you'll see my bra."

"Especially designed to enhance boobage," Paul pointed out. "It goes with the dress."

"That's okay," Bridget said beaming. "Lori is two sizes smaller than you. She'll look like a princess in it." Ignoring Lindsay's small frown, she looked a little closer. "Wait a minute. Is that a Vera Wang?"

"But of course," Paul replied, fussing with the train.

"Paul, we can't afford a Vera Wang!" Cici said, dismayed.

Paul peeked around Lindsay. "What part of 'sample' did you not understand, sweetness? I can get this for a steal, if this is the one our princess chooses. And . . ." He stood back to critique his work. "Why wouldn't she?"

Cici glanced at Bridget, and a secret smile tugged at her lips. "She would look like a princess, wouldn't she?"

"I don't know." Lindsay tugged uncomfortably at the top of the dress. "Now I'm starting to think you're right. Maybe this bra is too much."

"You look gorgeous," Derrick assured her from the bottom of the stairs, "bra or no bra."

"I'll say." Another male voice joined the murmurs of agreement, and Lindsay looked up from tugging at the bodice to see Dominic standing at the arched entrance that led to the dining room. He held a potted plant of some sort in his hand, and his expression was both bemused and appreciative. "Is there something I should know?"

Lindsay reached behind her to grasp the two parts of her dress, exclaiming "Dominic! I didn't know you were here. I was just helping Lori pick a dress . . . I mean, helping Cici help Lori pick a dress . . ."

Bridget turned to Dominic, smiling as she gestured to the plant he held. "What's this?"

It took him a moment to pull his attention away from Lindsay. "Umm, it's a rose bush. I forced the buds so it should bloom the rest of the winter in your sunroom. You can plant it as soon as the ground warms up."

"How sweet," Cici exclaimed, extending her hands for it. There was a teasing twinkle in her eyes as she lowered her voice a fraction and added, "But you really don't have to court us all, Dominic. Bridget and I already like you."

"So do we," volunteered Derrick, deadpan. "Don't we Paul?"

"Well, that depends," replied Paul, peeking around Lindsay. "What kind of rose is it?"

The corner of Dominic's mouth turned down dryly, proving he could take a joke. "The kind a man gives to the lady he's hoping to take to dinner on Valentine's Day."

Lindsay drew a breath for a reply, but Paul

interceded with a disapproving look. "You're asking her to dinner at ten in the morning? On Valentine's Day? I doubt very much she's available."

Lindsay spared Paul a quick scowl and a little backwards kick with her bare foot.

Dominic held the plant up toward Lindsay. "I know how you enjoy your rose garden," he said. "I grafted this last fall from American Beauty stock with two different floribundas. It has a blossom that's almost the color of your hair. So I'm calling it the Lindsay rose."

"Now that," admitted Paul, "is what I call a romantic gesture. Maybe she's available for dinner after all."

A faint pleased flush came to Lindsay's cheeks when he said that, and it made Dominic smile. Lindsay started down the stairs, but Paul caught a handful of fabric in his fist, holding her back. "Bra," he reminded her.

She tugged away from him, and with one hand pulling at the front of the dress and the other holding it together in back, she came down the stairs. When she reached Dominic, he said softly, "Now that is a pretty sight." Lindsay started to reach for the flower with her left hand and then with her right and was saved from an embarrassing slip of fabric when Bridget stepped in and scooped the plant from Dominic's hands.

"I'll put it in the sunroom," she said.

"That was nice," Lindsay told him. "I never had a rose named after me before."

"And I think that's a crime," Dominic replied.

They stood smiling at each other for a moment, and everyone else stood watching them indulgently, until Cici cleared her throat and stepped forward purposefully.

"Come have some coffee while Lindsay changes." Cici slipped her arm through Dominic's and turned him toward the parlor. "We didn't hear you drive up."

Lindsay cast her a grateful look and turned to hurry up the stairs, while Paul gallantly spread his arms to shield her bare back.

"I probably should have called first," Dominic said, "but I got a text from Lori asking me to meet her here at ten. She's awfully excited about something. I figured she cleared it with you."

"You text," observed Cici with an admiring expression. "I've got to learn how to do that."

"Where are you taking Lindsay for dinner?" Derrick asked.

"Wherever it is, I hope they serve red food," added Bridget, returning. Then, "Lori just drove up."

Cici's eyebrows flew to her bangs. "What do you know about that? She's on time!"

Lori blew in on a gust of cold damp air, swirling off her rain cape, tossing aside her hat, and leaving puddles wherever she moved. "Every time

I come home it rains," she announced cheerfully. "Why isn't the roof fixed yet?"

There was a flurry of activity while she dropped her overnight bag in the foyer, distributed kisses all around, and relayed Mark's greetings. Cici hung up her cape, Paul carried her bag upstairs, and Lindsay, now dressed again in sweater and jeans, begged Lori to come and try on the gown she'd just taken off.

"In a minute," Lori promised. Her eyes were shining with a secret delight as she slipped the strap of her oversized tapestry messenger bag off her shoulder and placed it carefully on the ottoman. "First I have something to show you. We need a corkscrew. And Ida Mae."

"Two phrases I never thought I'd hear uttered together," observed Derrick.

Cici held up her hands in protest as Lori, with a flourish, pulled a bottle of wine from her bag. "Lori, you're not going to open that now, are you? How long does it need to breathe, anyway?"

"Ida Mae!" Lori called. "We're not only going to open it," she told her mother. "We're going to drink it."

Bridget made a face. "At this time of morning?"

And Lindsay added, "I see we've been a very bad influence on you."

Lori held the bottle up with both hands, showing the label. "This," she told them, "is last year's shiraz from the Three Ponds winery, from where we're going to order our crush. You've got to taste this."

Derrick shrugged. "I'm game." He crossed the room, where a decanter of sherry and a display of Murano cordial glasses were displayed on a Queen Anne console table. He removed the decanter and brought back the tray of glasses.

Dominic took the bottle and examined the label. "New York, huh? Old vines?"

"European stock," Lori assured him. She turned and called again, "Ida Mae!"

Dominic took his key chain from his pocket and flipped open a corkscrew. Lindsay gave him an admiring look. "I do like a man who's prepared."

He flashed her a grin and started opening the wine.

Ida Mae appeared at the door to the parlor in the rooster-print apron that Lori had given her for Christmas and a purple cardigan over her house-dress and jeans. "What's all the bellowing about?" she demanded with a scowl. "I'm too old to be running up and down this hall every time somebody hollers, and I've got a cake in the oven."

"What kind?" Paul wanted to know.

Ida Mae ignored him and slapped a stack of envelopes on the table by the door. "Here's the mail," she said and turned to leave.

Lori hurried to take Ida Mae by the arm, urging her back into the room. "Wait, Ida Mae. I need you to taste something."

Dominic pulled the cork free from the bottle and sniffed it, then lightly inhaled the fragrance of the bottle itself. A slight tilt of his head suggested nothing as he poured a tasting measure into each of the glasses on the tray. Ida Mae watched him suspiciously.

"What're you all up to, bringing out spirits this time of day? You're gonna burn in perdition, ever' last one of you."

"Not spirits," Lori insisted, bringing her a glass. "Wine. A very special wine."

Ida Mae threw up her hands and stepped back, looking as though she'd just been offered poison. "Are you crazy, girl?"

Cici said, "Lori, really, is this some kind of joke?"

"Really," Lori insisted, pressing the glass on Ida Mae, "just taste it. A tiny sip."

Derrick cast a wary look toward her. "Are we all going to suddenly start shrinking and fall through a rabbit hole?" Nonetheless, he took a glass and held it up to the light, examining the color, and then waved it cautiously under his nose.

Dominic did the same, then took a sip. Everyone watched as he rolled the flavor on his tongue for a moment and then swallowed. "Nice base notes," he admitted to Lori. "Chocolate, maybe a little raspberry . . . something else. Familiar, but I can't quite say what it is."

Lori pressed her hands together excitedly, watching as, one by one, the others tasted the wine . . . everyone, that was, except Ida Mae, who looked at them all as though they'd lost their minds.

"Well?" insisted Lori, eyes shining. "Do you taste it?"

Lindsay held out her glass. "I don't even taste the chocolate," she admitted. "Of course, I just brushed my teeth."

"Funny," observed Bridget, "how wine doesn't taste nearly as good before lunch as it does after dinner."

"Wait a minute," Paul said. He held out his glass, then brought it back to his face, inhaling the aroma. "There is something familiar about it." He looked at Derrick, who nodded.

"Loire valley Beaujolais?" he suggested.

"Not Beaujolais," Dominic disagreed, taking another sip. "It's young, but you almost think if it aged another few years . . ."

"What does it remind you of?" Lori insisted.

"Odd," said Cici, examining the glass. "It's not sweet, but it makes me think of something sweet."

"Chocolate?" suggested Lindsay.

"Ida Mae's fruitcakes!" Lori exclaimed impatiently. "The Blackwell Farms'63!"

The Blackwell Farms Winery had become famous for its '63 shiraz, the last bottle of which had sold at open auction for in excess of $8,000. Ida Mae, oblivious to this, had been using it to marinate her Christmas fruitcakes for years—thus gaining the well deserved reputation for the most exquisite fruitcakes in the county, perhaps the world. The last of the '63 shiraz, however, had been used on the last fruitcake the year the ladies moved into the house.

For a moment, everyone stared at her and then re-tasted their wine. Even Ida Mae took a careful sniff, frowning. "Don't smell a thing like fruit-cake," she declared.

"Maybe." Paul took another sip. "There's something there."

"I knew it was familiar," Derrick agreed. He smiled at Ida Mae. "The best thing I ever tasted at Christmas!"

"Not quite there," Dominic said thoughtfully, gazing at Lori. "But close."

Cici said, "I don't know how you expect us to taste anything this time of morning." But she took another sip anyway.

"No, he's right." Bridget sniffed the wine again, then re-tasted. "It's . . . reminiscent."

"Sorry," Lindsay told Lori, setting aside her glass. "Tastes like toothpaste to me."

All eyes turned to Ida Mae as she sniffed the cordial glass again, stared at it, and then took one small, very careful taste. She smacked her lips. She looked at the glass. She set it down with a clack on the side table. "It ain't Blackwell Farms wine," she pronounced. "But," she added as she turned to go, "it's close."

Lori whirled back to them, beaming. "See? Was I right?"

Dominic smiled, lifted his glass to her in a small salute, and put it on the side table beside Ida Mae's. "You did good, kid," he told her. "You're starting to develop a real palate, and that's not something that comes with a college degree."

She glowed under his praise, and then he added, "But you know, last year's vintage has nothing to do with this year's crush."

"I think it does," Lori replied confidently. "Especially if you blend Ladybug Farm wine into it. Don't you see it's perfect?" She turned from one to the other of them, her excitement all but sparking in the air. "You wanted a unique wine brand, and this is it—the taste of the glory days of the Blackwell Farms winery with the jazz of the contemporary Ladybug Farm grape! Wait, I have to write that down. That could be our marketing copy."

Cici gave a weak, uncertain chuckle. "Lori, I don't know anything about wine-making but I'm pretty sure that mixing fresh grapes into aged wine is probably not a good idea. And we don't have any actual wine. We won't even have grapes until fall. Maybe."

"Except she's not talking about this year,"

Dominic said, with an approving glance toward Lori.

"Right." Lori gave a single adamant nod of her head. "This year, we bottle and label the wine we make from the crush. But we hold some in reserve. Next year . . ."

"We blend our own wine into the reserve," added Dominic thoughtfully. "A special edition."

"Exactly! And a winery is born." Lori held up her palm for a high-five, and Dominic slapped it with a grin.

Then he grew serious. "You asked them about fermentation and pump overs? What about ML inoculation? Did they use CO_2 in the cold soak?"

Bridget, Lindsay, and Cici exchanged blank looks while Lori and Dominic engaged in a few intense moments of technical conversation. Paul murmured, "I think we need to renew our subscription to *Wine Spectator*." And Derrick nodded agreement.

"Young lady," Dominic decided after a few more moments of rapid-fire questions and answers, "I think you just might have a future in the wine business. California's gain is our loss."

Lori's cheeks colored with gratification, and Cici gave her daughter's shoulders an affectionate squeeze. "I agree," she said.

"Good," said Lori. "Because they said they'd waive storage fees if we ordered before the end of the month, so I told them they could ship two hundred barrels."

"Two hundred!"

"Lori, are you crazy?"

"Lori, we can't possibly—"

Dominic held up a quick, placating hand. "It's okay," he assured them. "We can accommodate that, and she's right—the sooner we get the new wine into our own barrels, the more control we have over the outcome. As long . . ." He gave Lori a meaningful look. "As they don't expect payment in advance."

"I held it on my credit card," she assured him blithely. "They're mailing the contract. Here's what I negotiated." She took several typed papers from her bag and handed them over to Dominic.

Cici took a long, slow breath. "Lori," she said carefully, "you do realize that you're not actually an officer in this corporation, don't you?"

Lori had spotted the box of Valentine candy, and she headed toward it happily. "Not a problem, Mom. My pleasure."

Dominic examined the papers with an appreciative lift of his brow. "Pity we can't hire that girl," he murmured to Cici. And to Lori he said, "You could have gotten a better price on shipping."

"Not for that small amount," she assured him, biting into a caramel, and Dominic winked at Cici and handed her the papers.

"We'll take this up at the next board of directors meeting," he said, "which should be, what? In a couple of hours? Meanwhile, you all have wedding dresses to look at, and I want to check that pump again. We may need to order a new valve." He gave Lindsay a look that was obviously meant to be casual and which no one in the room could be persuaded to believe, and added, "Walk out with me?"

"I'll get my coat."

Cici went to take Lori's papers to the office, gathering up the mail on her way. "Oh, wait," she said, pulling out an envelope. "It's from the bank. What do you know about that? These must be the final papers on our loan. Perfect timing, huh?" She opened the envelope and pulled out a paper.

"Well, you know what they say," Lori replied cheerfully. "When you're doing what you're meant to do, the universe smiles on you."

"Now there, you see?" Derrick agreed. "There's always a reward in it when you get up at six in the morning to slog through the mud and take pictures of the groundbreaking ceremony for a friend's new house." Lindsay came back from the foyer, pulling on her rain jacket. "If we sign everything now, Dominic and I can run into town before the bank closes."

Cici looked up from reading the paper. There was an odd expression on her face. "What does the universe do when you screw up?" Her tone was dull; her eyes looked stunned.

"They turned us down," she said. "We didn't get the loan."

Chapter Eight

In Search of an Angel

Remember the lilies of the field," Noah advised somberly.

The seven pairs of eyes that turned on him were neither appreciative nor encouraging. Nonetheless, he explained, "They toil not, neither do they reap."

Noah, who had a half-day on Wednesdays, had come home for lunch to find everyone glumly picking over turkey sandwiches and searching for options. An hour later, Ida Mae cleared the table, but still they sat, the embers of the fire dying behind them, the bottle of Montrachet half-empty before them, the box of Valentine candy open in the center of the table.

"Thank you, Noah," Lindsay said before he could go on.

Lori gave him an impatient look. "Don't you know any verses about vineyards? There's lots of stuff in the Bible about vineyards. Quote something helpful."

Noah shrugged and reached for a chocolate.

Ida Mae rattled plates and saucers in the background, muttering to herself. Bridget twisted in her chair to look at her. "What's that, Ida Mae?"

"I said, the only thing you folks know about wine is how to drink it," Ida Mae replied. She scooped coffee into the coffee maker. "Shame on you, sitting here at the kitchen table, guzzling and moaning this time of day. Ain't you got anyplace better to be?"

"Actually," said Bridget with a sigh, "no."

"Although, I did sketch out a cute design for the winery office," Lindsay said wistfully, "where we could have had our meetings, instead of at the kitchen table. If we had a winery, that is. Right there in the west corner of the barn, next to the restaurant. There was room for a gift shop, too. We could have sold your wine jams and gift baskets, and on the front wall, right over the cash register, I was going to do a six-foot-tall canvas with a single cluster of grapes. With the tall ceilings in there it would've looked fabulous."

"Could've done a tin ceiling," added Noah, "and left the beams exposed so that it still looked like a barn. People would've liked that."

"We could have decorated the restaurant with your art," Bridget said, "and sold it there, too, just like they're doing at the B&B."

Derrick smothered a groan. "Restaurants and B&Bs sell food, not art. Lindsay, darling, we really must talk about what you're doing with your life. Not to mention Noah's."

She returned a steady gaze. "What I *was* going to do with my life was operate a winery and sell my paintings in the restaurant. Now I don't *know* what I'm going to do with it."

Cici took a breath. "I think it's important to remember that we weren't rejected because of our credit, or because of the idea. The bank just doesn't have the money."

"It's the economy," agreed Bridget.

"Which will never get better if banks don't start loaning money," said Lindsay angrily.

"The point being," interrupted Cici firmly, sensing a tirade, "that this is just one bank. We can try others."

The coffee pot gurgled in the silence that followed, filling the room with its rich aroma. Cici looked around the table for encouragement and found none. Dominic put it into words. "Your local bank is always your best chance for a small business loan," he said. "If they turn you down . . . Well, it's like a black mark for everybody else."

Bridget took a deep breath and let it out. "It's funny," she said. "Until now, I don't think I realized how much I wanted this. I mean, I didn't even think it was a good idea at first. But The Tasting Table." She smiled wanly. "That *was* a good name for a restaurant, wasn't it?"

Lindsay reached over and patted her hand. Noah

took another chocolate. Derrick refilled his glass.

"You know," he said, "Noah may be on the right track. What you need is an Angel."

Noah frowned, apparently trying to remember a verse that referenced angels, and everyone else looked at Derrick curiously.

"He's right," Dominic said. "We talked about this before. Failing cash or credit, we need investors. Or an investor. An Angel."

Lindsay slouched down in her chair until she could rest her head against the back rail, her demeanor a metaphor for the defeat they all felt. "We're talking hundreds of thousands of dollars. I don't know anyone with that kind of money. And even if I did, how could I ask them to risk it on a winery we haven't even established yet?"

Lori said without hesitation, "Dad is sending me a check for the wedding. You can use that."

"Absolutely not," said Cici.

Derrick and Paul exchanged a look. Paul said, "If we took out the pool . . ."

"And the radiant heat in the bathrooms . . ."

"And the terraced landscaping . . ."

"Stop it." Bridget reached across the table and grasped both their hands. "Thank you," she said sincerely. "But we don't want you to sacrifice your dream for ours." She smiled at Lori. "Either of you."

"Besides," said Lindsay with a sigh, "it wouldn't be enough."

Cici kicked her under the table.

"If only we could sell the house on Huntington Lane," Paul said, frowning. "Cici, are you sure you couldn't get your real estate license reinstated in Maryland for just a few months? No one ever moved property like you."

"All that custom crush," Lori said, dejected. "The base notes of chocolate and raspberry . . . Gone."

"I could call Kevin," Bridget suggested uneasily. "He's always talking about the hit his stock portfolio took last year. Maybe he'd like to invest in something more substantial."

Lori looked at her mother. "If you won't call Daddy, I will. He has plenty of money."

"Honey, no one has plenty of money these days." But she looked a little uncertain as she glanced at Bridget and then at Lindsay. "Besides, I hate being in debt to Richard."

"It wouldn't be debt. It would be business."

"Even more fun."

Lori pushed back her chair, her eyes suddenly alight. "I'll call Mark's parents! They were wild about this place. They would love—"

"No you won't!" All three ladies objected at once.

"We barely know them," Bridget added. "We're not going to ask them for money!"

"What kind of family will they think their son is marrying into?" Cici said, horrified. "No.

Absolutely not." She looked at Lindsay for support.

"It's never a good idea to go into business with relatives," Lindsay agreed. "Or to owe them money."

"Which is why you're not going to ask Kevin," Cici said to Bridget. "He's your only son. What if something goes wrong and we lose everything? Who's going to take you in if he loses everything, too?"

Bridget pulled a dry face, which nonetheless held a note of concession. "Which is a perfect argument for why you shouldn't involve Richard. Despite the fact that I know you'd love to see him lose everything, who would take care of Lori?"

Lori said, "Why is it that old people always look on the dark side?"

Noah offered gallantly, "They're not that old."

Lindsay inclined her head toward him. "Thank you, Noah." And to Lori she said, "It's not that we look on the dark side. It's just that, at your age, more things have turned out for better than worse for you, percentage wise. The older you get, the more experiences you have, and the percentage goes down. Therefore, you learn that it pays to be prepared."

That made Dominic smile. "Spoken like a practiced teacher. At any rate, Lori, they're right. You know it will take five years for any investor to start seeing a return, and that's if everything goes according to plan. In agriculture, things rarely go according to plan."

Noah said to Derrick, "Have you all been out to that B&B? Our stuff looks nice there. I've got one of that big old rooster . . ."

But at the slow looks that were turned on him, he trailed off. "I guess I've got homework to do." He pushed up from the table.

Ida Mae set a frosted cake on the table with a thunk. "Red velvet," she said. "If you're gonna be taking up space at my table, you might as well be eating."

Noah sat back down again. "Not that much homework," he said.

Ida Mae plucked the wine bottle off the table and replaced it with the coffee pot. She began distributing cups and saucers. Bridget cut the cake.

"I don't see what the real big deal is," Noah said, spearing a forkful of cake. "You've got all those cuttings that I helped Dominic bury last month. You said they were going to be your vines, right? And there were an awful lot of them."

"That's true," Bridget said, stirring sugar into her coffee. "But it will take two years before those vines even start producing fruit."

"Always does," acknowledged Noah. "Good cake, Ida Mae."

Dominic said, "I think what Noah is trying to

say is that you're no worse off now than you were this time last year. And he's right. Wonderful cake, Ida Mae. Thank you."

Paul said, "Good point. You could look on the bright side. You have a vineyard with old vines that still produce and cuttings that are ready to go in the ground. That's a lot more than most people have when they start out. The cake is out of this world, Ida Mae. You are a genius."

"It could even be a blessing in disguise," Derrick agreed. "You wanted to reproduce the Blackwell Farms wine, and the only way to do that is to start with Blackwell Farms grapes. Pure heaven, Ida Mae."

Ida Mae scowled at him. "You're not supposed to be eating that." Then she glared at Lindsay. "I thought you was on a diet."

"Cocoa is excellent for heart health," Derrick assured her.

"It's okay; it's red," Lindsay said, carefully scraping the white frosting off the cake. "It's on my list. Thank you so much. It's heavenly."

"It's just," said Cici, pushing around a small piece of cake on her plate, "I really wanted to do something big. Something important, like a legacy, you know? And . . ." She cast a sad half-smile toward Lori. "I wanted to toast my daughter's wedding with Ladybug Farm wine."

Bridget said, "I know we don't have anything to complain about. We really do have everything we could ask for . . . this wonderful house, good friends . . ."

"Plenty of wood in the bin," added Lindsay, "thanks to the tornado."

"A roof over our heads, more or less," supplied Cici.

"The animals," Noah added helpfully.

"Ida Mae's cake," offered Lori.

"And it's not like we can't still go through with the plan," Dominic pointed out, "in a few years. The economy could turn around, and one good harvest will set us up."

"I know," Bridget agreed, but she still looked wistful. "It's just that, after a certain age, you start to wonder how many more chances at success you have, and postponing them is hard. And wouldn't it be great if, just once, something actually worked out for us?"

No one knew how to reply to that, and they finished their cake and coffee in silence.

In Ida Mae's Kitchen

Lori cut herself another thin sliver of cake—because everyone knew the calories didn't count as long as the slices were small enough, no matter how many slices you actually had—and scraped the frosting off the knife with her finger, popping it into her mouth absently. Everyone else had adjourned to separate parts of the house to make phone calls or try to work on some kind of plan. Lori lingered at the kitchen table, absently eating cake with one hand and tapping intently on the keypad of her electronic tablet with the other. Thank heavens Wi-Fi had finally come to Ladybug Farm. Otherwise, they would all be standing in line to use the phone or the computer. It had broken her heart, but she'd already called to cancel the order of custom crush.

Ida Mae snatched her plate away, and Lori looked up from the tablet with an indignant, "Hey!"

"You keep on eating cake and you won't be able to fit in that wedding dress—if you even had one, that is." Ida Mae marched the plate to the sink, tossing over her shoulder, "Or maybe that's not something you're worried about."

Lori blew out a breath. "To tell the truth, I'm a lot more worried about what's going to happen to the winery today than I am about how I'm going to look in a dress in September."

"That winery ain't none of your business," Ida Mae informed her. "What is your business is getting married."

Lori didn't look up from her tablet. "Oh, Ida Mae, that's so old-fashioned."

"Nothing wrong with that."

"I can be married and still have a career."

Ida Mae slid her a shrew look. "Can you still be married and fool around with that Italian fellow on that fancy toy of yours?"

Lori's hand immediately flew out to cover the screen of her tablet, and color shot to her cheeks. "It's not like that. Sergio is interested in what's happening with the winery, that's all. I thought he might have some ideas."

Ida Mae said nothing.

"Besides, it's good to talk to somebody who understands." She hesitated. "Probably best not to mention this to Mom, though. I don't think she ever really liked Sergio."

"And that boy that gave you the rock you're wearing," said Ida Mae, using a bottle brush to clean a tall glass, "what does he think about this Sergio?"

Lori tried to look insulted. "Mark knows Sergio and I are just friends. It's not like I'm keeping secrets from him."

To which Ida Mae replied simply, "Hmph."

"I'm going to call my dad," Lori announced with resolve.

"Your mama told you not to."

"Maybe. But she didn't . . ."

"She's a grown woman who doesn't want your daddy lordin' it over her head that she messed up again," Ida Mae said, removing Lori's coffee cup just as Lori was reaching for it. "And I guess she's got that right. Now you put that thing away and go find something to do. Look at wedding books."

Lori hesitated and then reluctantly turned the tablet off. She watched Ida Mae wash the last of the dishes for a moment. "How old were you when you got married, Ida Mae?"

"I was sixteen."

"Wow. I guess he was your childhood sweetheart, huh?"

"Nope."

Ida Mae turned from the sink and thrust a dishtowel at Lori. Lori got up and took it from her, drying the dishes that were stacked on the drain board.

"So how long had you known him?"

"Less than a month. It was war time."

"But it worked out okay, right? I mean, you were married a long time."

" 'Til death do us part. That's what I said; that's what I meant."

Lori said, frowning a little, "My parents weren't married a long time. I'm going to do better than that."

Ida Mae concentrated on scrubbing the cake pans.

"I mean, it's not like I don't want to move to California. I'm practically *from* California. I spent a whole year there at UCLA. My dad is in California. I'm basically a bicoastal girl. And Mark really wants to get married. You should have seen how sweet he was when he proposed."

Her face softened with the memory and she hugged the dish she'd been drying to her chest. "He did it in front of the whole restaurant, down on one knee, and his speech was so sweet. Then everyone applauded—I mean, really, could anybody ask for more?"

She sighed, seemed to remember the damp dish in her hands, and finished drying it. "It's just that I didn't know so much would be going on here, I guess. And Mark . . . well, he tries to pretend he's interested in winemaking and viniculture, but he's really not, no more than I'm interested in all those algorithms he's all the time fooling around with." She smiled a little uncertainly. "But that's okay. That's a good thing, really. It's just . . . I don't know. It seems as though everything is happening so fast, and I hate leaving everybody in such a mess."

"It ain't like you're leaving tomorrow," said Ida Mae gruffly. "You gonna dry that dish or stand there playing with it?"

"I think," said Lori thoughtfully, "I could get more done on a desktop computer." She thrust the dish back to Ida Mae with a decisive nod. "Thanks, Ida Mae. You've been a big help."

She left the room, leaving Ida Mae gazing after her in a mixture of dismay and annoyance, clutching the previously dried dish in her wet hands.

———— ❖❀❖ ————

Chapter Nine

Valentine

Lindsay didn't feel like going out for dinner, and Dominic didn't try very hard to change her mind, although he also made very little effort to hide his disappointment. When he had gone, Derrick scolded her, "That is *not* the way to find and fascinate a man, my darling. Shame on you."

Lindsay gazed glumly out the window, watching Dominic's tail lights disappear through the chill, gray rain and fog. "Who wants to go out on a nasty day like this? Besides, the roads might ice tonight." But then she glanced at Derrick anxiously. "You don't think I hurt his feelings, do you?"

Derrick just rolled his eyes.

It took some persuading, but Lori finally agreed to abandon the computer—where she was futilely trying to rework the start-up cost figures into a number with less than four zeroes after it—and try on wedding gowns. For a short time, everyone was cheered by the fashion show, and even Noah paused on his way out the door for his date with Amy to grin at Lori as she came down the stairs in a froth of lace.

"You look like a Christmas catalogue Barbie doll," he told her. And when her brows drew together, he assured her quickly, "That's a good thing."

Noah, sensing his luck was about to turn, hurried to the door, and Lindsay called after him, "Home by 10:30! It's a school night!"

"Yes, ma'am," he called back.

"And drive carefully!" added Bridget.

"And take that girl a box of chocolates," Derrick called as he swung open the door on the cold night.

"I will, don't worry!" The door closed after him and he clattered down the front steps.

Lori wrinkled her nose as she reached the bottom of the stairs, plucking at the chiffon overlay. "I don't know. I don't think I'm a wedding gown kind of girl."

"Everyone is a wedding gown kind of girl on her special day," Paul assured her, adjusting the ruffle of a cap sleeve. "But you may be right. A bit much froth, I think."

The next one had too much shine, another too many little buttons, the next pooched out in the middle. Eventually, she allowed that the Vera Wang might be made to suit if they cut off the train, six inches of hem, and the satin bow. At this point, Paul, who was on the verge of going into respiratory distress at the mere thought of slaughtering a Vera Wang original, suggested they postpone the selection for another time.

"Maybe a denim jacket," suggested Lori,

examining her reflection critically in the dark windowpane, and the fashion show was definitely over.

Derrick proposed to take everyone out for a Valentine's Day dinner to cheer them up, but forgot this wasn't Baltimore. The only place besides the Pizza Inn that was serving dinner on this bleak February night was the Holiday Inn an hour outside of town, which was overrun with people who had the foresight to make reservations. They stayed home for hearty meatloaf with brussels sprouts and mashed potatoes, which was a fine winter meal, to be sure. But it wasn't very romantic.

After supper, Paul recovered from the wedding dress debacle enough to bring out his color chart and *Bride* magazines. "The important thing is color scheme," he explained patiently to Lori, who was properly fortified with a glass of Montrachet and a previous forty-five minute conversation with Mark, which, to those overhearing, had consisted greatly of I love yous and I love you mores. "Once you incorporate your color scheme into your theme, everything just falls into place—the bridesmaids' dresses, the table settings, the invitations . . ."

"We really need to get the invitation design to the printer as soon as possible," Bridget said. "These people get completely backed up in the spring."

"First we need to know how many invitations to print," Cici said. "It would help if we had a guest list. Even the beginning of one."

"Do you know what would be adorable?" Derrick put in. "OMG, I am seeing it now: grapevine runners on the tables, goes without saying, right, entwined with tiny white lights and clusters of fall-turning grape leaves, yes? And a huge, I'm talking twelve foot, grapevine chandelier—"

"Twelve feet?" exclaimed Cici. "That's bigger than our whole dance gazebo!"

"Six foot," conceded Derrick. "And of course, monogrammed wineglasses for each guest to take home, filled with—are you ready?—wine-flavored jellybeans! I know this company that makes cabernet, chardonnay, pinot noir . . ."

"Love it!" exclaimed Paul. "And, oh my God, too perfect—a wine-flavored ice cream bar!"

Lindsay scrunched up her face. "Wine ice cream? I don't know."

Derrick continued blithely, "So, obviously, I mean, *clearly,* you'll do the invitations in a grapevine motif. I'm thinking a simple card—"

"Parchment," supplied Paul.

Derrick nodded his head. "Parchment with deckle edge."

"And a vellum overlay," Paul added.

"Right. Held together with an interwoven grapevine twig . . ."

"Oh my God, right?" exclaimed Paul. "And delivered in an embossed velvet—"

"Wine bag!" declared Paul and Derrick together, and Derrick added, "Do you love it?"

Paul said, "So you see, as soon as you choose the color theme, we'll know what to go with for the colors of the wine bags . . ."

"And the tablecloths," Derrick added.

"And the flowers," Lindsay pointed out.

"And the bridesmaids' dresses."

"And the cake," added Bridget expectantly.

"So, sweetie," said Cici, watching her daughter carefully. "Have you decided on the bridesmaids yet?"

Lori said, looking from one to the other, "You know my dad could buy a whole winery for what this wedding is costing, right?"

"Not even close!" Paul scoffed.

And Derrick insisted, "Grapevines? You pick them up off the ground!"

Cici said, "Seriously, Lori, not the same thing at all. This is your day. The sky's the limit . . . within reason, of course."

"Colors, sweetie," Lindsay urged. "Just pick the colors."

Lori sighed. "I don't know. I'm not really a colors sort of girl." She sipped her wine and turned a page. "This is nice. Peaches and cream."

"How did that get in there? So 1996!" Paul swooped in immediately with an overlay. "This year's Pantone colors, sweetkins. Let's keep it in the decade, shall we?"

"Really?" Lindsay leaned over Lori's shoulder. "Let me see."

Bridget scrunched in on the other side of Lori. "Margarita," she said, "love that."

"I like cockatoo." Lindsay took the chart and held it up for Cici. "That would look gorgeous on the mother of the bride."

"We don't want to get too literal," cautioned Paul as Cici reached for the chart. "Personally, if I see one more tangerine tango bridesmaid dress . . ."

"Oooh," said Cici, pulling her chair closer, "I love the lilac. And the belleflower. Bridget, wouldn't those colors look fabulous cascading down a wedding cake?"

Lori murmured, "I think I'll get more wine." She wriggled out of the crush and Lindsay took her place, turning pages, matching colors, holding up choices for approval. It was some time before anyone noticed the bride-to-be hadn't returned. By that time, Lori had already gone to bed.

The weather cleared overnight into a bright, crisp morning, and the mood at the Ladybug Farm breakfast table was a remarkable improvement from the day before. "You know," Bridget said when the platter of whole-wheat waffles topped with fruit compote had been devoured and the last of the coffee had been poured, "if you think about it, everything probably worked out for the best. I mean, two graduations and a wedding within six months of each other . . . Who has time to open a new business?"

"Not to mention helping your friends move," Paul pointed out with a wink.

"That's right," agreed Lindsay. "There's more than enough excitement around here just watching you guys put that house together."

"And I don't think we ever really thought about the kind of work that would be involved just setting up," Cici added. "I mean, we're talking some major construction here if we were going to remodel the barn into a restaurant."

"And don't forget the gift shop," Lindsay added.

"Not to mention the real work with a winery," Lori said. "The marketing, the management decisions . . . You guys haven't even designed your label yet, much less thought about bottle color, oak or steel barrels—and if you go with oak, you'll probably have to send to France for them. And without me here to help you . . ." She shrugged. "It would probably be more than you could handle."

"Well, if you all don't take the cake," observed Ida Mae sourly. "Yesterday, all you could do was fill up my kitchen with your dark thunderclouds because you didn't get your way, and now it's all sunshine and rosebuds because you ain't got time to put in the work anyhow. I wish you'd make up your mind what it is you want, because you're just about to give me a headache."

" 'All things work together for good to those that love the Lord'," Noah said, rising to clear the table. "Romans 8:28."

"The Lord helps them that help themselves," Ida Mae muttered, wiping down the countertop. "Ida Mae Simpson."

Noah didn't notice the smothered grins that went around the table as he started scooping up the dishes and platters. One of his chores was to clear the breakfast dishes before he left for school in the mornings, and he did this now with dispatch, causing Paul to reach protectively for the waffle he hadn't quite finished eating. "Sorry, folks, I've got to hustle. Assembly this morning and all the seniors are supposed to do something."

"What are they supposed to do?" asked Lindsay, handing him her plate and Cici's.

He shrugged, building an efficient tower of dishes. "Dunno. That's why I've got to get there early." He carried the swaying stack of dishes to the sink without breaking a single one and slid them into the soapy water with a flourish. "See ya!" He pulled on his jacket and backpack, snagged a set of keys from the hook by the door, and was gone before anyone at the table could draw breath for a reply. A cacophony of wild border collie barking followed his progress across the yard.

"He certainly is a busy young man," observed Derrick, sipping his coffee. "Always rushing here and there."

"All boys his age are like that," said Lori sagely. "They only have one speed—full." She glanced at her watch and gulped down the last of her juice. "Well, I guess I'd better get on the road. I don't want to hit traffic coming into Charlottesville."

Cici hid her smile with her coffee cup. "Some girls are like that, too."

Lori tossed her a quick apologetic smile. "Sorry we didn't get very far with the wedding. I promise I'll put a guest list together before I see you next time, and I'll tell Mark's mother to fax you hers."

She stopped by Paul's chair and dropped a kiss atop his head. "Thanks for bringing the dresses down, Uncle Paul. They just weren't me, you know?"

"I do. A bride's gown should be her every dream come true." He caught her fingers as she passed and kissed them. "What do you say we make a date to go shopping in D.C. in a month or so?"

"Sounds fabulous."

"I'll say!" exclaimed Lindsay. "Now that's something to look forward to."

"We'll get our hair and nails done," said Bridget, clapping her hands together like a girl. "And have sushi for lunch."

"And get our own dresses for the wedding while we're there," added Cici. "And shoes."

"We might have to stay over," cautioned Lindsay, looking pleased.

"We have guest rooms in the suburbs," Derrick volunteered.

"See?" declared Bridget happily. "Who even needs a winery anyway?"

Lori laughed. "Well, I guess it's a date, then. Thanks for breakfast, Ida Mae. I'm going to get my things together and let Mark know I'm on my way. What *is* that dog still barking about?"

But no sooner had she said it than there was a quick light rap on the back door and Dominic poked his head inside. "Good morning, everyone. I hope I'm not calling too early."

Lindsay quickly smoothed back her ponytail and straightened the cowl neck of her sweater. "Dominic! What are you doing here?"

"We didn't expect you," clarified Bridget, standing to welcome him.

"You missed breakfast," said Ida Mae, taking down the coffee canister. "I'll put on another pot."

"No, don't," he insisted. He unzipped his fleece-lined denim jacket as he came inside, rubbing the cold from his hands. "I'm not staying. I just came to bring some news I didn't think could wait."

"Uh-oh," said Lindsay, regarding him cautiously. "News that can't wait is hardly ever a good thing around here."

But his eyes were sparkling and the flush on his cheeks might have been from more than the cold. From his inside jacket pocket he took a sheet of paper, unfolded it, and spread it out in the center of the table. Lindsay got up to read over Bridget's shoulder, and Bridget put on her reading glasses. Cici squinted at the paper.

"Wait a minute," she said. "This looks like it's from the bank."

"Ladybug Farm Winery, Inc.," agreed Bridget, and then she gasped softly. "It's a balance sheet."

Cici rubbed her eyes. "That can't be right."

Lindsay snatched Bridget's glasses and put them on, peering at the paper. "Oh my God!" she exclaimed.

Lori grabbed the paper away, scrutinizing it. Her face lit up like a thousand Christmases. "It's true! This is actual money! In our account! Your account, I mean. More than enough money to . . ." Her eyes went big as she stared at Dominic accusingly. "This had better not be a mistake. Tell me it's not a mistake."

Paul and Derrick got up to read over Lori's shoulder. "It looks real enough to me," Paul declared, and Derrick agreed. "Ladies, you're rich!"

"We got the loan!" Cici cried, leaping to her feet. "The bank came through after all. The letter we got must have been a mistake."

Lori said uncertainly, "That doesn't sound like something a bank would do."

Lindsay whirled and threw her arms around Dominic. "Thank you, thank you! This is the best surprise ever."

Cici hugged Lori and Bridget hugged Paul and Derrick hugged Ida Mae, who shrugged away irritably. All of them were laughing from sheer relief mixed with more than a little astonishment that, for once, the strange and unpredictable twists of fortune had somehow managed to actually favor them.

And then Dominic said, "Okay, I will definitely try to be the bearer of good news more often. But . . ." He gave Lindsay's shoulders a final, one-armed squeeze and looked around the room. "The bank didn't come through. They were as surprised as I was. Happy for us, of course. But surprised."

The laughter left their eyes to be replaced by puzzlement. "What?" said Cici.

Lindsay stepped away from him. "I don't understand."

Lori said, "I told you banks don't make that kind of mistake."

Ida Mae gave what might have been a grunt of satisfaction. "Guess you'll be wanting that coffee now. "

Everyone sat back down. Dominic pulled out a chair. "Frank Adams asked me to stop by and see him this morning. I figured he'd gotten a copy of the loan letter, his office being on file with the bank for all the paperwork, and he'd want to know what our plans were. But that wasn't it. What he wanted was to let me know that late yesterday afternoon an anonymous investor—those were his words, anonymous investor—had transferred $100,000 into the Ladybug Farm Winery account. I knew you'd want to see it for yourself, so I had the bank print out a balance sheet for you."

Every pair of eyes at the table was fixed on him. In the background, the coffee pot gurgled.

Lindsay was the first to speak. "Anonymous? What do you mean anonymous?"

"It means," supplied Derrick, "unknown or unnamed, as in . . ."

"I know what it means! What I mean is—"

"Who?" said Bridget, looking stunned. "Who just gives someone else that kind of money?"

"Someone they don't even know?"

Lori said shrewdly, "But Mr. Adams, the lawyer, *he* knows who it is, doesn't he?"

"He's 'not at liberty to say,'" replied Dominic with a wry turn of his mouth. "But my guess is yes."

"Bizarre," said Paul.

"Certainly is," agreed Derrick.

Three pairs of eyes turned to them, one by one, each in varying degrees of speculation. "Guys," said Cici, "it's not that we wouldn't love you more than words if you did—"

"And be forever grateful," put in Bridget.

"Not to mention forever in your debt," added Lindsay.

"But," said Cici, "you didn't . . . ?"

For a moment they looked baffled, and then Derrick held up his hands in protest. "Not that we didn't wish we could—"

"You know we'd give the world for you, darlings," added Paul.

"But it couldn't have been them," said Lori practically. "They didn't have time. I mean, we were with them every single minute yesterday, and that kind of transaction takes at least a phone call."

"Sorry," said Paul, and Derrick looked genuinely disappointed.

"I've always wanted to be a hero," he sighed.

Lindsay slid an uncertain glance toward Dominic. "Dominic, you'd tell us, wouldn't you, if we asked? Because there's no need to be shy about it, if it was, you know—you. We're already proud to have you as a partner, and it wouldn't be awkward, if that's what you're thinking."

But he stopped her with a rueful shake of his head. "I don't know what kind of pension you think I have, but it's not that much. All I can afford to invest in this business is my time. And yes." He looked at Lindsay steadily. "I'd tell you."

Cici blew out a breath. "Wow. Just imagine. Someone gives you enough money to change your life, and you wouldn't even know them if you passed them on the street."

Ida Mae plopped a coffee cup in front of Dominic and filled it, then went around the table, refilling the others. "Looks to me like you'd be counting your lucky stars instead of looking for faces on the street. Or maybe I forgot. You're too busy to run a winery, right?"

"Oh my God!" Lori bolted up from the table. "The custom crush—I told them to cancel it!"

She ran through the house for the telephone, and in a moment, they heard her say, "Hello, this is Lori from Ladybug Farm Winery . . ." And everyone smiled.

Then Derrick said speculatively, "You don't suppose that fiancé of hers, the one with the rich parents . . . ?"

"The ones who loved our house," added Bridget.

"And dreamed of owning a winery," said Cici, sinking back into her chair. "That's it; it has to be." And then, "Oh dear." She glanced around the table uncertainly. "I don't know how I feel about that."

"I know," said Lindsay, frowning. "I mean, what's the protocol? Do we send them a thank you card?"

"At least, I should think," offered Paul.

"We could name a vintage after them," suggested Bridget.

Cici pulled a skeptical face. "Diane or Jonathon?"

"It wasn't Mark's parents," Lori announced, returning to the room. "I just got off the phone with him. He said they've been over the Pacific since yesterday afternoon and he couldn't have called them if he wanted to . . . which he did," she assured them. "He wanted me to tell you that. The crush is being delivered next Friday," she added without drawing a breath, "providing they receive a deposit by Monday. They're emailing the invoice. Gotta go, really, love you all." She blew kisses all around. "So happy for you. This is the best thing *ever!*"

She was gone in a flurry of whirling cape and rolling luggage and hugs all around. Then, just as she was getting into her car, she turned and called back, "Cabernet! Cabernet and rosé, those are my colors!"

She blew another kiss and got into the car, leaving everyone standing on the porch, shivering and waving and celebrating their triumph with shared grins.

"Next Friday!" exclaimed Bridget when she was gone, hugging her arms. "That doesn't give us much time to get the place cleaned up."

Dominic said, "We need to start sanitizing the tanks as soon as possible. I can get most of the supplies we need in town."

"That definitely sounds like our cue to leave," announced Paul, holding the door for Bridget and Derrick as they hurried inside.

Cici murmured thoughtfully, "I have to make a phone call," and followed them in.

Lindsay lingered, stuffing her hands into the pockets of her jeans and hunching her shoulders against the chill as she smiled up at Dominic. "Pretty exciting, huh? It's really going to happen."

Dominic nodded, but his expression was somber. "I'm glad we have a chance to talk privately," he said, "because now that we're officially business partners, there's something I've been meaning to talk to you about. It's a little delicate."

"Oh." The excitement in Lindsay's eyes faded into disappointment, which she quickly tried to neutralize. She straightened her shoulders and cleared her throat, trying to look mature and relaxed. "I know. I'm glad you brought it up. I've been wanting to talk to you about the same thing."

He tilted his head slightly. "Have you now?"

She nodded, digging her hands more deeply into her pockets. "Dominic, I really like you," she began.

"I'm glad," he said. "Because I really like you, too."

"But there's an awful lot at stake here, for all of us, and I wouldn't want to do anything to jeopardize our working relationship."

He nodded thoughtfully. "Me, either. Which is why I think it's best we get this out in the open now and come up with a plan. You like plans, am I right?"

"Absolutely." Her tone was vigorous. "There's nothing you can't do if you just have a plan."

"So what would you say is the first step in solving this little problem we seem to have?"

"The first step is always acknowledging the problem," she said confidently.

"I thought so. So the problem is . . ." He looked at her, assessing. "How am I going to concentrate on my work and do my partners justice, if all I can think about is kissing you?"

Surprised color came to her cheeks, and he insisted in mock earnestness, "That is the problem you were talking about, isn't it?"

Lindsay fought and lost the battle against the smile that dimpled the corners of her mouth. "I'm starting to understand why Frenchmen have the reputation they do."

"Fortunately," he said, musing, "I think I may have a solution to this dilemma. For the good of the company, of course."

"Of course," she agreed, tilting her head in amusement.

"My plan is this," he said. "We solve the problem by dispensing with the awkwardness and simply get the kiss over with. With your permission, of course."

Her breath was coming a little unsteadily now, and her voice was not as strong as she might have liked. But she admitted, "Sounds reasonable."

The spark that danced in his eyes was both

tender and delightfully amused. "When do you think might be a good time?"

"For what?"

"To get it over with."

She said, with her heart beating so loudly the words were barely audible, "How about now?"

She stepped forward and wrapped her arms about his neck and kissed him.

Cici didn't reach her ex-husband until after supper, 7:00 Eastern Time, 4:00 in L.A. At first, she was a little awkward. "Listen, Richard," she said, lowering her voice so as not to be overheard by Ida Mae, who was clearing up dishes in the other room, or her housemates, who were busy getting themselves settled for the evening, "I don't know what got into you, but . . . thank you."

"For what?" he sounded distracted.

"You know." She glanced around, trying hard not to be overheard. "Yesterday. I know we have our differences, but in one way, nobody's better than you. I just wanted to make sure you knew that I . . . well, I appreciate that."

"For God's sake, Cici, you're on speaker phone." A click and he sounded exasperated as he demanded, "What are you talking about?"

Now she was exasperated, too. "You know, the money! Lori must have called you. I told her not to, but—"

"Oh, cripes." He groaned. "I forgot. Tell her the

185

check's in the mail. I'll make sure it goes out today."

Cici blinked. "The check?"

"For the wedding. And listen; don't try to hold me up for more. We agreed when Lori started college to put aside twenty thousand for her wedding, and if it's more than that, you'll just have to figure it out. That's what I told her, and that's what I'm telling you. I'm not an ATM, you know."

Cici's head was spinning. "Wait a minute. You haven't talked to Lori since you talked about the wedding?"

He said, "Okay, listen, I already feel like crap about this, so just don't go off the deep end, okay? I was going to call her tonight. I'm not going to make it back east for her graduation. I'll be there to walk her down the aisle, I'll be there as long as she wants me for the wedding, but I've got this hot new client in Australia, and he starts shooting a blockbuster in May—so top secret I can't even say the director's name on the phone—and if I don't babysit him the whole first week, the whole damn thing might blow up. So I'm sorry, but graduation isn't going to happen for me, and if you think you can make me feel any worse than I already do, you just go ahead and try."

"Are you kidding me?" Cici's voice rose to a screech, the reason for her original phone call all but forgotten. "Are you really kidding me? Your

186

only daughter, her only college graduation—do you have any idea how hard she's worked for this? How hard I've worked? And you can't even be bothered to show up? Do you know how this is going to make her feel? The child worships you, although why, I can't begin to imagine! And this is how you react to the greatest accomplishment of her life?"

He said darkly, "True to form, Cici. I knew you just had to try to make me feel worse."

And for the next quarter hour, that was exactly what she did.

"Well, it wasn't Richard." Cici blew out a heavy sigh and dropped into a wing chair, swinging her feet up on to the ottoman. She held out her wine glass for a refill.

Bridget obliged, but her expression was dismayed. "You didn't call him?"

"Well, who else could put together that kind of money on such short notice?"

"The boys," said Lindsay thoughtfully, gazing at the reflection the dancing fireplace flames made in the ruby depths of her wine. "If it wasn't Richard, and it wasn't Mark's parents, they're the only ones left with money."

"I don't think so." Bridget shook her head. "They don't have any reason to keep it a secret."

"And besides," Cici added, "Lori was right. Their hearts may have been in the right place, but they just didn't have the time to make the transfer."

"It's just weird, isn't it?" Lindsay frowned and sipped her wine. "To think that somebody has done something that big for us, and we don't even know who it is."

"It's going to drive me crazy," Cici said. "Who *does* that?"

"Maybe that's the point," Bridget said. Her expression was ruminative in the firelight. "Maybe we don't need to know." She glanced at them. "Think about it. If we knew, we *would* feel weird. Obligated. But not knowing, we can think the best about everybody."

Cici considered that for a moment. "Well, except Richard."

"Except Richard," Bridget agreed, and Lindsay saluted her with her glass.

They sat for a time in the silence of the winter evening, listening to the crackle of the fire and the sigh and creak of the old house settling in for the night. Then Lindsay said, "I kissed Dominic."

Cici said, "We know."

Bridget gave an apologetic shrug of her shoulder. "It was broad daylight. You were right on the porch."

Lindsay tried to scowl but couldn't pull it off. Instead, a secret smile played with her lips as she gazed into her wine.

"And?" prompted Cici.

"How was it?" Bridget urged.

Lindsay thought about that for a moment, and her smile deepened. "It was okay," she said and sipped her wine. "It was really . . . okay." But as she turned her gaze toward the fire, her smile suggested that it had been a great deal more than that.

And that was okay, too.

TWO

Bigger Dreams

Chapter Ten

Blossoms

It was generally agreed that there had not been a more spectacular April in recent memory. On Ladybug Farm snowy pear blossoms danced against a bright blue sky and cast lacy shadows over the new lawn. The distant mountains were a thousand shades of green, ranging from the base notes of deep blue to the treble of bright yellow. Lilacs burst into extravagant bloom and daffodils bathed the hillside in yellow. The windows and doors were flung open, and the house was suffused with the taste and smell and the balmy breezes of spring.

March had been bleak and muddy, with temperatures mild enough to be unseasonable but just cold enough to be miserable. The ladies had spent days in the cool wine cellar, dressed in layered sweat suits, gloves, and wool socks, sweeping, vacuuming, and polishing. They hauled buckets of hot soapy water down the stairs and used stiff brushes to scrub every inch of the floor, the walls, behind the sinks, under the tanks. Dominic cleaned and repaired the tanks and, with Noah's help, cleared the steel door that opened onto the vineyard, which over the years had become so overgrown it was inoperable.

Farley brought his tractor and cleared the path that Dominic said once had been a road that led from the vineyard to the barn. Then Dominic called in trucks to reinforce the new roadbed with gravel. When the tanker pulled up on that road with their order of custom crush wine, the three ladies stood in the rain, holding hands and grinning like children, their hearts beating so hard with excitement they could barely speak. Lindsay took photographs and emailed them to Lori, who posted them on Facebook with multiple exclamation marks.

But after the initial thrill, the ladies soon learned that owning a winery consisted in great part of paperwork and waiting. Cici spent hours on the computer, ordering supplies and tracking orders. Bridget spent hours on the phone, tracking down permits and licenses. Lindsay spent a lot of time in her studio, working on the label design and sketching out the mural for The Tasting Table. Sometimes Dominic joined her there, helping, as Lindsay explained blithely, with the design. Bridget and Cici exchanged secret looks and asked as few questions as possible.

The last days of winter limped out on tired legs, drawing out its final exit interminably. When the first weeks of April burst into bloom so lavishly, the energy in the house, and in its occupants, was palpable. Dominic planted cuttings; Bridget planted broccoli. Cici fought with roofers;

Lindsay fought with printers. Ida Mae embarked upon her annual spring cleaning campaign, which consisted mostly of giving orders to the other three women. The house shone with beeswax and sparkled with lemon oil.

Cici began striding around the house, making notes of what needed to be painted and repaired before the wedding. Bridget began measuring and marking off sections of the barn that might be suitable for her restaurant, much to the dismay of the barn's current residents. The chickens laid golden-yolked eggs. The sheep grew fat with fleece that was almost white, and the nanny goat munched grass in the sun. Lori called six times a day. Noah spent most of his free time chasing Bambi out of the garden.

Lindsay planted her rose bush next to the ladybug-painted bench that Noah had built for them in the garden on his first Mother's Day at Ladybug Farm. Dominic helped her, and Lindsay kept a wary eye on Bambi, who pretended to only be interested in munching the shoots of new grass that were sprouting up along the garden paths.

"There," Lindsay declared, stripping off her gardening gloves and admiring her work. "Perfect. Look, it's even starting to bud again, and that rusty-red color in between the Peace rose and the Mr. Lincoln is going to be stunning."

Dominic extended his hand to help her to her

feet again. "Do you know the story of the Peace rose?"

She dusted the mud off the knees of her jeans, glancing up at him. "It has something to do with World War II, doesn't it?"

He nodded, taking her gloves and the gardening spade in one hand and resting the other easily on her waist as they walked toward the potting shed. "It was cultivated by a Frenchman . . ." His eyes twinkled as he glanced at her. "Naturally, by the name of Monsieur Meilland. When he saw the German invasion of his homeland was inevitable, he knew he couldn't keep the rose safe, so he sent cuttings to his colleagues all over Europe and in the United States. In fact, one story says that the rose escaped France on the last flight to the US before the invasion. When France was liberated, Monsieur Meilland wanted to name the rose after Field Marshal Alan Brooke, who had played such a crucial role in bringing the war to an end, but Brooke was a modest man and suggested the name "Peace" instead. The name of the rose was officially announced on the day Berlin fell, and Peace roses were given to the delegates at the first ever meeting of the United Nations later that year. Thousands of Peace roses were planted around the world over the next few years in memory of fallen soldiers."

He nodded over his shoulder down the path they had just left. "Those two there, on either side of the fountain, were in memory of Miss Emily Blackwell's two sons, buried somewhere in France."

Lindsay gave a small shake of her head. "I forget sometimes."

"What's that?" He opened the door of the small cedar potting shed, releasing the odor of cool musty earth and well-oiled tools.

"That you were here before us. How much you know about this place. It must feel strange, having other people live here."

"Not really." He smiled at her. "Actually, I kind of like it." He hung the spade on a hook by the door and placed Lindsay's gloves neatly on a shelf. "I spent some happy days here, yes." He closed the door and held out his hand. "Shall I show you my favorite place?"

Lindsay opened her mouth to protest that she really couldn't spare the time, she had far too much to do, she really should get back and help with lunch, but what came out was, "Okay." And she slipped her hand into his.

They walked around the barn and took the path into the woods that curved by the sheep meadow. Bambi followed for a while, occasionally lingering to strip the leaves off a bush or a low-hanging branch, and Dominic observed, "That buck of yours is getting quite a rack on him."

"I guess he is a buck now," Lindsay said, a little surprised. "I still think of him as a fawn."

"I don't guess I'll ever get used to it, seeing a wild creature roam around here like a pet."

"He is a pet," Lindsay objected. But a small frown pinched her brow briefly as she added, "Even though he's a lot more trouble than most."

And then her face cleared and she laughed out loud with delight as she suddenly realized where they were going. "Oh, I love this place, too!"

Her pace quickened until she was running the last few steps, tugging Dominic behind, and in a moment it came into view: the circular, tin-turreted folly with its decaying gingerbread scrollwork, its sagging walls, its broken windows. The rusty-hinged door stood half open, too swollen with moisture to fit the frame, and there were boards missing from the charming porch that surrounded it. Lindsay clapped her hands together and beamed, gazing at it.

"It's like a little piece of magic from another time, isn't it?" she said. "The glade, the stream . . . It always makes me think of girls in white dresses and gentlemen with bow ties. Can you imagine the trysts that must have taken place here over the years?"

He replied with a slight quirk of his brow, "Not only can I imagine, I may have actually had a few."

In a single graceful step, he bounded up onto the porch and swept open the door. He extended his hand to her. "My lady."

She closed her fingers around his wrist and he pulled her up with a firm grip. She glanced at him askance. "Trysts? Really?"

"Well," he admitted, "as a teenager I mostly came here to smoke—" He caught himself with a small, amused compression of his lips and finished simply, "to smoke."

At her look of pretend shock, he gave a negligent lift of one shoulder. "It was the sixties, after all."

Lindsay laughed softly, holding on to his arm as she picked her way carefully across the debris-strewn floor. "Nice to know you were once a bad boy, actually."

He turned her to him with one hand lightly on her back, the other cupping her neck. Everything he did was like a dance. He said, "I can still be a bad boy, when it's called for." And he kissed her.

He made her feel like a teenager: silly and delirious and completely clueless. She melted into that feeling, every single time. When the kiss ended in sweet, soft surrender, she leaned back from him and smiled into his eyes. "You're very good at this."

"What's that, chérie?" His voice was a bit husky, and he traced the shape of her eyebrow with a delicate fingertip.

"Flirting," she replied. "You make me feel all giddy and gooey-eyed."

The smile in his eyes deepened, crinkling at the

corners. "A lifetime ambition, to make a beautiful woman feel gooey-eyed. But I think we have both seen too many summers to waste time with flirting, am I right?"

Lindsay caught her breath and turned away from him, gesturing toward the tangled vista beyond the bank of east-facing windows, where the creek could be heard gurgling and splashing only a few feet away. "I've always fantasized about renovating this place. This is where Noah used to camp out when he was living on the run. Did I tell you that? And even after he moved into the house with us, he wanted to live out here and have a place of his own. Since then, I've been toying with the idea of what I would do with it. It wouldn't take much, you know. Replacing a few floorboards on the porch, glass in the windows . . . The roof is still good, even if it is a little rusted, and the floor inside is solid marble, not to mention that darling marble fireplace. I think some simple canvas curtains, maybe a really plush daybed with tons of cushions, a couple chairs and a table, a new coat of paint. Wouldn't it be a perfect summer house?"

She turned with a bright and rather shallow smile, and his hand fell lightly upon the crown of her head, smoothing back her hair. He was not smiling at all. "Love," he said softly, "enough."

She looked up at him, her throat tight, her heart beating slow and hard.

"Enough flirting," he said, "enough dancing, enough pretending we're both sixteen with a lifetime of mistakes yet to be made. I don't know about you, but I've made all the mistakes I can afford to make." Gently, he smoothed a strand of hair behind her ear. "I need to know, chérie. Either we go forward, or this stops now. But I need to know. Is that unfair?"

Lindsay swallowed hard. She could feel everything inside her quivering, yet her voice was surprisingly steady. She had known this moment would come. It always did.

She said, "I'm never leaving here."

No surprise showed in his eyes. "Okay."

"What I mean is . . ." Now she was uncertain, casting about for the right words. "I've had a lot of boyfriends." Flushing, she corrected herself. "I mean, not a lot, in the sense of a *lot* . . ." And then she lifted her chin and met his eyes and repeated simply, "I've had a lot of boyfriends, and it took me a long time to understand this, but none of them have made me feel as comfortable and safe and at *home* as I do now, at Ladybug Farm. Cici and Bridget are my family. This is what I want. I'm not leaving them; I'm not leaving this place, not for a man, not for anything." She drew a breath. "You need to know that."

He said cautiously, "Okay."

She sucked in another sharp breath. "I like you,

Dominic. I might even . . . I might even like you more than any man I've ever known, and I might even, I mean it's possible I might even have . . . but at this point in my life I'm just not looking for anything more. At the end of the day the only place I really want to be is on the front porch with Cici and Bridget and a glass of wine, watching the sunset. And that's the truth."

He said gently, "It's a big porch."

She looked up into his eyes and the slow twisting pain she felt in her chest might have been her heart trying not to break. She replied simply, "But there are only three chairs."

Dominic dropped his gaze, and his fingers, resting so lightly against her neck, gave her skin one last butterfly caress before drifting away. He said, "I understand."

Lindsay searched his face. "Do you? Do you really? Because I thought it was important that you know."

He nodded somberly. "And I think it is important that you know this. I am quite hopelessly in love with you. I hope that won't be a problem."

Lindsay looked at him, barely breathing. Somehow she managed to shake her head. "No," escaped hoarsely. "Not a problem."

He smiled and touched her shoulder. "And now I think we've malingered long enough, eh? Tomorrow we begin planting the vines and between now and then, we both have work to do. We had best get to it."

They walked back to the house together, but neither had much to say along the way.

Chapter Eleven

Labors of Love

April twenty-third," Bridget announced. "That's when the ancient Romans held their spring festival to honor Venus, the goddess of the fruit. They called it *venalia prima*. The blessing of the vines. So I think that's when we should hold our blessing. On April twenty-third."

Her words were a little choppy with exertion as she struggled to wind a length of wire cable tightly around a clamp on a support post. They were all, at that moment, laboring in the vineyard among the vines that were waiting to be blessed. Dominic and Noah worked a row or so ahead of them, digging post holes and pounding uprights into the ground. It was Cici's and Bridget's job to string and tighten the wire between the posts while Lindsay dug the holes and carefully placed the new vines in the ground. It was dirty, sweaty, back breaking work, but on this glorious spring day, it was also a labor of love.

Lindsay straightened up now, arching a pain out of her back, and said, "I don't know, Bridge, seems to me these vines are already blessed enough with my blood, sweat, and tears." But her gaze was on the two men who worked on the row beyond them, and her expression was vaguely troubled. Noah, in muddy jeans and T-shirt with his sweatshirt tied around his waist, steadied a post while Dominic pounded it into the ground with a short-handled sledge. Dominic had his hair tied back with a bandanna and wore a plain black T-shirt, now stained with sweat. He had the muscles of a man half his age.

Cici noted the direction of her gaze. "Can you imagine if we had tried to do this by ourselves?"

Lindsay gave a short, quick shake of her head, as though to clear her thoughts, and picked up her shovel again. "I didn't even know you were supposed to tie up the vines. I mean, I guess I did because I can see someone else did it here with the old vines, but I wouldn't have the faintest idea how to begin."

"Not just that. Everything." Cici used a screwdriver to tighten down the clamp that held the wire, gritting her teeth with the effort. When she was done, she pushed back her baseball cap and wiped the sweat from her forehead, leaving a smear of mud from the back of her glove. "Maybe Bridget is right. We have an awful lot of be grateful for. A little show of appreciation to the gods might not be a bad idea."

"Seriously," agreed Bridget. She carefully

removed one of her gloves to examine a blister that was beginning to form on her palm. "After all this, are you willing to take a chance on *not* blessing them?"

Once again, Lindsay found her gaze straying toward the two men who worked ahead of them, and she quickly brought it back to her work. "So what did the Romans do at this festival?" she asked.

"Well," said Bridget, pulling her glove back on, "they drank, of course, and danced and had food. And then they blessed the wine from the previous year before releasing it to be served, and they asked the weather gods and the fruit gods to bless the vines that would produce this year's harvest. It was really very sweet, when you think about it." She bent to pick up the heavy spool of wire and dragged it to the next post. "Kind of symbolic of the full cycle of nature and the humble role of man within it."

"You read that on the Internet, right?" Cici screwed in another clamp.

"Right."

"Hey, ladies!" Domnic called back to them, grinning. "A little less conversation, a little more action, eh? We're getting ahead of you."

Cici and Bridget grinned back and waved to him, but Lindsay's answering smile was brief and the other two women noticed she didn't quite meet Dominic's gaze as she dug her shovel into the ground. "Well, a party sounds like fun," Lindsay admitted. "I just don't know where you're going to find anyone to bless the vines. The Episcopals used to do a blessing of the animals back in Baltimore, remember? We took Lori's cat to it one year. But I don't know anyone who blesses vines."

Bridget grunted as she grabbed the wire and pulled it taut, while Cici tightened the clamp. "I'm sure," she said, digging in her heels, "there's someone . . ." She pulled harder. "On the Internet."

Bridget slipped backwards and almost fell; Lindsay shoved her hard in the small of the back and Bridget righted herself, casting Lindsay a grateful look.

Cici reached out a hand to steady her. "I don't know if we're up to a big party," she said. "Not that soon, anyway. We still have a hole in our roof, remember?"

"It wouldn't have to be big," Bridget said, breathing easier as Cici finished tightening the clamp and she could release the tension on the wire. "I'm thinking just us, and Derrick and Paul, and Lori and Mark of course, Dominic, Frank Adams and his wife, and maybe Farley. Everyone who's helped us with the winery."

"Then we'd better include Mark's parents," said Lindsay, tamping the last of the soil around the cutting she'd just planted. "I still think they're our secret investors."

"Oh great, how awkward would that be?" said Cici.

"Of course," added Bridget innocently, "we'd give tours of the winery, and it *would* be the perfect time to preview The Tasting Table."

Cici stared at her. "Bridget,"—her voice was incredulous—"we've spent four months trying to get a hole in our roof repaired, and you think we can build a restaurant in two weeks?"

"It doesn't have to be *built*," Bridget insisted. "Remember, technically I'm just catering events. I don't have to have a real restaurant or a restaurant license or anything like that. Just a place."

Cici and Lindsay exchanged a glance and a wry smile. "Well," Cici said, "as long as it's just a place . . ."

"Ladies!" Dominic swiped the back of his arm over his wet face. "Daylight's burning!"

Bridget bent to pick up the spool of wire again and Cici centered another clamp. "So glad we found him," she muttered.

But Lindsay, glancing quickly across the row at the two men, only smiled vaguely and did not reply.

In Ida Mae's Kitchen

Lindsay was stirring up a pot of cabbage soup—*Guaranteed to lose ten pounds the first week!* according to the testimonials on the web site—and trying not to hold her nose at the smell when Ida Mae came in from the porch with a basket of fresh mint in one hand and a collection of envelopes in the other. Ida Mae wrinkled her nose and shrank back from the odor emanating from the stove.

"What are you stinking up my kitchen with now?" she demanded.

Lindsay abandoned the soup and came over to her eagerly. "Is that the mail?"

"That's what it looks like to me."

Lindsay took the envelopes and sorted through them quickly, her expression falling as she failed to find what she was looking for. "I just don't understand," she said, placing the envelopes on the table for someone else to deal with. "We should have heard *something* by now. I checked with all the websites, and none of them are running behind."

Ida Mae covered the soup pot with a lid, trying to fan away some of the odor with her apron. "If you're gonna keep this on simmer, you better start opening some windows."

"Ida Mae, are you *sure* we haven't gotten something official looking from a college? It would probably have an emblem or watermark or something on the envelope and say 'university' somewhere."

Ida Mae gave her a dry look as she spread out the mint in a colander and ran it under water. "I reckon I know what a college is."

Lindsay wrestled with the stubborn lock on the east-facing window. "All the colleges get their replies out by April. They just can't say nothing. They have to send something—yes or no. They *have* to."

Ida Mae said, "I didn't say they hadn't."

The window flew up on its sash with a rattle, and Lindsay staggered back a little. She whirled to Ida Mae. "Do you mean we *did* get something from a college?"

"Got four or five of them, as near as I can tell. Course, I don't always see the mail first."

Lindsay stared at her. "What? Why didn't you tell me? Where are they?"

Ida Mae shook the water off the mint placidly. "Weren't addressed to you."

"But . . ." Lindsay fell back with a puzzled frown. "You mean Noah has them?"

"That'd be my guess. Seeing as how his name was on them."

"But why wouldn't he tell me?"

"Why should he?"

"Well, because . . . Why shouldn't he?"

"Maybe because it don't involve you."

"Well, of course it does!" She was indignant. "I'm his mother, even if I haven't been for very long, and more importantly, his teacher! I have a right to know what college he's been accepted into. Of course I do! Do you know how worried I've been? Do you know how important this is?

You just wait until he gets home from school. I'll get to the bottom of this!" She turned on her heel to go.

Ida Mae blew out a long-suffering sigh. "Well, if that ain't just like you to go prancing off in your high-heeled shoes to fix the world without giving thought one to whether or not it *needs* fixing. Or wants fixing, for that matter."

Lindsay looked down at her sneakers, puzzled. "I'm not wearing high heels. What are you talking about?"

"You took in a wild boy," said Ida Mae, "and you didn't do a half-bad job taming him; I'll give you that. But he took care of hisself for more years than you been taking care of him; you remember that." She stacked the mint on the cutting board and sliced off the stems in one efficient roll of the knife. "Maybe he don't want to be ruled over by a pack of women. Maybe he likes to keep some things to hisself. Maybe he feels like he needs to hold on to that part that took care of hisself for all that time, just in case he ever needs it again. And maybe you're forgetting he ain't a boy no more. He's already got one foot over the line of being a man. And maybe this here ain't as much of your business as you think it is."

Lindsay was quiet for a moment. Then she said, "I forget sometimes, who he is and what he's been through. I guess if I were him I'd want to guard a little independence for myself, too. It really is his decision. He's earned it. Thanks, Ida Mae." She turned to leave.

Ida Mae didn't look up from mincing the mint. "And if you think for one minute you're going to go off and leave that mess simmering on my stove, you got another think coming."

Abashed, Lindsay murmured, "Yes, ma'am," and returned to stir the soup.

The planting and staking of the new vines took the remainder of the week, and the women went to bed aching with exhaustion each night, too tired even to complain. But at the end of the week, their bedraggled, neglected, winter-torn vineyard looked like a picture postcard. Neat orderly rows curved down the hillside, trellises stood tall and straight; baby grapevines hugged each post; and mature vines began putting out sweet green shoots. The white gravel road swept from the driveway to the vineyard entrance to the winery below the barn, and a new cedar sign glistened in the dew of early morning: Ladybug Farm Winery. Cici, Bridget, and Lindsay stood on the side porch in their pajamas and robes with their morning coffee as the mist was rising off the vines, and they simply admired the view.

"Funny," observed Bridget, "I can hardly even remember how much my back hurts now."

"I should get my camera," Lindsay said, sipping her coffee. "This would be a perfect picture for our brochure." But she made no move to actually go inside.

"We can afford brochures," said Cici, wonderingly. "Life is good."

"Well, almost." Lindsay frowned a little. "I just wish Noah would talk to me about his college choice."

"It's a big decision," Bridget said. "The first step toward being an adult."

"Remember what I went through with Lori?" Cici said.

"I just don't understand why he would be so secretive about it," Lindsay said. "Why he wouldn't want to at least discuss it with me."

Both women were deliberately silent, gazing at their cups.

Lindsay's expression sharpened. "What?" she demanded. "What are you thinking? I know that look."

Cici and Bridget tried not to roll their eyes as they shared a glance. "Well," said Bridget carefully, "you know you can be a little hands-on, particularly when it comes to matters of education."

And as Lindsay's eyes widened to the point of bulging out of her head, Cici added quickly, "Not that there's anything wrong with that. You're a teacher. Listen, it's hard to let go. It's the hardest thing about parenting. But the best thing about you—the thing I admire most about you—is how hard you've tried to respect Noah's boundaries. I don't think he could have grown up to be as responsible as he has if you hadn't done that, so . . . just a little longer, okay?"

"You really *did* make such a big deal on his birthday about giving him the choice," Bridget reminded her. "I think he might be taking that a little too seriously. Just give him some time."

Lindsay took a deep breath and blew it out slowly. "I never had to take care of anything before," she admitted. "Not even a parakeet. I just want to do it right."

Cici saluted her with her coffee cup. "You're doing great," she assured her.

And Bridget added, raising her own cup, "Really."

Before Lindsay could even muster a smile in reply, Rebel darted out from under the porch in a furious cacophony of barking. He raced down the drive in a blur of black-and-white feet, and in another moment they heard the sound of tires on the drive. Lindsay straightened up and pushed back her hair as the truck rounded the curve, because Dominic often came to check the wine or work in the vineyard this time of morning. It wasn't that he was unaccustomed to seeing any of them in their pajamas, and Cici and Bridget were as comfortable around him as they would have been with a brother. But they couldn't help notice that Lindsay's sleepwear had gotten quite a bit cuter over the past few weeks, and often, she came to breakfast wearing lip gloss, just in case.

Lindsay relaxed as they all saw it was only the battered red pickup of the roofing crew. Rebel veered off, as disappointed as Lindsay, and raced toward the meadow to torment the sheep.

Cici heaved a huge sigh. "And so the day begins."

The roofers had finally begun replacing sheets of blue tarp with sheets of actual plywood, happily banging away from seven in the morning until noon, then disappearing until the notion struck them once again to continue the job. Rebel barked himself hoarse every morning, circling the trucks and the ladders, snapping at tires and lunging at toolboxes, until finally Cici yelled out the window, "You can bite them if you want to, Rebel!" After that, Rebel seemed to lose interest and trotted away in search of something to do. The roofers, however, looked at her with new respect and generally made themselves scarce when they saw her coming.

"I guess Bridge and I will get started in the barn while you torture the roofers," Lindsay told Cici, turning to go inside. "But first, breakfast. I think I smell wild berry muffins."

Bridget followed her. "I thought you were on a diet."

"It's okay," Lindsay assured her, though she sounded a little morose. "I can eat anything I want as long as I drink a quart of grapefruit juice first."

"A quart!"

"To tell the truth," Lindsay confessed, "I don't have much of an appetite after that."

Cici started to follow them inside, then turned back at the sound of more tires on the driveway. Lindsay pushed past her to peer around the corner. They heard the truck stop in front and then move on. Cici shrugged. "Probably the mail," she said.

And then Dominic's truck came into view.

He slowed at the steps and rolled down his window. "Good morning, ladies," he said pleasantly.

Cici watched Lindsay. Lindsay tried very hard not to have any expression at all.

Bridget called, "Hi, Dominic! We were just going in for breakfast. Will you join us?"

"No, thank you kindly. I can't stay. I just stopped by to drop off a little something for you. I saw it in town and thought you could use it. I left it on the front porch." He put the truck in gear and waved as he drove off. "Have a good day, now!"

Cici looked at Bridget, eyebrows raised in question. Lindsay swallowed hard. They all walked around the porch to the front of the house.

There, sitting in alignment with the three white

rocking chairs, was a new rocker, freshly painted white, with a big red bow on it. Pinned to the bow was a note. It said: *Just in case you ever want to have company.*

"Well, my goodness," said Bridget, reading the note. "How sweet!"

"Thoughtful," agreed Cici. "But then, he's that kind of guy."

Lindsay just stood there, smiling and smiling, and didn't say a word.

"What a bunch of idiots," Cici fumed, pulling on a pair of work gloves as she entered the barn half an hour later. "You won't believe what they've done now. They've got half the shingles torn off the front porch roof—without even asking me, mind you!—and they're planning to replace them with tin! Tin! This is an historic house. You don't just go ripping off handmade tile shingles and tossing them in the trash pile. And you certainly don't replace them with tin!"

"Tin roofs are kind of nice," Bridget said, but when Cici turned her glare on her, she added quickly, "but not on Federal-style houses, of course." She grasped the handle of the wheelbarrow and pushed it across the stone barn floor.

"Why don't you call Paul and Derrick's builder?" Lindsay suggested.

"Oh, I don't know. Paul says they're already behind because of all the rain we had, and I'd feel awful if I stole their builder just when they were starting to make some progress."

"We're going to have to find a builder anyway," Bridget pointed out, "to remodel the barn for the restaurant and gift shop and build the office."

"I suppose," agreed Cici with a sigh. "So." She looked around the dustily sunlit barn with her hands on her jeaned hips. "What's the plan here?"

"Well." Bridget dropped a box filled with loose nuts and bolts into the wheelbarrow and straightened up, dusting off her hands. "I know it's hard to picture now, but I thought if we could move all this stuff out of the way, this corner here would be easy to section off. With the big doors open, there would be plenty of light, and we could set up a buffet station over here . . ." She crossed the floor with half-running steps and sketched a wide horseshoe shape in the air. "And tables . . ." Again a few running steps. "From here to here. I think we can get six in here easily, don't you? And maybe half-walls . . ." More quick steps, more gestures. "Here, here, here. I mean, this is just a suggestion, right, of what the finished product will look like. Just for the party."

Cici nodded thoughtfully, looking around. "It's kind of quaint, having lunch in the barn. I like it. But, Bridge, I don't think you should count on getting real walls up between now and then—even half walls. Maybe some kind of screen . . ."

"We could do trellis," suggested Lindsay.

"We've got all that trellis leftover from the wedding last year, and it's already painted."

"Perfect," exclaimed Bridget. "We could back it with fabric . . ."

"And maybe wind some artificial grape leaf garlands through it," Lindsay said. "I'll bet they have some at the dollar store in town."

"If not, I know they have silk roses."

"Paul will die when he sees fake flowers."

"Well, he's just going to have to figure out some way to make roses bloom in April, then. Or grape leaves, for that matter."

"We'll have real flowers on the tables," Lindsay assured her. "The tulips will be in bloom next week, and we've got plenty of daffodils."

"Better—lilacs," declared Bridget. Her eyes lit up as she looked around, picturing it. "In keeping with the whole vineyard theme, right? Lilac blossoms do kind of resemble grape clusters, and I could make napkins out of some of that lavender calico I found last year . . ."

"We have so many lilac bushes, we could bank the buffet with lilac branches. Of course, keeping them from wilting will be a problem. Do you know," added Lindsay thoughtfully, "and just to keep Paul from making a scene, mind you—we *could* take cuttings from the pear tree, with all those gorgeous white blossoms and wind them through the trellis, mixed in with just a few lilac blossoms for symmetry, you know and—oh, I know! We'll mix in some white Christmas lights for sparkle and maybe have Noah tack some on the underside of the loft. We could cover the lights with a drape of cheesecloth—they have it by the bolt at Family Hardware—and it would be absolutely heavenly! I know it won't be as dramatic as if it were nighttime, but still, details are important."

"Burlap!" Bridget clapped her hands together happily. "I'm going to use burlap for the tablecloths and the buffet and contrast it with lavender satin runners . . ."

"And the napkins," Lindsay put in. "Satin for the napkins."

"Of course! How cute will that be? Oh my God!" Bridget pressed her hands to her flushed cheeks, her eyes bright. "I think I've just come up with the décor for my restaurant!"

Lindsay grinned and gave her a quick one-armed hug, and Cici said, "How are you going to plug them in?"

The other two women looked at her blankly. "The lights," explained Cici practically. Her gaze traveled from the loft, around the walls, and across the boundaries of Bridget's imaginary restaurant, assessing. "How are you going to plug them in? The only outlet is on the other side of the barn, fifty feet away. You could run an extension cord, but it would be kind of ugly. And Bridge, you know that with all the hay we have stored in the loft there's bound to be, well, mice. And the sun really heats this place up by the middle of the afternoon. You'll need a fan to keep the air circulating, which brings up the question of where you're going to plug that in, and when you do, there's no telling what kind of dust and debris it'll stir up. With all that food out . . ."

It was at that point that Cici noticed the excitement of her friend's anticipation was deflating like a balloon with a slow leak with every word she spoke. She glanced at Lindsay, who moved protectively closer to Bridget, and she said brightly, "But, hey, it's April. What are the chances we'll need a fan, anyway? And we can spray-paint the extension cord white; you'll never even notice it. So let's get this corner cleaned out and start bringing in the trellis. What do you say?"

Like sunshine from behind a cloud, Bridget's grin returned and so did her enthusiasm. She rubbed her hands together in glee. "I say, what are we waiting for?"

In Ida Mae's Kitchen

Cici sat at the kitchen counter, scowling as she flipped through *A History of Blackwell Farms*. The kitchen was redolent of the sharp odor of spring greens and new potatoes roasting in pork fat and the faint aroma of turned earth and spring flowers that wafted through the open window.

"Ida Mae," Cici said, turning a page, "I don't see anything in here about the Blackwell Farms tasting events. I don't see how they could've been held in that barn. In the first place, there was no refrigeration, and they would've had to pull from the house for electricity. In the second place, there was no lighting. I know it was the sixties, but there had to be some sanitation codes and at least a *few* regulations about serving food to the public. Where did they wash dishes? Didn't anyone need to go to the bathroom?" She sighed and closed the book. "I just don't know what to do."

Ida Mae sprinkled a generous handful of flour over the pie dough she was rolling out, and Cici brushed the residue off the cover of the book. "Bridget has her heart set on opening a restaurant in that barn," she said, "but there's no way it's going to work. Even without a health department permit—I mean, let's just assume we're calling this a catering business—it's just not practical. The ceilings are twenty feet high. To lower and insulate them would be a major construction job—like that's something that's easy to do around here!—and to try to heat and cool that space the way it is would cost a fortune. And let's not even talk about building the walls—you'd have to trench out those gorgeous stone floors—

and putting in HVAC. There is no plumbing whatsoever, and if we try to tie into the house I *know* we're going to have to apply to the health department for a permit, and you just can't imagine what kind of can of worms that opens. And did I even mention the electrical situation? Even if all we're talking about is warming trays and steam tables . . . I mean, for heaven's sake, you've got to have more than one outlet!" She dropped her head to her hands. "What was I thinking? I never should've let her get her hopes up. I should've been paying more attention."

Ida Mae flipped the pie dough and applied the rolling pin with vigor.

"The truth is," Cici confessed, dragging her fingers down her face as she straightened up, "it would be cheaper to build a separate building for the restaurant than to try to convert the barn. I mean seriously, at $120 per square foot for a commercial building . . . Oh, what am I thinking? That would take every bit of our windfall, and we're supposed to be running a winery, not a restaurant."

She squared her shoulders and pushed back from the table. "On the other hand, it's just a party, right? And why not hold it in the barn? It's going to be cute. I mean, we don't even have a vintage, for heaven's sake. It's not like we're going to be doing a tasting *today*. The restaurant is the last item on the business plan, right? We have months to figure it out." She sighed. "It's just that I feel so bad. I don't know what to tell her."

Cici pinched a piece of pie dough from the rolling board and popped it in her mouth. "Umm." She was thoughtful for a moment. "You know, Ida Mae," she decided, "I think you're right. What's the point in breaking her heart? Not yet anyway. We'll have the party. I'll figure something out. Who knows? Maybe the vine blessing will bring us luck."

She plucked off another piece of pie dough. "Good," she observed, pushing away from the counter. "What kind of pie are you making?"

"Peach," said Ida Mae, glaring at her. "If I have any crust left."

"I love peach," said Cici, closing the book as she stood. "Thanks, Ida Mae. You've been a big help."

Ida Mae said, "Hmph." And she didn't look up as Cici left the kitchen.

Bridget said, "The bad news is, no one within fifty miles is available to bless our vines." She sank down into her rocking chair, cradling a glass of wine, resting her head momentarily against the back rail of the chair. "Can you believe that? What kind of world do we live in? Reverend Holland was appalled. You'd think I'd asked him to sanction public drunkenness. And

Pastor Winfred was conveniently noncommittal. This is not, and I quote, 'in the purview of the Methodist church.' So I found an Episcopal in Staunton, but he has a wedding that day. Then I had to go all the way to Charlottesville to find a Catholic priest, and it turns out I was in luck. He's done dozens of blessing of the vines ceremonies. In fact, he's doing one next weekend . . . in France. So that pretty much lets him out for our event."

She sipped her wine and slid a glance, from one side to the other, to her friends. Neither of them missed the secretive sparkle in her eyes. "The good news is," she said, "Paul and Derrick sold their house!"

Over the exclamations of delight and excitement, she raised her voice. "They have to be out in two weeks. They're coming to our blessing of the vines, but . . ." She waited for the excitement to die down. "They're staying in the B&B until their house is finished."

"Are you kidding?" Cici declared, insulted. "We have all these empty rooms and they're not good enough? I'm calling them right now."

"The B&B?" Lindsay repeated, frowning. "Whatever gave them that idea?"

"And," declared Bridget firmly, the sparkle unrelenting, "they have a priest for our ceremony! So the blessing of the vines is on for April twenty-third."

"Oh, Bridge!" exclaimed Lindsay sincerely, "I'm so glad. That's fabulous news."

But Cici's frown was unrelenting. "I still don't understand why they don't want to stay here."

"Come on, Cici," said Bridget, "it'll be weeks, if not months, before their house is finished. Why would they want to move in with somebody else for that long? They're going to have a nice vacation at the B&B, so good for them."

Cici thought about that for a moment, and then agreed, "Well, I guess it can get a little hectic around here with Noah in and out, and all the animals, and Lori back and forth between here and Charlottesville. Speaking of which, I invited Lori and Mark for the weekend, but not his parents. I'm just too embarrassed that, not only is the roof still not fixed, the hole has actually gotten bigger. So let's just keep it to people who already know we don't really live like squatters, okay?"

"Not a problem," declared Bridget. "Just people we know. I invited everyone from the bank who helped out with the loan—even though they didn't come through, their intentions were good—and the entire Friends of the Library Book Club, because I *know* they drink, and Jonesie and his wife from the hardware store, and all the real estate agents because we definitely need them to spread the word, and the president of the Chamber of Commerce . . . I figure about thirty people."

Cici tried not to show her alarm. "Bridget, that's a lot of people."

"The barn is a big place," she replied happily. "Not a problem."

Lindsay said, "You're not planning to do a full lunch for all of them, are you?"

"Just heavy hors d'oeuvres," she assured her. "Spring rolls and pepper shrimp . . ."

"Shrimp!" exclaimed Cici before she could stop herself.

"It's a business expense," Bridget informed her archly. "Besides, it's important to set the tone for what the future of The Tasting Table is going to be. Upscale casual with a touch of country nouveau cuisine."

Lindsay looked at her curiously. "What is country nouveau cuisine?"

"You know. New potatoes stuffed with fresh herbs and manchego, tossed in olive oil. Crispy battered green beans served with a chipotle dipping sauce. Grilled peaches drizzled with balsamic and sprinkled with ground black pepper. Fresh raspberries . . ."

"Okay, enough." Lindsay held up a hand in protest. "I can't believe I just finished dinner and I'm hungry again."

"Sounds pretty ambitious, Bridge," Cici said cautiously. "Thirty people and all."

She gave a dismissive wave of her hand. "It's practically done. Everything I need is in the freezer, and our Christmas party is twice as big as this. I'll toss it all together that morning. Oh! And the best part is that Dominic was able to get a couple of cases of wine from the very winery we ordered our crush from. He says it's perfectly acceptable to serve another winery's vintage at our blessing of the vines. Although . . ." Her expression fell slightly. "It's against the rules to put our label on it."

"Bambi!" Lindsay exclaimed, surging up from her chair as the deer wandered close to the house and began stripping leaves off a hydrangea bush. The deer looked up with interest, then returned to nibbling the hydrangea.

Cici clapped her hands loudly, which attracted the attention of Rebel, who darted out from under the porch, barking madly. Bambi bounded away in one direction, and Rebel scrambled off in the other, looking for something else to bark at. Lindsay sank back into her chair.

"I don't know what's gotten into that deer," she said. "Noah is going to have to keep a better eye on him."

"He's a deer," Bridget pointed out. "He eats hydrangeas."

"He used to eat the carrots and cabbages we fed him, and a few weeds and maple leaves. Now he eats everything."

"We're going to have to build some kind of fence if we expect to have any flowers left at all this year," Cici said. "And what about your roses?"

"Speaking of roses," Bridget said, glancing at her, "I haven't seen Dominic in a couple of days."

"So?" Lindsay sipped her wine, staring deliberately across the meadow where the sheep bunched lazily, their fleece glowing faintly pink in the setting sun. "He doesn't live here, you know. He has a life."

Bridget shrugged. "I know. But I've gotten kind of used to having him around. And he usually does stop by once or twice a day to do whatever it is he does with the wine." She glanced at the rocking chair, which had been relegated to a lone place on the opposite side of the door. "It was nice of him to give us the chair," she observed innocently. "You know, in case Ida Mae ever wants to sit with us."

Lindsay frowned into her wine. "She never does."

"Or for when Lori comes," added Bridget. Then she corrected herself, "But now there's Mark. So I guess that doesn't work. But Paul and Derrick will visit."

"When they get tired of the B&B," observed Cici darkly.

Bridget gave a quick, bright smile. "I guess he really should have given us *two* chairs. It seems as though everyone is a couple!"

Cici tossed her an impatient look. "Oh, for heaven's sake." She turned to Lindsay and demanded frankly, "Are you ever going to tell us what's going on with you two?"

Lindsay rocked and sipped her wine and said nothing. Rebel sailed over the pasture fence, circled the flock twice, and jumped back over the fence. She said finally, "We worked so hard to get here. I don't just mean here." She gestured vaguely to include the house, farm, the sheep, the dog, the deer. "I mean *here*. In this moment. Do you know what it *takes* to reach a dream? I mean, of course you do, because you did it, too; we did it together. But do you know how many people never get to do that? And now here I am, *finally,* with everything just the way I want it, and somebody has to come along and complicate things. It's not fair."

Bridget smiled kindly. "War isn't fair," she said. "Children who never call aren't fair. Famine, poverty, politics, post-menopausal weight gain, wrinkles on your neck—those are not fair. This is just . . . interesting."

Lindsay frowned. "You know what I mean. I like things the way they are. I don't want them to change."

"They're changing already," Cici pointed out. "Noah is going to college. Lori is getting married. Nothing will be the same after that." Her tone fell a little as she gazed into her glass. "Nothing."

Melancholy settled over the porch like the lavender shadows of the evening, sweet and gentle and cool to the touch.

"You're right," said Lindsay sadly. "Nothing stays the same."

"Sometimes that's a good thing," Bridget said. "Remember, the reason we started the winery was because we wanted a change."

"I guess it's all a matter of how you look at it," Cici said.

Lindsay tried to smile. "Adapt or die, huh?"

"It's always better to adapt," Bridget assured her.

Lindsay sighed. "It's just that I was so happy."

Bridget reached across and placed her hand gently atop Lindsay's, and Cici smiled at her sympathetically. "We know," she said.

Chapter Twelve

Surprise

Lindsay leaned on the broom. Cici put down the nail gun. Both of them stepped back to assess what two days of labor had wrought.

Even with the back doors open, the sixteen by twenty section of barn that had been blocked off was dim and shadowy. There hadn't been quite enough trellis panels to completely enclose the area, so they staggered them at odd intervals, hoping to give the impression of a garden wall. They hadn't quite succeeded. The dime store grape leaves that Lindsay hoped to use as a backdrop for real lilac blossoms looked like a child's craft project as they wound in and out of the trellis, and the Christmas lights that were tacked up everywhere looked . . . well, tacky.

They spent all morning building an L-shaped buffet table from sawhorses and plywood, and scavenged every spare table and chair from every storage area and unused room in the house to make six different dining tables. Bridget had gone to Family Hardware to purchase the burlap and lace that she was certain would transform the tables into charming vignettes. Meanwhile, The Tasting Table looked like nothing so much as a sad little display in the junk section of a public flea market.

"A few flowers, some candles," Cici offered hopefully.

"The tablecloths will make a huge difference," Lindsay added.

"After all, it's just for practice," Cici said. "It's not like this is the real restaurant."

Lindsay looked at her with a sigh. "This is never going to work, is it?"

Cici looked at her in despair. "Lindsay, it smells like manure in here."

"It's right next to the goat house."

"How can she not see it?"

"I think she sees it," Lindsay said sadly. "She just doesn't want to admit it."

"Thirty people." Cici's voice held a note of despair. "The book club, the bank president, the chamber of commerce . . ."

"Shrimp," Lindsay reminded her.

Cici groaned. "In two days."

"Ladies, good morning."

They both turned at the sound of the voice behind them—Lindsay with perhaps a bit more alacrity than Cici. Dominic stood for a moment, silhouetted in the sun-glare of the open doors, and then came inside, glancing around.

"You all planning on a yard sale?" he inquired.

Cici gave Lindsay a helpless "I told you so" look and turned back to Dominic. "No, Dominic," she said wearily. "No yard sale. Just a project that didn't work out. Did you need us for something?"

Dominic's eyes were on Lindsay, who suddenly decided it was very important to finish up the sweeping. He said, "I just wanted to let you know that your license to sell came in. I've got the papers in my truck."

Cici smiled gratefully. "We have got to get you an office."

His gaze lingered on Lindsay just a half a moment longer, and then he smiled at Cici. "One of these days," he answered easily. "Meanwhile, I'm going to walk down and look at the vines. "We haven't had as much rain as I'd hoped and I want to make sure they're not stressed. Do you want me to just leave the papers at the house?"

"That would be great," Cici said. "Thanks, Dominic."

Lindsay looked up and flashed him a quick, shallow smile. "Thanks, Dominic," she echoed.

"See you ladies later."

Lindsay watched him until he was out of sight, and then she turned back to Cici, a determined look on her face. "We cannot," she said simply, "let Bridget do this."

"I don't know that we have a choice." Cici's expression was a mixture of desperation and dismay. "The party is in two days. She's already started cooking. She's invited everyone we know. Paul and Derrick are bringing a priest. How are we going to stop her?"

Lindsay's lips tightened in sudden resolve, and she thrust the broom to Cici. "Okay, when Bridget gets back, make sure she stays busy sewing the tablecloths. Whatever you do, don't let her come back out here."

Cici's eyes widened. "Me? How am I going to keep her—"

"And as soon as Noah gets home, send him to me. Meanwhile, start taking this crap down and moving the tables out. I've got a plan!"

"What plan? What—"

But Lindsay was already dashing out of the barn.

Dominic was crossing the barnyard toward the vineyard when Lindsay reached him, breathing hard, and caught his arm. "Are you any good with your hands?" she demanded.

He turned to her, his expression both surprised and amused. "I've been told," he admitted modestly, "I'm quite good."

"Then grab a hammer and follow me." She raced away again, but turned after a few feet, running backwards, and called, "But first, stop by the barn and get the sawhorses."

He opened his mouth for a question, wisely closed it again, and followed her.

In Ida Mae's Kitchen

Noah sat at the kitchen counter, barefoot and shirtless, hunched over a bowl of bananas and milk, absently reading *A History of Blackwell Farms* by the light of the open refrigerator door. It was four-thirty in the morning. Lindsay had kept him working until after ten the night before. Not that he minded; it was just painting and stuff, and besides, he'd do whatever she needed to help out. That was just the way it was. Still, he'd fallen asleep before his head hit the pillow and then had come wide awake a half hour ago with too much running through his head to go back to sleep. So he had come downstairs in search of something to eat. All he could find was some bananas on the counter and some leftover cauliflower from the night before in the fridge. He wasn't wild about cauliflower, so he made the best of it.

The overhead lights suddenly sprang on, and he whirled, mouth full of bananas, flinging up a forearm to shield his squinting eyes.

Ida Mae stood beside the stove in a flowered quilted robe and a multi-pocketed hunting vest, an iron skillet held over her shoulder like a baseball bat. He swallowed hard, trying not to choke, and exclaimed, "Hey!" Ida Mae lowered the skillet to the stove with a clatter, glaring at him.

"What you doing sitting in my kitchen like a naked savage in the middle of the night, boy?" she demanded. She marched to the refrigerator and slammed the door shut, then turned with her hands on her hips, demanding an answer.

Noah turned back to his bowl of bananas. "I was hungry," he muttered. "Couldn't find the cereal."

Ida Mae strode to the pantry and returned in a moment with a box of cornflakes, which she plopped on the counter before him, and a navy windbreaker, which she thrust at him. "Nobody sits at my table with no clothes on," she told him. "Have some respect."

Meekly, he pulled on the windbreaker and zipped it up.

She gave a short nod of semi-satisfaction and

returned to the refrigerator, removing a bowl of brown eggs and a pound of butter. "Seems to me you'd be taking every chance you can get to sleep in, with all you got going on."

He gave a small, uncomfortable shrug and poured cornflakes into his bowl. "I've got stuff on my mind."

"I know the kind of stuff boys your age've got on their minds, and it ain't worth mentioning." Ida Mae scooped flour from a glass canister into a big bowl, sparing him a slow sideways glance. "That mama of yours knows about them envelopes you've been getting from the universities."

He paused with the cornflakes box in midair, then set the box on the counter. "That's okay," he said, smashing the cornflakes into the bananas and milk in his bowl. "I was gonna tell her anyhow."

"Well, you better make it soon. She's about to drive everybody in this house crazy, wondering and worrying about you and what it is you're going to do. I've never seen such a fuss in my life about nothing."

He was about to shove a big spoonful of cornflakes and bananas in his mouth, but instead, he lowered the spoon to the bowl and simply looked at it. Ida Mae returned to the refrigerator and took out a bottle of milk.

He said, without looking up, "You ever had somebody love you more than you deserved?"

Ida Mae frowned as she poured a measure of

milk into a saucepan and set it on the stove. "If you're talking about that little gal you've been sparkin', you're too young to know a thing in this world about love, both of you."

He turned the spoon over and over in the bowl. "Nah. I'm not talking about Amy. We're breaking up after graduation anyway. She's going to missionary school."

Ida Mae turned the milk on simmer and measured yeast into a small bowl.

Noah took the spoon and started drawing an absent design in the mush of bananas and cornflakes with it. "What if a person loves you more than you deserve and dreams a dream for you bigger than you want? What're you supposed to do then?"

Ida Mae's steps were slow and deliberate as she replaced the milk in the refrigerator, returned to the stove, sprinkled sugar over the milk that was warming there. For all intents and purposes, she might not have heard Noah at all.

Noah pushed up from the table. "Maybe I'll go work in the studio for a while," he said.

He reached the door before she spoke. "Every born soul has got just one job to do," she said, cracking eggs into a bowl, "and that's to figure out who you are in this world. Then be that. Nobody can do it for you. It's up to you."

Noah stood there for another moment, thinking about it, and then he smiled, just a little. "Yeah," he said quietly. And then, with more conviction, "Yeah."

He opened the door.

"And don't you even think about going out in that yard in the dark without your shoes," Ida Mae said sharply.

He closed the door. "Yes, ma'am."

He went in search of shoes.

The Mountain Laurel Bed and Breakfast was not exactly what Paul and Derrick had expected, and they were connoisseurs of B&Bs. The building was big and brown and rambling, with more of a lodge feel than the quaint antebellum charm they had for some reason expected. On the front of the building alone there were four doors, each painted a different color—red, green, lavender, and yellow—which was probably an attempt to make the best out of someone's bad design decision. There was a koi pond in front, with a small stone bridge and a cheerfully splashing waterfall, and the long, low-roofed front porch was hung with lush baskets of ferns at every pillar. There was a blowsy wildflower garden bisected by a stone path and dotted with colorful folk art bird feeders and a big oak tree with a kissing bench encircling it. There was not, however, a stick of mountain laurel in sight.

They followed the gravel drive around to the side of the building, where a neat parking lot was framed by railroad ties and surrounded by beds of bright daffodils and deep purple hyacinths. Red glass hummingbird feeders were suspended from shepherd's crooks at uneven intervals throughout the garden, clashing with the color palette. Theirs was the only car in the lot.

"I still think we should've stayed with the girls," Derrick complained as they got out of the car. "I know we hurt their feelings by moving in here."

"And *I* still say we should've stayed over and driven down in the morning with Father Mike. Bridget is counting on us to bring the priest, and we should've actually brought the priest."

"I don't know how we could've done that when everything we own is at this moment being packed into giant storage pods and carted off to who knows where." Derrick looked around curiously. "Shouldn't there be more cars? Are we the only ones here?"

"Well, it's early in the season." Paul opened the back of the car and removed the first of two oversized rolling suitcases.

Derrick took out the garment bags and draped them atop the suitcase. "The view is nice," he observed.

"Peaceful," agreed Paul, gazing around. "The hyacinths are to die for."

Derrick ducked suddenly as something buzzed

past his ear, his expression astonished. "What the—?"

Paul swatted the air as another one of the creatures zoomed so close to his face he could feel the stirring of its wings. "Was that a mosquito?"

"If that was a mosquito," Derrick said, "we're getting back in the car and going to stay to with the girls."

Paul frowned a little as his gaze returned to the building. "A little signage wouldn't hurt. I wonder where the entrance is?"

The air buzzed again and Derrick threw up his arm in self-defense. "Good Lord," he exclaimed, following the path of the iridescent winged rocket toward one of the red glass globes in the garden. "I think those are hummingbirds!"

They dragged the giant suitcases up the steps, dodging hummingbirds as they went, and around the porch to the first door they saw, a bright blue one. It was locked. The suitcases thundered behind them as they followed the porch around to a second door, fuchsia pink. Also locked.

"Aha," declared Derrick as they reached the third, deep red, door. "A sign."

It was actually less of a sign than a note pinned to the door. Paul took it down and read it out loud.

Dear Paul and Derrick,
Welcome to the Mountain Laurel B&B!
So sorry I couldn't be here to greet you,

but I had a family emergency. Please come in and make yourselves at home. Your room is the first one down the long hall to the right.

Amelia Wriggly

P.S. Help yourselves to anything in the fridge

Paul looked at Derrick. Derrick lifted his eyebrows. "Welcome to the country?" he suggested, by way of explanation.

Paul tried the door. It opened. Very cautiously, they went inside.

The shrimp were marinating. The miniature pizzas were drizzled with olive oil and topped with sun-dried tomatoes, herbs, and Ladybug Farm goat cheese, waiting only to be popped into the oven when the guests arrived. Fresh melons and berries had been tossed with a champagne dressing and feta cheese, and the traditional cheddar biscuits were sliced and spread with pepper jam and wafer-thin slices of ham. Crisp stalks of blanched asparagus wrapped in thin slices of smoked turkey were arranged on platters lined with dandelion greens and sprinkled with chopped roasted walnuts. Ida Mae's sheet cake was beautifully frosted and decorated with fondant grape leaves. Bridget had already posted pictures of it to the Ladybug Farm website.

Everything was ready for the guests, who were scheduled to arrive for the blessing of the vines in approximately twenty hours. And Bridget was in a panic.

One thing or another had kept her away from the barn for the past day and a half. First, something had gone wrong in the winery—a cask exploded or something—and Dominic declared the entire area off limits to everyone until it was repaired. This hadn't concerned Bridget very much, since he seemed to have the emergency under control and she was, frankly, busy sewing tablecloths and marinating shrimp. But when she arrived bright and early the next morning, ready to start painting chairs, Lindsay and Cici assured her it was all taken care of and sent her on a wild goose chase for plastic ivy. Meanwhile, the sound of buzz saws and nail guns was unceasing. Noah clattered up and down the stairs so many times with cardboard boxes in his arms that Bridget was persuaded to poke her head out of the kitchen and inquire in alarm, "Noah, are you moving out?"

"No, ma'am," he replied over his shoulder, hurrying off. "Just redecorating!"

Bridget was no fool. She knew her friends were planning a surprise for her. She just hoped it would be finished in time for the blessing of the vines.

There were only twenty hours left before the first guests started to arrive and she needed to set up the bar, stage the tables, arrange the buffet. And all her tablecloths were missing.

"I'm not kidding, Ida Mae. I've got to have time to run that burlap through the washer and dryer for shrinkage," she said, trying to keep the hysteria out of her voice. "I know I left everything in the laundry room, so if you accidently ran it through with another load, it's okay. I just need to know where you put it. Everything will have to be ironed, and it's not like I have a whole lot of time."

Ida Mae said, scrubbing down the counter top, "I don't mess with your stuff; you don't mess with mine."

"But twenty-two yards of burlap and muslin tablecloths do not just disappear!" Bridget cried. "Do you know how long it took me to sew those lace runners? Ida Mae, *think,* for heaven's sake!"

Ida Mae glared at her. "I'm not your mama."

Bridget drew her breath for a virulent reply, and Cici pushed open the door from the dining room. "Everything okay in here?"

Bridget whirled on her, Ida Mae scowled at her, and before either could speak, Cici said, "By the way, Bridge, we found the tablecloths and went ahead and put them on the tables. Do you want to see?"

"Oh, thank goodness." Bridget placed a hand over her heart and heaved a huge sigh of relief. "But they really needed to be washed first."

Cici beckoned her to follow. "I think they'll be okay. After all, this is just practice, right?"

"Well, we want to make a good impression." Bridget hurried through the house after her. "And listen, Cici, do you think it would be too much to ask Noah—or even Lindsay—to paint a sign for tomorrow—it wouldn't have to be very big—that said 'The Tasting Table,' just to give people the impression it was a real restaurant? I know it's pretty last minute, but . . ."

"I'm sure they'd be fine with it," Cici said, skipping down the front steps. "After all, how long could it take?"

"I know you guys have been working overtime getting things ready," Bridget confessed, "while I was busy sewing the tablecloths and preparing the food. I want you to know that I . . ."

She started to turn toward the barn, but Cici gently grasped her arm and turned her in the other direction, around the house and toward the east. Bridget cast her a puzzled, questioning look, but Cici just smiled. "We figured," she said, "that if you're going to do this thing, you need to do it right."

Bridget looked back toward the barn, confused and reluctant. "Cici, we have an awful lot to do before tomorrow . . ."

Cici tugged her forward. "Maybe not."

They rounded the house, past the gardens, and approached the stone dairy, which was now

Lindsay's art studio. Lindsay, Dominic, and Noah stood in front of it, all of them with odd, subdued expressions on their faces, as though someone had told them a secret and dared them to keep it. But the strangest thing, the thing that immediately caught Bridget's eye as she drew up in front of the building, was that someone seemed to have tacked a sheet above the doorway, for no apparent reason whatsoever.

Bridget said uncertainly, "Hi, guys." She glanced at Dominic. "Is everything okay at the winery? Can we go back into the barn to start decorating now? What's going on?"

Dominic just smiled.

Noah reached up and tugged on a string. The sheet fell away and the three of them stepped back, grinning. Above the door of Lindsay's art studio was a scrolled wooden pub sign with "The Tasting Table" painted in elaborate gold script between two wine glasses that were tilted toward each other. Bridget stared at it.

"I did the sign work," Noah said, making no effort to hide his pride. "What do you think?"

"I—I think it's beautiful, Noah," Bridget said, her eyes widening with delight. "But shouldn't it be . . . ?" She gestured back toward the barn.

Cici gave her a little push forward. "Check it out," she said.

Dominic swung open the door to the studio and made a broad sweeping gesture to usher Bridget inside. Lindsay stood aside, her steepled fingers pressed to her lips, her eyes dancing with anticipation as she watched her friend enter. "Welcome," she said, "to The Tasting Table."

Bridget took an uncertain step inside and then caught her breath, looking around in astonishment. "Oh my goodness," she said softly. "What have you done?"

The long room was flooded with light from the skylights overhead and the rows of high windows that lined the creamy walls, and the stone floors had been waxed until they sparkled. To the right of the entrance a cubby had been created with a tall console that held a computer station and an adding machine. On the wall behind it there was a display of black-and-white photographs of Blackwell Farms from the early days that Lindsay had reproduced from tintypes she found in the attic. On the opposite side of the entrance, one of the former dairy stalls had been opened up into a small gift shop, with spotlights highlighting Bridget's gift baskets, jams, and homemade potpourris, and art lights illuminating some of Noah's and Lindsay's framed paintings. On either side of the room, private tables, each appropriately dressed in burlap and lace with a centerpiece spray of lilac, were nestled into the nooks that had once been stalls, and a different piece of framed art was spotlighted in each one.

But the most striking feature was the long trestle

table that was arranged beneath the skylights, running almost the length of the room. It was flanked on either side by a row of black lacquered chairs and set with stylish square white plates and black napkins. A runner of plain burlap ran down the center of the table, topped with candles in glass jars and lilac blossoms in colored glass bottles. All of it led the eye toward the ten-by-ten foot mural that covered the back wall.

The painting was a *trompe l'oeil* depiction of Ladybug Farm as seen through two swagged black velvet curtains: the sweep of lawn, the stately house, the sheep meadow, the rose garden, the vineyard in the distance, the barn and the gravel drive that curved toward the winery with its wooden sign: Ladybug Farm Winery. And if one looked very closely, a faint cloud formation in the eastern corner bore a very distinct resemblance to a feathery flying horse.

Bridget approached it with her hands pressed to her cheeks, her eyes wide and glistening, unable, for a moment, to even speak. Cici beamed at Lindsay. Dominic dropped a hand lightly on Lindsay's shoulder, and Noah nudged her affectionately with his elbow, grinning. Lindsay impatiently struck a tear from her eye, not wanting to miss a moment.

"It's . . ." Bridget finally managed. She half turned to them, choked on an exclamation that was part laugh and part sob, then whirled back.

"Oh, look!" she cried, stretching out a hand. "There's Rebel under the porch."

"I painted him in," Noah said. "Bambi, too, over there by the barn."

"We've been working on the panels all winter," Lindsay admitted, trying to sound casual. The glow of pleasure on her face betrayed her. "I was going to surprise you and move them in to the barn when you got your restaurant set up there, but as it turns out . . ." She shrugged. "This was a better place."

Bridget turned back to them, one hand still shielding her trembling lips, her face flushed and her eyes full. "You . . . these last couple of days . . . you did all this? For me?"

"Dominic and Noah helped move all the art stuff to the loft," Lindsay replied, casting a quick grateful smile from one to the other of them, "and they helped Cici build the table."

"What luck Family Hardware had sixteen matching chairs out in their storehouse," Cici put in. "They're just plain pine, but they look nice painted like that, don't they?"

"I can't believe we were able to sneak them in here without you noticing," Dominic added. "Didn't you hear Farley's truck yesterday morning?"

"And the dishes," Noah said. "Don't forget the dishes."

"I saw them in Staunton when I was Christmas

shopping," Cici said, "so I called the shop and luckily they still had two sets. I had them keep the store open last night while Noah drove in to get them. Of course, we'll order a lot more."

"And I had all those glass bottles in the attic," Noah added. "You know, picked up here and there around the place while we were planting stuff. Some of them are real antiques."

"And see? We brought in some of the other artifacts from the house and the old barn to use as art." Lindsay gazed around proudly at the polished-steel dairy cans that held fresh daffodils, the age-darkened chicken crate mounted on the wall, the horse collar that framed a mirror. "I know it's not finished, but we were running out of time. And it does look a little like a real restaurant, doesn't it?"

Bridget said, still struggling to get the words out, "It looks . . . it looks perfect! But Lindsay, your art studio." She looked at her helplessly. "You can't do this. Did Lori talk to you? I told her not to. This is your studio!"

Lindsay looked momentarily confused. "I think it was Ida Mae who first mentioned the idea to me," she said, "but I didn't give it much thought until I saw the barn. Bridget, really, what worked fifty years ago simply will not fly today." She looked at Dominic for reassurance, and he nodded.

"The entire set-up of the farm was different back

then," he said. "It was practical to have the tasting room upstairs because it was unused space. But now you're using it for a different purpose. There's no sense in trying to make something work for you just because it worked for someone else."

"Seriously, Bridge, the expense of converting the barn would be enormous," Cici said.

"Not to mention the smell," added Noah.

Lindsay said, "And this place already has good lighting, a new electrical box, heating, plumbing, and a real bathroom with another one roughed in. And did you see the serving area Cici walled off for you? Right there by the sinks so you can do prep and clean up and with six—count them, six!—electrical outlets."

Dominic cleared his throat. "Farley did the wiring," he pointed out. "You might want to have it checked by a licensed electrician."

Bridget looked from one to the other of them, brimming with hope and despair. "But, Lindsay, it's your studio! It's your dream. Where will you paint? Where will you have your classes?"

She shrugged it off cavalierly. "So now I have a better dream. My classes are down to practically nothing, and I never needed this much room for myself. The important thing is now I have a place to *sell* my paintings—with actual people coming through here to look at them. I can always paint upstairs in the loft when you're not using the downstairs, right? The light is better up there anyway."

Bridget ran to her and embraced her in a hug so fierce it almost knocked her down. Lindsay was laughing; Bridget was crying. "I love you!" she cried. "Thank you!"

She turned her embrace on Noah, and then on Cici, and then on Dominic. "Thank you! Thank you! Thank you!" She stepped back and wiped her damp face with both hands. "You're the best friends in all the history of friends. I don't deserve this."

"Maybe not," replied Cici with a grin, "but we wanted to do it anyway."

Lindsay draped her arm around Bridget's shoulders and gave them a squeeze. "Because we love you, too."

Cici caught her hand. "Come here, let me show you where I thought you could set up your buffet station."

Noah hurried after them. "Did you see the grape leaves I painted on the doors?"

Dominic, smiling, watched them for another moment, and then he turned and quietly left the building.

Paul looked around the entrance of the B&B, with its polished plank floors and country-bright décor, and observed, "I may be taking a risk here, but at first glance it doesn't look a thing like the Bates Motel. Always a good sign."

251

Derrick called out, "Hello?" His voice echoed.

Paul opened the door to a small, cluttered room marked "Office" and found it empty. Derrick looked around until he spotted a painting of a deer and another of a basket of wildflowers, each on opposite walls. "Aha," he said, going over to them. "Noah and Lindsay Wright. I would know their work anywhere, however badly displayed. And I don't see price cards on either one of them. Very bad marketing."

"If it were me," Paul said, "I'd turn this entire area into a gallery wall, get some proper lighting in here . . ."

"Lose the quilts and the tchotchkes." Derrick bent to peer inside an old-fashioned glass-fronted hutch. "Really? Miniature teapots?"

"Tell me that's not a wallpaper border," said Paul, looking up toward the ceiling.

"I like the chandelier, though," said Derrick. "Painted antlers. Just retro enough to be amusing."

Paul went over to a pink birdcage displayed on an ornamented pedestal and lifted an eyebrow. "Someone has a sense of humor."

"Now this room is not bad." They left their luggage behind and wandered into the sitting room adjacent to the entrance. There was a tall stacked-stone fireplace and French doors leading out onto a stone patio and a walled garden just coming into bloom.

"I could do without the velvet settee," suggested Derrick.

"And I would so paint that ceiling white," said Paul, craning his head backwards, "beams and all. That dark wood just brings the whole thing crashing down."

They made their way through the house, randomly opening doors and critiquing choices, occasionally fluffing a pillow or rearranging a candy dish, and pronouncing it on the whole acceptable. In the room that had been assigned to them there was a decanter of sherry and two glasses, which was a nice touch, and in the big, granite-and-steel kitchen there was a covered platter of chocolate chip cookies. They helped themselves to both and returned to the front room.

"We should call the girls," said Paul.

"Maybe they'll invite us to dinner."

"You're right. It might sound a bit needy to call them before dinner."

"We could drive out and look at the house site."

"And leave this place unlocked?"

"It was unlocked when we got here," Derrick reminded him.

"But it didn't have any of our possessions in it."

"Good point."

They spent a moment sipping sherry and contemplating the dilemma. Then Paul said, "Dinner on the terrace?"

"I saw some camembert and eggs in the refrigerator."

"And fresh spinach for a salad."

"We could open the bottle of Malbec we brought."

"I'll get the candles," Derrick said.

"I'll start the omelet," said Paul.

Later, they lingered in the garden over wine and the dying candles, watching the dart and dive of the hummingbirds from a safe distance, until the garden disappeared into shadows. The stars appeared, one by one, like distant fireflies behind the gossamer veil of twilight, and they agreed that the evening was one of the nicest surprises they'd had in a long time.

Evening shadows were deep upon the porch when the three women finally settled into their chairs, muscles aching, thoughts peaceful. The sound of Farley's tractor working in the vineyard had gone on long past suppertime, but now was quiet. They sat and watched the pink paint the sky, sipping cabernet, and Bridget said softly, "Is this the most beautiful sunset ever?"

A bright blue indigo stopped by the bird feeder, looked at them alertly, then helped himself to dinner and whisked away. Cici said, "Lori picked her bridesmaids."

Lindsay looked at her in surprise. "Cool. Who are they?"

"She didn't say."

"Paul called from the B&B," Bridget said. "They're all settled in."

"I thought they were driving down tomorrow."

"Change of plans."

"Hmm," said Lindsay, rocking and sipping thoughtfully.

In the distance, they heard the sound of Dominic's truck engine starting and saw the flash of his headlights behind the winery. Rebel gave an obligatory bark or two, then lost interest.

"I do believe that dog is getting tame," observed Cici. "I'm not sure I can get used to that."

"You can get used to anything," argued Bridget placidly, "if you live long enough."

They all watched as the truck rounded the curved gravel drive and slowed in front of the porch. Dominic waved at them through his open window.

"Good evening, ladies," he said. "Rest well! A big today tomorrow, eh?"

Bridget said, "We were just having a glass of wine to celebrate our big day. Won't you join us, Dominic?"

He glanced at Lindsay, but almost before he did, she said, clearly, "Yes, won't you join us?"

He turned off the engine. Cici poured wine into a fourth glass. He smiled as he opened the door.

"Thanks," he said. "I believe I will."

He came up the steps and took the chair that was waiting for him.

Chapter Thirteen

Blessings

"It serves you right, if you ask me," Cici observed archly. She sipped her wine and gazed out over the festivities, pretending to be unimpressed by Derrick's story of their night at the B&B. "You choose to move in with strangers when we have a perfectly good guest room going completely unused . . ."

Derrick cast his eyes to the heavens. "I knew you would be mad. I knew they would be mad," he told Paul, who dropped an arm around Cici's shoulders and kissed her on the cheek.

"Darling, you know we'd never take advantage of you like that," he assured her earnestly. "Not when we're counting on every ounce of your goodwill to help us put our house together when it finally is finished. Why, hanging the draperies alone will put us so far in your debt we'll have to have you over for dinner every night for the rest of the year to pay it off."

Cici looked at him skeptically, then relented with subdued reluctance. "Well, as long as there's dinner involved . . ."

The mint-green lawn was awash in early afternoon sunshine and dotted with the pastel colors of all their guests. Some wore their Sunday best ("I've never been to a vine blessing before," declared Maggie Woodall of Woodall Realty, clutching to her head a wide-brimmed flowered hat that wouldn't have looked out of place at the Kentucky Derby. "Am I overdressed?") and others were in shirt-sleeves and jeans. Lori floated about in a flowered chiffon maxi-dress with ribbons in her hair, looking like a fairytale princess—sans Prince Charming, as it turned out, who was tied up with "some app or something for work," as Lori explained vaguely. Everyone exclaimed over The Tasting Table, where Bridget, who wanted to conduct a Grand Reveal, had finally been persuaded to set up the bar. Dominic and Lori took turns pouring the wine, while Noah collected and washed the empty glasses. He was by now resigned to the fact that, no matter what the occasion, he would sooner or later end up bussing tables. And Bridget was paying him fifty cents a glass.

"At any rate," Derrick concluded, "it all worked out well. Our hostess returned in time to make apple pancakes for breakfast . . ."

"Exquisite," added Paul, kissing his fingers to the air.

"And she couldn't have been sweeter. She refused to charge us for the night—"

"Although, of course, there will be a little something extra under the pillow when we leave."

"And insisted on making a casserole for us to

heat up for dinner tonight before she left, even though dinner isn't included in the price."

"She left again?" Cici said.

"Her daughter had triplets," Paul explained. "That was the emergency."

"Ah," said Cici. "How long will you be there? How is the progress on the house?"

Paul and Derrick exchanged a glance. "Actually, we wanted to talk to you about that," Paul said. "Doesn't 'dried in' mean under a roof?"

Cici's eyes widened. "Do you mean you're not even dried in yet?"

"Not entirely," Derrick admitted. "We do have walls."

"Of a sort," corrected Paul. "More like a skeleton of walls."

"And floors."

"Here and there."

"To be fair," Derrick said, "we didn't have a lot of time to look around this morning. It was awfully muddy, and we were wearing Italian loafers."

"What did your contractor say?" Cici asked.

"There wasn't actually anyone there this morning, but when we talked to him last month, he assured us everything goes much faster once they get the roof on."

Paul tried to look hopeful. "You know about these things, Cici. Do you think it will be finished in time for Lori's engagement party?"

Cici said carefully, "Well, that depends."

The engaged person in question flitted by just then, greeted both men with a quick kiss, and turned to her mother. "Have you seen Aunt Bridget? I'm supposed to find out how much longer before the blessing and whether or not we should open more wine. Personally, I think we should save the good stuff for after the blessing, but Dominic says . . ."

Paul held up his glass, surprised. "This isn't the good stuff?"

Derrick tasted his wine again, more carefully this time.

Cici drew a breath to answer her daughter and then turned back to Paul, frowning. "We haven't had rain all week. Why would it be muddy?"

"Oh, there she is!"

Bridget was coming toward them, managing to look at once both charming and authoritative in a white pantsuit with a flirty red polka-dot scarf at the throat. She also looked, at the moment, a little concerned.

Lori said, "Aunt Bridget, how much longer until the ceremony? I don't think we should open more wine until you put the food out, do you?"

Bridget said, "It's past two. I told everyone the ceremony would be at two. I've already started warming the pizzas." She looked around anxiously. "Is he here yet?"

For a moment, Paul, who was still focused on

Cici's question about the mud, looked blank. And then he said, casting a quick glance through the crowd. "Oh, Father Mike. Don't worry. He must have run into a patch of traffic. He's very reliable, and he has directions."

"And GPS," added Derrick.

"I'm sure he would've called if he was going to be more than a few minutes late," Paul said.

Derrick glanced at him. "Is your phone on?"

"Of course." But Paul took it out to check.

Bridget stared at him. "You gave him your cell phone number?"

"No cell service," Lori reminded him sympathetically.

"Sometimes we have cell service," Cici protested.

Lori made a face. "When the moon is full and Venus is retrograde in Scorpio. That's why Mark couldn't come today—he can't get anything done without his phone."

Paul said, trying not to look worried, "Maybe I'd better make a call on the land line."

Bridget hurried away with him, and Lori said, "I'll tell Dominic to hold up on opening more wine."

Derrick took Cici's arm and turned to walk toward the vineyard. "Tell me," he invited, "more about this drying-in stage."

When Lori entered The Tasting Table, there was no one there but Lindsay and Dominic, and they stood with their heads close together, his hand lightly cupping her hair. Lori couldn't help noticing that Lindsay was dressed for the occasion in a strapless print sundress, with a nipped-in waist and a flowing skirt that flirted with her knees, and cute strappy sandals with two-inch heels. She even curled her hair, which she almost never did.

Lindsay stepped away immediately when she heard Lori, of course, and took a sip of her wine, her expression completely neutral. Dominic just smiled.

"The priest is running late," Lori said, "but Aunt Bridget isn't ready to bring out the food yet. So how drunk do people generally get at these things? I say we hold off on pouring more wine."

Dominic looked at her ruefully. "I say the first rule of a good wine tasting is never to run out of wine. I'm going to bring up another case."

"I'll mind the bar," Lori volunteered. "But I'm not pouring the good stuff."

"Chérie," Dominic assured her, giving her cheek a quick pat as he passed, "it's *all* good stuff."

Lori returned a grin and moved behind the lace-covered table that served as a bar. "I really like Dominic," she said, and slid Lindsay a sly look. "Or should I start calling him *Uncle* Dominic?"

Lindsay fought with amusement as she rolled her eyes. "I'm sure I don't know what you're talking about, you obnoxious child."

Lori poured herself a glass of wine. "He's awfully good-looking, too. I mean, if you go for that type."

Lindsay replied, "Hmm." But the softening of her eyes as she tried to hide a smile gave her away.

Lori came around the table, leaning against it casually, and sipped her wine. "This place is fantastic," she said, gazing around. "Even better than I pictured. Look how those floors shined up. Noah said you guys worked till midnight on them."

"That was Dominic's idea. We used marble sealer. I was afraid it wouldn't dry in time, but he turned on the big fans in the loft overnight. Perfect."

"I love that cream color on the walls. Everything looks so bright and cheerful. And the mural! Unbelievable."

"It's not exactly like the one Dominic remembers," Lindsay admitted, "but we all thought we should update it to make it Ladybug Farm, not Blackwell Farms."

"So." Lori smiled at Lindsay over the rim of her glass and bumped her shoulder with her own. "You and Dominic. Tell all."

Lindsay's expression was a study in complacency as she sipped her wine. "Tell what?"

"Oh, come on, Aunt Lindsay. It's not as though you haven't found a way to get his name into every sentence you've spoken all day. That's the first sign."

"I have not." She looked at her with a frown. "The first sign of what?"

"You know. Are you and he . . . ?" She grinned a little. "Doing the deed?"

Lindsay's eyes flew open wide, whether with real or feigned shock, and color tinted her cheeks. "In the first place, that's an incredibly rude question," she replied in her school-teacher voice, "and in the second, it's none of your business."

"That means the answer is yes." Lori fought bubbling delight.

"It does not!"

"Then it means you want to."

Lindsay looked at her warily. "You," she told her, "are much older than I remember." She sipped her wine and tried a quick change of subject. "Your mother said you've picked your brides-maids. Anyone we know?"

She shrugged. "Probably not. Just some girls from school, and Mark has two sisters. I think four bridesmaids are enough, don't you?"

"I think it's your wedding and you should choose. But four sounds like plenty."

Lori glanced at her curiously. "Why did you never get married, Aunt Lindsay? I always wondered."

"I was married," Lindsay reminded her, "and didn't like it enough to try it again." She shrugged. "I don't know. I think over the years you get used to being your own person and making your own decisions. I never met a man I cared for enough to put his needs before my own."

Lori was thoughtful, gazing into her glass. "Don't you think," she offered in a moment, "that the right man wouldn't ask you to?"

Lindsay looked at her, a question forming on her lips, but just then, Dominic returned with the case of wine. "Everyone seems to be heading toward the vineyard," he said, "so the problem of the tardy priest must have been solved. Either that, or the crowd is growing impatient." He slid the box under the table and straightened up, smiling at the two ladies. "Shall we join them for the ceremony?"

"Oh good!" exclaimed Lori. "This will be my first vine blessing. You'll have to explain everything to me." And then, catching the expression on Lindsay's face, she added quickly, "Maybe I'll just meet you there."

She hurried off and Lindsay laughed softly to herself. She and Dominic followed, at a much slower pace.

"Darling, I'm wretched, just wretched," declared Paul as he followed Bridget into the kitchen, and the emotion on his face was genuine. "Derrick said we should've waited and driven down with Father Mike this morning, and he was right. This is my fault, all of it. How can I ever make it up to you?"

Bridget chewed her bottom lip and glanced around the kitchen distractedly, as though a solution might be plucked from the air. "Don't be silly, Paul. It's not your fault the poor man had a flat tire."

"Who had a flat tire?" Noah came through the back door with a tray full of glasses. "You need somebody to go fix it?"

"Thank you, Noah, but someone is already fixing it. The problem is that the priest is still two hours away."

"Biggest bunch of foolishness I ever heard, anyway," Ida Mae grumbled, "having a preacher incant over grape vines. You're not going to let that shrimp sit out like that much longer, are you?"

Noah sighed heavily and slid the glasses into a sink filled with soapy water. "Too bad. I'm a lot better at fixing tires than I am at washing glasses. 'The Lord gave, and the Lord has taken away. Blessed be the name of the Lord.' Job 1:21."

Bridget whirled on him, her eyes alight with a kind of fierce determination. "You!" she exclaimed. "You can do it!"

"Do what?"

She caught his arm, tugging him away from the sink. "The blessing!"

Noah dug his heels in and his eyes went big.

"Me? Talk in front of all those people? Why me? I'm not a preacher!"

"Well, you're practically one. And you will be as soon as you finish seminary. May as well get some practice in now."

He stared at her. "Seminary? What seminary?"

"Oh, Noah." Her expression was torn between impatience and tenderness. "I don't mean to spoil your surprise, but it's pretty obvious. All the Bible verses, the secrecy about college . . . It's okay if you'd rather go to seminary than art school, really, and I know Lindsay would agree. So don't you see, this is a heaven-sent opportunity."

He looked at her for a moment as though she were speaking a foreign language. "The Bible verses were for a contest," he said. "I don't want to go to seminary. I just wanted to go to the rodeo. And . . ." He took a step back from her, shaking his head adamantly. "I'm not giving any blessing."

While Bridget was struggling to absorb this, Paul volunteered quickly, "Fear not, fair lady, I'll be delighted to step up. I've been told I have an excellent orator's voice. And I'm sure there's something you can pull off the Internet that would be appropriate . . ."

Bridget looked at him distractedly. "I appreciate it, Paul, but I think it only works if the person who says the blessing is ordained. Or . . ." she glanced at Noah. "At least, you know, *called*."

Noah turned quickly back to washing the glasses.

Ida Mae gave a disgusted shake of her head and put the shrimp back in the refrigerator.

There was a tap on the open back door and Farley poked his head inside. For the occasion, he wore his Sunday jacket over his work shirt and the camouflage print cap without the stains on it. He had also temporarily left the tobacco behind, which he often did when he knew he'd be seeing Bridget in a social context.

He said, "'Scuse me, Miss Bridget, but I was wondering, didn't y'all keep any guns up here at the house?"

"Guns?" Bridget looked blank, and Noah turned away from the sink with interest.

"What kind of guns?" he wanted to know, and Bridget shot him an alarmed look.

"Don't have to be nothing fancy," allowed Farley. "A .22 ought to do her. Don't want to kill anything, it being out of season and all."

"Kill?" exclaimed Bridget, and now she could hear, faintly, the sound of distant excited voices through the door. "What are you trying to kill?"

"Reckon it'd be that deer down yonder eating your grape vines," Ida Mae said sourly, gazing out the back window.

"Deer!"

"Bambi!" Noah bounded out the back door, shouting, "Hey! Hey!"

Paul looked at Bridget in alarm. "In the grape vines?"

Bridget started to run after Noah, but stopped when Farley inquired, "Did I hear y'all was looking for a preacher? Somebody getting married?"

She said, "Um, no, not married. We just need someone to say a blessing over our grape vines."

She touched his arm urgently to move past him, and he nodded thoughtfully. "Reckon I could do that. Got me one of them mail order certifications to do weddings and funerals. Guess it's good for blessings, too. Cost you ten dollar," he added.

Bridget gazed at him for a moment in disbelief, shared an incredulous look with Paul, and then was distracted by the shouting from the vineyard. "You're hired!" she cried, and raced to help the others save the unblessed vines from the appetite of a pet deer.

"All in all," declared Derrick, watching the dust of the last vehicle disappear down the drive, "one of the most memorable blessings of the vines it has ever been my pleasure to attend." He gave Bridget's shoulders a squeeze and kissed her cheek. "Well done, my dear."

She looked uncertain, pushing back a damp strand of hair from her face. "Well," she admitted, "I suppose we did pull it off."

"My favorite part," put in Lori, "I mean my

absolutely *favorite* part, was when Farley raised his hands like Moses and said, 'I declare thee vines to be blessed . . .' "

Even Bridget, who hadn't found it the least bit funny at the time, had to grin at that. "Who would've guessed?" she admitted. "Farley, a mail order minister."

They'd gathered outside the entrance to The Tasting Table to say good-bye to the guests, who, as the sun sank low behind the mountains, had finally departed. Paul, with his sleeves rolled up above the elbows, volunteered to carry the dishes to the dishwasher—his way of atoning—and Lindsay and Cici bundled up the tablecloths while Noah swept out the room.

"Really, Bridget," Cici assured her, stuffing tablecloths into an oversized laundry bag, "I thought it was fabulous. And everyone loved The Tasting Table."

"Who wouldn't?" Paul was quick to put in. "The food was to die for, and who could ask for more charm?"

"And you heard Carlene say she was going to do a special write up about it in the next Chamber of Commerce bulletin," Lindsay added, stuffing another handful of napkins into the laundry bag.

Bridget smiled, pleased. "She did, didn't she?"

"Of course she did, darling," Paul said, moving past her with a plastic tub filled with dishes. "This kind of upscale establishment is exactly what this community needs to bring in a little class. Note for future, however: an onsite dishwasher wouldn't hurt."

"And really," Derrick added, "the whole thing with the deer was just local color."

Noah said anxiously, "I would've locked him in the barn, but I couldn't find him. I thought he was out in the woods, you know, like he is most of the time. I'm really sorry."

Dominic said, "It's okay, he didn't have a chance to do much damage. But . . ." He cast a glance around the three women that looked serious. "We need to do something about deer fencing."

"Fencing?" Cici looked dismayed. "For the whole vineyard? How much will that cost?"

"You should count on about $1.50 a linear foot," he said.

The three women exchanged a disheartened look. "Well, Bridge," said Lindsay, "guess you'd better start planning some really spectacular menus for The Tasting Table, because we're going to need the customers."

Cici thrust the laundry bag to Noah to carry, and they started walking back toward the house. "Seriously," said Lori, "the only thing you missed was press. If you had a radio station broadcasting from here, or at the very least, someone from the newspaper . . ."

As one, the ladies groaned out loud.

"She has a point," Paul said. "The whole deer debacle was a missed opportunity, from a journalist's standpoint . . ."

Dominic touched Lindsay's arm and the others moved ahead, laughing and talking, as she turned a questioning gaze on him. "I know it's been a long day," he said, "and you're probably tired. But if you could spare a few minutes, I'd like to show you something."

She tilted her head toward him, smiling. "Well, given that the alternative is washing dishes, maybe I could take a minute or two."

While the others walked toward the house, he guided her around the barn and down the path that led through the vineyard. "Oh!" she exclaimed softly, noting the mulch-lined path that encircled the vines. "This is what Farley was doing with the tractor this past week. I was so busy getting the restaurant ready I didn't even notice."

Dominic laughed quietly. "It's amazing how much you can sneak past a busy woman," he said. He lifted his arm and pointed the way down the path. She responded with amazement.

"Oh my goodness," she said on a breath. "Did you do what I think you did?"

She quickened her step and started to run down the path that led into the woods. He called, "Mind your step in those shoes!"

Lindsay clapped her hands and laughed out loud with delight when she came upon the folly. The tractor path had been extended to a cleared circular area landscaped with pine straw and pink azaleas that were just coming into bloom. And the folly had been brought back to life. The broken glass was repaired in the windows, and a new yellow door had replaced the sagging, rotting one. The missing floorboards were replaced and the circular porch had been painted a bright, shiny white. The folly itself was restored to its original forest-green color, and the lacy gingerbread trim that decorated the eaves had been painted white to match the porch.

Lindsay turned to him, her hands pressed to her flushed cheeks, her eyes shining. "It's like going back in time. It's just like it used to be! How did you do that? You must have looked in the book."

He smiled and tapped his head. "No. I just looked in here."

"Oh. I—of course you did!" She looked around in amazement, her eyes hardly knowing where to turn next. "I had no idea—I thought you might've cleared out the weeds with the tractor, but this! How did you do it? How could you possibly have found the time?"

"It wasn't that much," he admitted modestly. "Noah helped a lot, until you called him away to work on your project. The old place was still solid. It was just a matter of replacing a few boards and some glass, and we brought a compressor down here to paint that day you all thought we were spraying the vines."

He reached for her hand. "Come look at the inside. But first . . ."

He bent down and for the first time Lindsay noticed a green extension cord lying along the mulched ground. He plugged it in and the octagonal outline of the building sprang to life with a thousand miniature white lights. Lindsay gave a cry of astonishment and pleasure, and her words came out in a gasp of delight. "It's a fairy house in the woods." Then she turned to him, laughing. "So this is what happened to all those Christmas lights we put up in the barn."

"Farley did the wiring," he cautioned. "So—"

"We'll have it checked out by a licensed electrician," she assured him.

He took her hand and guided her up the one step to the porch, then opened the door and gestured her inside. Lindsay walked into the room and stood there for a long moment, too overwhelmed to speak.

Though a deep-woods twilight pressed against the windows that encircled the little house, the lights from outside shed a sparkling glow over everything. The marble floor glistened with a subtle hue, and all of the old, broken furniture had been removed. The cherub-flanked fireplace had been scrubbed clean of years of smoke damage and firewood was laid neatly inside, waiting to be lit. On one wall was a wicker daybed, piled high with cushions and soft throws and next to it a matching wicker rocking chair. In the center of the room, a small round table with two ice-cream parlor chairs held a candle, a bottle of wine, and two glasses. But the thing that caused moisture to spring to Lindsay's eyes was the easel that was set up before the window that overlooked the spring, with one of her blank canvases on it. She bit down hard on her lip.

Dominic came up behind her. "What you did for your friend was beautiful," he said simply. "But I thought it might be good for you to have a place of your own, to come and paint when you wanted to."

Lindsay blinked hard and walked over to the daybed, absently touching the soft woven throw that was draped over one arm. "I can't believe you did all this," she said thickly.

"Actually," he admitted ruefully, "the fluff and feathers were supplied by little Miss Lori. I asked her for some ideas, and she drove down with a car full of this stuff this morning. That's why I needed to get the tractor path cleared, so we could get vehicles in and out."

Lindsay choked on a laugh. "That girl is an imp. But she has a nice flair."

"The wine, however . . ." She heard the slide of a cork from its bottle. "Was all my idea."

She turned, eyes wet, her face aching with

smiles. "Are you real? I mean, can you possibly be for real?"

"Funny," he said, and the tenderness in his eyes took her breath away. "I often ask myself the same thing about you."

He handed her a glass of wine and raised his own in a salute. "To the rest of your life, Lindsay Sue Wright. May it only get happier."

She said, "Right now, I don't see how that's possible." They drank, and her heart felt as though it was filling up her entire chest. If she had ever known this kind of sheer, simple pleasure in the presence of another person, she couldn't remember it. It was a lovely, peaceful feeling, a feeling of rightness with the condition of the world and all those in it.

She looked up at him. "Now I'd like to make a toast." She raised her glass. "To the only man," she said, and she met his eyes steadily, "I would ever leave Ladybug Farm for."

He smiled at her and cupped his hand gently around her neck. "My darling girl," he said, "don't you know by now that I'm the one man who would never ask you to?"

She drew in a breath and closed her eyes and sank into his embrace. For the longest time they simply stood there, holding each other, her head against the beat of his heart, his face against her hair, swaying together softly to the rhythm of a music only they could hear. Then Lindsay stepped away, letting her hand slide down his arm until her fingers entwined with his.

"Why don't you light the fire?" she suggested huskily. "Let's stay a while."

Throughout the night, the fairy lights of the little folly in the woods didn't dim, and the soft light of morning found the two lovers still wrapped in each other's arms.

Chapter Fourteen

Graduation Day

The weeks that followed were filled with a frenetic celebratory energy: baccalaureate dinners and dress rehearsals; good-bye parties and final exams; inspirational speeches and sailing mortarboards and proud tears and heartfelt hugs. Lori sold her textbooks and packed up her winter clothes. Noah signed yearbooks and was voted "most fun to be around" by his classmates. He remained stubbornly secretive about his college choice, and Lindsay grew more anxious every day.

"It's not like it's an open-ended invitation," she said, worrying over coffee on the morning of his graduation. "These places have a deadline for acceptance. And I have to make arrangements."

"Did you tell him that?" Cici asked practically.

"You bet I did. I'm tired of tiptoeing around the subject. He said he had it under control."

"Well, we know for sure it's not seminary," Bridget said with a small sigh. "Too bad. That would've been interesting."

"I think it's UVA," said Cici. She chose a strawberry from the bowl on the table and popped it in her mouth. "He's probably already sent in his acceptance letter and he's waiting to surprise you. Probably tonight at dinner, after graduation."

Lindsay frowned a little, helping herself to a strawberry. "Why do you think that?"

"It makes sense," Bridget answered for Cici. "That's the only decision that wouldn't cause any drama—he would be close to home, the tuition is low, they have a good arts program—so he feels safe keeping it a surprise."

"Well, maybe." Lindsay took another strawberry, looking unconvinced. "I would've felt a lot better if he let me be a part of the decision, though. It doesn't feel fair somehow."

Ida Mae snatched the bowl of strawberries away. "I'm saving these for a shortcake."

"It's Noah's favorite," Bridget reminded her. "We thought we'd have all his favorites for his graduation dinner. He's got a lot to celebrate."

Cici said to Lindsay. "Anyway, I thought you were on a diet. No carbs?"

"Oh, that was last week. This week it's the all fruit diet. I like it a lot better. And . . ." She cheered considerably. "I can eat the filling out of the shortcake."

The sound of rattling wheels reached them through the open window and Lindsay sprang to her feet, her eyes alight with excitement. "Oh good!"

"What in the world?" Bridget and Cici got up to follow Lindsay to the back door.

"I didn't want to say anything in case it didn't come through, but Farley found this '92 Mustang for $500, and Dominic said he thought he could get it running . . ."

"Is there anything that man can't do?" inquired Cici innocently, and she and Bridget shared a grin.

Lindsay ignored them. "I was hoping to surprise Noah for graduation and the timing is perfect. I was afraid they wouldn't get it finished by today. Where is Noah, anyway?"

"If you all ain't a sight to be seen, running out the door in your underwear." Ida Mae scolded as they all rushed out onto the porch, slippers scuffing and bathrobes billowing. "Get back in here and put on some clothes!"

Bridget was about to defend their attire, which consisted mostly of perfectly acceptable capri pajamas and below-the-knee nightgowns, when the vehicle they'd been expecting rounded the corner of the house. It was neither a '92 Mustang nor a car trailer carrying a '92 Mustang. It was a white pickup truck with lettering on the side, towing what appeared to be an empty horse trailer. It did not stop at the back steps, but continued bouncing around the rutted drive toward the barn.

"Wait," said Bridget in confusion. "When you said 'mustang' you meant *car*, right?"

Cici squinted after the vehicle. "Did that say 'Department of Natural Resources' on the truck?"

And Lindsay said, "They must be in the wrong place."

That was when they saw Noah coming out of the barn, leading Bambi with a rope around his neck. A man got out of the truck and shook Noah's hand.

Lindsay murmured, "What in the world?"

She caught the belt of her open bathrobe, fastened it securely, and started off across the yard at a determined pace. Bridget and Cici followed.

By the time they reached the barn, the back of the trailer was open and the man was locking down a ramp. Noah, with a bunch of garden carrots in his hand, led Bambi toward the ramp.

"Hey!" Lindsay cried, and broke into a run. "Hey, what are you doing?"

The man turned to Lindsay and touched the wide brim of his hat. "Good morning, ma'am. I'm Roger Killian from the DNR, wildlife relocation. I'm here to take care of your deer."

Bridget, whose shorter legs had trouble keeping up with the other two, gasped, "What?"

Lindsay grabbed for the rope that Noah was now transferring to the officer. "I'll take care of my deer, thank you very much! Noah, what is this all about?"

Noah's jaw had a firm, stubborn set to it and he stepped between Lindsay and the deer. Bambi reached around Noah's arm and started nibbling the carrots. His rack caught Noah's shirt, jostling him off-balance a little. "He's too old and too big to be hanging out around here. I'm sending him off."

"You're *what?*"

Bridget said, "Noah, it's okay about the grape vines. We're getting a fence—"

"You don't have to. A wild deer's got no place on a farm." He handed the rope to the officer.

"He's not a wild deer!" Lindsay cried. "He's a pet. Noah, what are you thinking?"

Cici turned to the officer. "We have a license to keep him. I can go find it if you want me to . . ."

The man gave a small shake of his head. "Ma'am, all I know is I got a call about removing domesticated wildlife from this property, and that's what I'm bound to do."

"You can't do that," Lindsay said. "He's my deer! I found him as a fawn; he followed me home—"

"And I raised him, didn't I?" Noah said fiercely. "I fed him and made sure he was in the barn at night and kept him out of the gardens all these years, didn't I? Well, who do you think is going to do that now? I'm not going to be here anymore, and you all have got enough to do." He drew a breath, his jaw knotting again, his gaze fixed deliberately over her shoulder. "This is the way it's got to be."

A silence fell that was thick and painful, choking with words unspoken. The officer took the carrots from Noah and led Bambi up the ramp into the hay-lined trailer. The sound of his hooves on the metal echoed. Bridget clutched Cici's arm. Lindsay looked at Noah helplessly.

"I can't believe you're doing this," she said. "You're just going to send him away?"

"Deer are territorial," he said stiffly. "If I turn him loose in the woods, he'll just come back."

"But—he's a pet! All he knows is how to live with people. He can't take care of himself in the woods. He'll be shot!"

Noah flinched. "They're going to try to get him in a wildlife park. He'll be fine." He looked much less sure than he sounded.

Lindsay looked from Cici to Bridget in desperation, and with their eyes they ached for her, and begged her to be strong. Yet they all jumped at the sound of the metallic clang of the trailer door being slammed shut.

Cici put a hand on Lindsay's shoulder. Bridget wound her hands around Lindsay's other arm. They stood together and watched as the truck and trailer bounced down the driveway.

Noah dashed a hand across his eyes. "I got

things to do," he said gruffly, and he walked away, back straight, shoulders tall.

"That was brave of Noah," Cici said softly.

Bridget pressed her head against Lindsay's shoulder in a firm, brief gesture of support. But she was blinking back her own tears.

Lindsay swallowed hard. "He's grown up," she said. There was wonder and sorrow and also a touch of pride in her voice. "How could I not have noticed?"

Cici gave her a quick, one-armed hug and turned back toward the house. "Come on," she said. "We've got things to do, too."

Lindsay cried all the way through the graduation ceremony. "Remember when he first came to us?" she whispered to Cici, beaming through her tears. "He was stealing vegetables from our garden to live and camping in the folly. Now look at him. Just look at him!" And to Bridget, sniffling, "Remember how he would spend his whole paycheck every week on building materials the year our barn burned down? Was there ever a better boy?"

By that time, the other two women were crying, too, and when the graduating class was introduced and the audience surged to its feet with applause, no one cheered louder than the three ladies in the third row.

Dominic called before they left to report that he

would have the car waiting in front when they returned, and Lindsay's excitement overcame her sentiment as she pushed her way through the milling crowd and flung herself on Noah, hugging him hard. "I'm so proud of you! So proud!"

Cici and Bridget wedged their way in for hugs, crying, "Congratulations!" and "We love you!"

Noah laughed off his embarrassment and hugged them back. "Bet you never thought you'd see the day, huh?"

And they all insisted fiercely, "We never doubted you, not for a minute."

Lindsay caught his hand. "Come on, Noah, let's go. It's so hot here. Let's finish celebrating at home."

He hung back, looking around uncertainly. "Well, you know, I'd kind of planned to go out with the guys . . ."

"After dinner," Lindsay insisted, tugging on his hand.

"We kind of planned something, too," Cici confessed.

"You're going to like it," Bridget promised, eyes sparkling.

He looked from one to the other of them, and then his better nature seemed to win out, although there was a bit more stoic resignation than pleasure in his eyes as he gave a nod. "Sure," he said. "I guess there's some stuff we should talk about anyway."

Cici tossed Lindsay a triumphant "I told you so" look, and Lindsay's excitement could barely be contained as she hurried Noah away.

The black Mustang, freshly washed and waxed, was sitting in front of the house when they pulled up, and Dominic was waiting on the porch. He came down the steps as they got out of Lindsay's car.

"Hey, man, cool car," Noah said, coming around to admire it. "When did you get this?"

"You like it?" Dominic replied easily. "It's got a few rust spots here and there and could use a complete engine overhaul. But it's got a new set of retreads on it, and I got it up to sixty on the highway."

"'92, right?" Noah ran his hand lovingly over the finish. "Man, they knew how to make 'em back then. Would I love to get under the hood of something like this."

Lindsay was practically bouncing with anticipation, her eyes sparkling like fireworks. Dominic said, "Hi, sweetheart,"—because they had long since given up pretense about their relationship— and kissed her cheek, slipping the keys into her hand. Cici and Bridget grinned at her.

"Say, I've got a buddy whose dad sells classic car parts and accessories on the Internet," Noah said. "I bet he could find you a sick set of mags for this thing. How about popping the hood?"

That was when Lindsay stepped forward. "Why don't you do it?" she suggested. "After all, it's your car." She held out the keys to him between her two fingers.

He stared at the keys. He stared at her. Lindsay laughed and thrust the keys into his hand. "Seriously, it's your car! Happy graduation, Noah."

For another moment he stared at the keys in disbelief and then an expression of sheer, incredulous delight washed over his face. "Are you kidding me? No way!"

Cici and Bridget burst into applause and laughter. "I'm kicking in the first year's insurance," Cici said, and Bridget stepped forward and slipped a gas card into his shirt pocket, giving him a quick, fierce hug.

"This ought to keep you on the road for a few months, anyway," she said.

The wonder in his eyes grew as he looked from one to the other of them. "You did this? For me?"

"Well," said Lindsay, trying very hard to pull a sober face, "it seemed like a practical thing for you to have. After all, we're going to be way too busy with the vineyard to be running back and forth to see you when you go away to college, so this way you can drive home on breaks. And, of course, when you're home, it sure will save wear and tear on our vehicles for you to have your own. So really, I guess the car is mostly for us."

But as she spoke the happiness in his eyes visibly faded by slow and reluctant degrees. He swallowed hard and looked down at the keys in his hand. "You shouldn't have done this."

Lindsay smiled. "Don't say that until you've checked it out. It hardly cost anything, and it wasn't even running until yesterday. It needs a lot of work. But I thought you could do that over the summer and use the money you've saved for parts. If you like it, that is," she added, a little anxiously.

Noah said, "Really. You shouldn't have." He held out the keys to her.

Cici said, "Noah?"

Bridget added, confused, "You can paint it if you don't like the color."

Even Dominic looked puzzled.

Noah looked from one to the other of them with a mixture of mounting dread and growing resolve, and by the time his eyes reached Lindsay, he had the look of a man who was about to cross a trestle in front of a speeding train. He said, "I don't need a car to go to college because I'm not going to college." He drew a breath. "I'm joining the Marines."

The silence that followed was absolute. The birds didn't chirp. The chickens didn't cluck. The sheep didn't baa. There was just stillness.

And then Lindsay gave a soft, incredulous exclamation of laughter and a single shake of her head. "I don't think so. We talked about this. You're going to college. You have scholarship offers. And don't think I don't know you have acceptance letters because—"

"No." He spoke over her firmly. His hand bunched into a fist around the keys. "We didn't talk about it. You talked about it. You decided. Well, now I've decided. I'm joining the Marines."

Lindsay looked quickly around the circle of her friends for support, and there might have been just the tiniest flicker of panic in her eyes. Cici spoke up for her.

"Noah, maybe we could all go inside and talk about this. It's a big decision, and I'm sure we'd all like to hear your thoughts . . ."

He said flatly, "Nothing to talk about. It's done. I report for basic in two weeks."

Bridget gasped softly. Lindsay didn't move.

Noah held out the car keys to Lindsay again. She didn't appear to see them. She said in a stunned voice, "But . . . your dream—of being an artist, of studying in a real university—"

Noah tossed back his head in a brief and helpless gesture of exasperation. "That wasn't my dream," he burst out. "That was yours! Look, I like to draw, okay? I like thinking up things and painting about them. But I'm never going to do it for a living. And I'm never going to stand up in front of a classroom and teach other people how to do it or wear a suit and tie to work and draw cartoon characters for ad agencies because that's not who I am. Don't you get it? That's who you *want* me to be and I'm not going to spend the rest of my life living out your dream for you!"

Lindsay reeled backward as though she'd been slapped. But the color in her cheeks and the flare of her nostrils was from anger, and she shot back, "So you think the way to fix that is to go out and play soldier?"

"For crying out loud, I've spent my whole life in this one stinking little county! I've never even been out of the state. This is a chance for me to see the world, to find out who I am and what I'm made of—"

"All you're going to see of the world is the back side of some African desert where people plant bombs on the side of the road and shoot at anything that moves! *That*'s how you're going to find yourself?" She looked at him in outrageous disdain. "The fact that you would even say that tells me you're not mature enough to make the decision."

"You told me I was." His cheeks were starting to stain red. "You told me the decision was mine."

Lindsay threw up her hands, palms out, and held them there firmly. "This discussion is over. It's not going to happen. I raised you to be an artist, not a warrior. You're not joining the Marines. Over. End of conversation."

"You didn't raise me to be anything!" he

exploded back at her. "You gave me a place to stay and three squares and okay, I get it, but I don't owe you my life for that, okay? It's my life! And you can just go to hell because it's already done!"

Bridget said, shocked, "Noah!"

He tossed the keys into the dirt at Lindsay's feet and turned and strode away.

Lindsay cried, "Then undo it, do you hear me? Do you know why they send eighteen-year-old boys to war? Because they're too stupid not to go, that's why! Noah!"

He threw up his hands and didn't stop walking.

"Noah, come back here! We're not finished!"

She lunged after him, but Dominic caught her arm. When she tore her arm away, he stepped in front of her and took her shoulders. His expression was grim. "Lindsay Sue," he said, "you know I've got more respect for you than any woman I know, but you need to hush, and you need to hush right now. Because if you don't, you're going to lose that boy forever."

Lindsay looked up at him, stricken, and he released her shoulders cautiously. "I'll talk to him," he said.

Lindsay raised a trembling hand to her lips as she watched him go. "He's just a boy," she said, and her voice was low and tight and strained with the effort of keeping it steady. "He doesn't know what he's doing. He doesn't know anything but here. He was supposed to go to college. All these years, that's all we worked for . . . He was supposed to go to college!" She drew a breath that sounded like a stifled sob. "He can't make it out there on his own, any more than . . . any more than that stupid deer can. He can't do this!"

Bridget reached for her, but Lindsay turned and ran into the house, letting the screen door slam behind her. She caught herself against the newel post at the bottom of the stairs, and then her knees buckled beneath her. She sank to the floor, holding onto the stair rail, weeping.

Cici and Bridget dropped down beside her on the floor and unfolded their wings of love over her. They held her and rocked her and didn't say a word.

Dominic came into the barn just as Noah threw a feed bucket against the wall. He stood and watched until the clatter died down, then moved forward. Noah turned on him with eyes that were defiant and wary.

"First off," Dominic said mildly, holding his gaze, "if you ever speak to the woman I love like that again, it's going to be between you and me, and it won't be pretty. Are we clear?"

Noah jerked his gaze away, jaw tightening.

"I said, are we clear?" His voice was like steel.

Noah swallowed and darted a quick glance at Dominic. "Yeah," he muttered.

Dominic relaxed his shoulders and leaned back

against one of the stalls. "Second, if you think a uniform is all it takes to make a man, you're even more of a boy than your mother thinks you are." He ignored the angry look Noah shot him and absently plucked a broken straw from the spider web in which it was caught against a post. "And she is your mother, not only legally, but because she's earned it. She's earned a lot of things from you, not the least of which is respect." He twirled the straw in his fingers for a moment, then let it float to the floor. "Anyway, I happen to think she's wrong about you. I think you're more of a man than she gives you credit for, but it's not running off and joining the Marines that's going to prove it to her—or to anybody else, for that matter. It's what you do when you leave this barn."

Noah looked at him for a moment, allowing a small amount of puzzlement to seep into his gaze, and Dominic's held steady. He said, "Isn't it?"

Noah scowled and looked away.

"So," Dominic said after a moment. "Two weeks, eh?"

Noah nodded cautiously.

Dominic gave a small, smothered chuckle and a shake of his head. "Parris Island, the paradise of the South. A vacation experience you'll never forget."

Noah looked at him cautiously. "You were in the Corps?"

"Semper Fi."

Noah studied him for a moment. "You're not going to try to talk me out of it?"

"It's not my place. Besides, son, if you've signed those papers, you're government property now. Like you said, it's done."

Noah said, relaxing a little, "It's what I want. Those women—and I'm not saying anything against them—they can't understand that. "

Dominic nodded.

He gave an uncomfortable shrug. "You know I didn't come from much. But my great grandpa was a hero in World War II, and I guess ever since I found that out, it's made me think a little different about myself." He darted a quick glance toward Dominic. "Maybe I'd like my kids to think different about themselves someday, too."

He was silent for a moment. "So I studied on it, and the more I thought about it, the more I couldn't see myself going to some fancy college and hanging out in art museums and when it was done, then what? All that money, when nobody around here has any to spare, and when it's done, you've got nothing. The only reason those colleges even wanted me was because I had a good story. You know, orphaned and uneducated and all that. It didn't seem like any of it had anything to do with *me,* or who I wanted to be.

"And then last summer, when I worked in Washington at Derrick's gallery, it all started to make a little more sense to me. The people that came in there, they weren't the kind of people I wanted to be, or even hang out with. I mean it was fun and all, and I learned a lot, but mostly what I learned was that the world was so much bigger than I ever thought it was. And there were important things to do in it I never thought about before."

Dominic just listened.

"And then I met this solider over Christmas, and we talked a lot. I guess that kind of stayed in my mind. But I knew how much my mom wanted me to go to college, and it's hard to disappoint somebody you . . ." He shrugged uncomfortably. "You know, care about. But when the recruiter came to school on Career Day a couple of months back, I took home the papers and studied them and got on the computer and studied more, then I went in to talk to them. It just felt right." He straightened his shoulders. "I'm sorry I hurt her. But I'm not sorry I signed up."

Dominic was thoughtful for a moment. "That might be something she'd like to hear."

Noah was silent for a long time. And then he glanced at Dominic. "You were really in the Marines?"

Dominic gave a rueful smile and pushed away from the wall. "I was. And let me tell you, boy, you sure picked a hell of a way to see the world." He started to leave the barn and then looked back. "Act like a man," he told him.

In a moment, Noah nodded.

• • •

Sunset. Lindsay stood alone at the edge of the vineyard, watching the breeze ruffle the pale undersides of the leaves, tasting the evening that crept into the air. A crow cawed overhead, and the shadows on the hillside lay still and purple. Dominic came up beside her and just stood there silently for a while, his hands clasped loosely behind his back.

He said, gazing over the vineyard, "I didn't talk him out of it. I wouldn't have if I could have. The boy wants to serve his country. It's his right. And if you want to hate me for that, it's your right."

Her makeup was worn off, her hair had come down from its pins, and her eyes were tired of crying. She still wore the ruffled blouse and flared skirt from the suit that she'd worn to graduation, but she was barefoot. The breeze caught her skirt and tangled it briefly around her legs. She reached into her pocket and took out a wrinkled paper.

"Noah's personal essay for college," she said, looking down at it. "The one he never would let me read. He gave it to me this afternoon. We had a talk." The smile that ghosted her lips was fleeting and filled with an achingly tender combination of pride and sorrow. "Do you know he got into every college he applied to?"

Dominic said, "They'll still want him in three years."

She glanced at him, then back at the paper. "The essay is all about us and this place and the life we've built here . . ." She smiled quietly to herself and the glance she gave him was on the border of being shy. "About me. I guess he was embarrassed to show it to me. Boys can be silly like that."

"Yes," agreed Dominic gently, "they can."

She looked back down at the paper. "The last part is, 'I don't know where my life will take me. I don't guess anyone does. But the one thing I do know is that, because of them, I'll always be able to find my way home.'"

She folded the paper, smiling sadly, and tucked it back into her pocket. They stood together for a long time, not touching, just standing and watching the vines.

Then she said, "I don't hate you."

He looked down at her. "I'm glad."

She turned to him. "I think I love you."

He said, softly, "I'm glad."

She went into his arms, and they held each other quietly until the evening leached all the color from the sky.

Chapter Fifteen

The Home Front

They planted their garden; they tended the vines; they picked berries. They fed the chickens and cleaned the coop and weeded the flower beds. They painted the steps and washed windows and polished floors. They focused on the things that didn't change, because they didn't want to look too closely at how much everything was about to change. And how soon.

Ladybug Farm entered a state of barely controlled chaos. Lori moved in for the summer while Mark attended orientation sessions for his new job and searched for apartments in San Francisco. Bridal magazines and color swatches were scattered all over the house. Noah was constantly in and out, slamming screen doors and thundering up and down the stairs as he tried to balance a dozen good-byes to people all over the county with the last minute details of packing up four years of his life and preparing to move on to his new one. Lindsay pretended to be on board, or at least supportive, but she spent far too much time on the USMC website, viciously clicking the mouse and muttering things like, "Savages!" and "Brutes!" Sometimes when she was in the midst of one of these self-tormenting tirades, Dominic would come looking for her on the pretense of needing help tying up vines or running hoses or aerating soil. He would put a shovel in her hand and dirt would fly, and before long, she was calm again and almost rational.

Bridget was in the midst of a jam-making frenzy, because if one thing was certain it was that time and fresh berries wait for no one. Ida Mae grumbled about the mess the two young people were making all over the house and spent more than the usual amount of time making cookies, which disappeared as fast as she served them. And Cici's battle with the roofers veered into the red zone.

"What I'm trying to tell you, Ms. Burke," explained Leroy L. Squire, head roofer, with an exaggerated show of patience, "is that they don't make these kind of tiles anymore and even if they did, you're not going to be able to get an exact color match for a roof that's over a hundred years old."

"And what I'm trying to tell you," said Cici through gritted teeth, "is that there is absolutely no excuse for a simple patch job to take five—count them, *five*—months to complete. We've lived through the banging and the sawing and the mess long enough. I'm not going to have tarps and piles of shingles all over the yard on the day of my daughter's wedding!"

He inquired politely, "When is she getting married?"

"That doesn't matter. What matters is that I want a roof on my house. And I want it now!"

He nodded sagely. "Well, now, as to that, the fact is, we've just about got her done. It wouldn't have taken near as long if we hadn't had to search all over the country for them matching tiles. Now, if you'd just let me go ahead and put tin on the porch all the way around, you'd have plenty of tiles left over to fix the main roof and it'd look real nice, too. You see that all the time on these old houses, nice tin roofs like that."

"You are not an architect!" she practically screamed at him. "You don't get to make design decisions. This is an historic house. This is a Jackson . . ." She struggled to remember the name Mark's father had rolled off so readily. "Jason, I mean, Jason Anderson original structure, a part of Virginia history, and you're not going to just throw a tin roof on it because it's convenient, is that clear?"

He said, gazing over her head at the problem in question. "Yes'm, I guess so. But I sure don't know what you expect me to do about it."

Cici drew a long, calming breath. "I'll tell you what you can do," she said. "You can pack up your tools and you can leave."

He looked surprised. "But don't you want us to—"

"No," she said. "I don't." She turned and marched up the steps. When she reached the porch, she looked back to where he still stood, agape, and repeated sternly, "Tools. Leave."

She stormed into the parlor and started scrambling through the highboy where Bridget kept odd notes, receipts, and business cards that hadn't yet been filed away in the office. Ida Mae was running a feather duster over the grand piano and looked up when Cici started unloading papers.

"What're you tearing up those drawers for?" she asked. "You lose a nail file?"

"I'm looking for that card Paul gave us. I know Bridget put it in here."

"Well, you're making a mess that I sure hope you plan on cleaning up."

"Wait a minute, here it is." She sank back in triumph, the business card in her hand. "Lincoln Crebbs, General Contractor. "

Ida Mae gave a snort of derision. "I hope you ain't planning on calling that crook."

"He's not a crook. He's Paul and Derrick's general contractor. And if he can't take the time out from building their Taj Mahal to come over and look at our roof, I'll bet he knows somebody who can."

Ida Mae grunted. "Yeah, well, good luck finding him. They already tried to put him in jail twice. Now I hear the police are hunting him down again for taking some poor woman's money and leaving her with a house falling down." She peered at Cici scornfully. "Don't y'all ever listen to the radio?"

Cici looked at the card in her hand, an awful feeling creeping over her. She repeated carefully, "Lincoln Crebbs."

"I heard you the first time."

Cici demanded, "Ida Mae, are you sure?"

"'Course I'm sure. Why would I make something like that up?"

"Umm," Cici murmured as she hurried out of the room, "I think I'd better call Paul."

Paul and Derrick had settled into the routine of the B&B with surprising ease, despite the fact—or perhaps because of the fact—that their hostess was rarely in evidence, and when she was around, she talked far too much and far too long about her precious grand-triplets. She made an excellent breakfast, however, which they often enjoyed on the garden patio, safely away from the flight path of the hummingbirds, and she always put out a platter of warm cookies in the afternoon, with wine and cheese in the baroque-velvet parlor, promptly at five every evening. In between times, she graciously offered them the use of her kitchen, and they were amazed by how much better a luncheon salad tasted when the lettuce was plucked from the garden twenty steps away, or how exquisite a simple supper of broiled fish and potatoes could be when the ingredients had been purchased fresh from a local market only hours previously. Paul speculated that he might take up gourmet cooking in his retirement. Derrick observed that gardening might not be nearly as pedestrian a hobby as he once imagined.

They had, of course, been devastated by Noah's announcement and had spent hours going back and forth about the matter—with Lindsay, with Cici, Bridget, and with each other. Finally, they agreed that, as tragic as the whole thing was, there was nothing they could do except to be there for Lindsay. And surprisingly, perhaps, their outrage seemed to have a steadying effect on Lindsay, as every time she talked to them she seemed to grow a little closer to acceptance. It was as though as long as she knew someone still was upset about it, she didn't have to be.

But with all that was going on at Ladybug Farm, they tried not to insert themselves into the confusion any more than necessary. They took Lori to lunch in Staunton but were dismayed when she spotted a white muslin beach shift in a store window that she claimed was exactly the kind of wedding dress she had in mind. They found a local organic wine and brought it to dinner at Ladybug Farm, and everyone seemed happy that it wasn't very good. Paul and Derrick were happy that the ladies always kept a bottle of drinkable wine in reserve for emergencies.

They wandered the countryside during the day, visiting the antique shops, photographing the

301

scenery, taking in the local color. In the afternoons, they enjoyed socializing with the other
guests, sharing a fine local cheese they found or
introducing a neophyte to a sophisticated new
wine. Sometimes they would dabble around in the
kitchen, experimenting with flavors, and come up
with a platter of hors d'oeuvres to serve in the
garden at cocktail hour. They met all kinds of
interesting people, which, being the social sort
themselves, was essential to their wellbeing.
Because Miss Amelia was always going out of her
way to accommodate them and often worked far
into the night trying to keep up with the needs of
her guests and the needs of her daughter's new
babies, they didn't mind helping her out now and
again by filling the bird feeders or taking
reservations when she was away from her office.
In fact, they rather enjoyed it.

As a gift to their hostess, Derrick bought proper
art lights and arranged the little gallery in the foyer
in a much more well-merchandized way. He even
picked up a couple of primitive paintings that he
liked from a local artist, added a zero to the price
he paid for them, and hung them for sale beside
Noah's and Lindsay's work. A young couple from
Atlanta bought one of the primitives three days
after he hung it, and that very weekend a woman
who was redecorating her country house bought
Lindsay's painting of the fox. Amelia was beside
herself with excitement and wanted to share the

profit with Derrick; Derrick just smiled and waved her away. "My dear," he assured her, "this is what I *do*." And he discreetly added another zero to the price of Lindsay's flower basket painting.

They thought they would be bored after a couple of days at the B&B but were amazed at how many ways they found to fill the days. They were a little anxious at first about the slow progress on the house, but the contractor assured them that once the marble arrived from Italy, things would go much faster. And he promised them they would be in their new house by the end of summer, so in truth, they really weren't much behind schedule at all.

And then Cici called.

They didn't panic until they tried to reach Lincoln Crebbs for two days and received nothing but a "voicemail is full" message. It was Cici's idea to have a certified building inspector come out and look at the place and, using all her charm, was able to persuade a local man to meet them there early Sunday morning. Cici agreed to come along for moral support.

Viewed from the car, the building site looked as it always did—a big rambling skeleton covered in blue house wrap, sitting in the middle of a giant mud hole. Parts of the roof were covered with strips of plywood and parts were not. They supposed that was why there were puddles of standing water on the concrete floor of what was to be their wine cellar.

This time they'd worn boots, and they got out of the car slowly, noting the official-looking man with the hardhat and the clipboard who was walking around the structure with a studious look on his face. "Guys," said Cici in a puzzled voice as she exited the back seat. "Wasn't this supposed to be a two story house?"

"With a wine cellar," Paul agreed. "Why?"

She gestured helplessly. "No floors."

Derrick frowned. "Don't they go in last?"

The look on Cici's face—a mixture of alarm and pity—told them they were in real trouble. The three of them scrambled down the muddy hill to meet the inspector.

"The upshot of it is," said Matthew Shaw, building inspector, when all the introductions were made, "you've got yourself some pretty shoddy construction here. It's framed twenty-six inches on center—whoever heard of that?—and the roof decking is quarter inch interior plywood; that's all going to have to be ripped off. And see here, where they started roughing in your plumbing? Both lines are plain PVC, which means the first time you turn on the hot water, it's all going to blow apart."

Paul said in a sick voice, "We paid for copper."

Cici squeezed his arm sympathetically. "I don't see any supports for the floor joists," she said, glancing around.

"That's because there aren't any," said Matthew Shaw, looking grim. "All in all, I'd say you all were lucky to catch this when you did . . . except for one thing." He walked over and scuffed his boot meaningfully through a three inch pool of standing water that covered a good half of the concrete floor.

"Poor drainage?" suggested Derrick, weakly.

Cici said, "Where's it coming from? We haven't had that much rain, and even without a roof, that much water shouldn't still be standing."

Wordlessly, the inspector led the way to the northeast corner of the block foundation. They followed in helpless dread, their footsteps echoing wetly on the floor. There they stood, staring in disbelief at the steady stream of water that was gurgling down the already-cracked wall.

"Looks to me," said the inspector simply, "like they built your house where your swimming pool was supposed to be."

In Ida Mae's Kitchen

"We're ruined," moaned Derrick from between his splayed fingers. "Absolutely ruined."

Paul gave him an absent pat on the arm. "We're not ruined."

Derrick looked at him bleakly. "We're homeless."

Paul slumped back in his chair as Derrick's dejection crept into his own eyes. "That we are," he admitted heavily.

Cici set a cup of coffee before each of them, and Lori, who stayed home from church to have the weekly apartment-hunting telephone conference with Mark, followed with a basket of the morning's leftover muffins. "Don't worry," she offered generously, giving each man a brief hug before she sat down. "I'll be moving soon, and you guys can have my room."

A pot roast was simmering in the Dutch oven, filling the kitchen with the fragrance of onions and carrots, and something sweet was baking in the oven. Ida Mae noisily chopped vegetables at the work island, occasionally muttering to herself. Sunday dinner at Ladybug Farm always smelled like heaven. And Paul and Derrick were too distraught to notice.

"We always have room for you," Cici assured them, cradling her own coffee as she took her chair. But she added, worried, "You didn't give him all the money up front, did you?"

"Not all of it," Paul admitted. "But he did have to order the marble . . ."

"And the polished granite for the pool cabana," Derrick reminded him.

"And the reclaimed oak beams for the great room, and the fixtures for the bathrooms were all special order . . ."

"And the light fixtures were custom made."

"And the water feature in the foyer had to be prepaid."

"And the kitchen appliances alone . . ."

Cici held up a hand, wincing. "Okay, I get it."

Lori reached for a muffin. "What did the sheriff say?"

"He said the scoundrel had left the county," replied Paul, angrily, "possibly the state. He also said there's some question as to whether this is a civil or criminal matter. *I* said we'll just see what our lawyers have to say about that."

"Not that it matters," Derrick said miserably. "We'll never get our money back. Or our house."

"Or our dream," said Paul sadly. And they just looked at each other, heavy with regret.

"Dad-blast it all!" exclaimed Ida Mae, slamming the oven door shut. "Now will you just look what you've done?"

She plopped a spring form pan down on the counter and stripped off her oven mitts, gazing at it in disgust. "Everybody knows an angel food cake won't rise with the devil in the kitchen, and that's what you all've done—brought the devil hisself marching right in here, twitching his tail and breathing hellfire."

Lori paused in the act of biting into the muffin, her eyes wide. Cici shrank back. Paul and Derrick looked at her, eyebrows raised to the ceiling. Ida Mae glared at them.

Lori squeaked, swallowing a bite of muffin, "What did we do?"

"You." Ida Mae pointed a boney, accusing finger at her. "What are you doing out here in Virginia when that boy you're supposed to marry is in California, trying to set up housekeeping for you? Seems to me you need to take a good long look at what it is that's important to you, instead of spending every spare minute down at that winery that ain't even yours in the first place, then hiding out in my kitchen mooning over what you don't have."

She turned her dark gaze and her accusing finger on Cici. "And you. Trying to make a hundred-year-old house into what it used to be and then filling up my ears with your whining and your sighing because it ain't never going to be what it used to be. Don't you know that's why God made the twenty-first century?"

She turned her glare on Paul and Derrick. "As for you two, what did you expect? You never wanted to build a house, nohows, and the last thing either one of you wanted to do was to retire. All that pissing and moaning about how this had to be just here and that had to be just there—nothing but an excuse because you were too afraid to leave your big city life and get on with the rest of your life. Lies are the devil's work, and every time I turn around, I see somebody else that wouldn't know the truth if it jumped up and bit them in the face." She placed her hands firmly on hips, her eyes afire. "Seems to me the only person in this house who knows what's right is that boy, and he's the one you're all chastising. Well, I'm done with it. Get on out of here, all of you. And don't you come back until you bring a smile to my kitchen. I mean it."

Lori started to sputter something, but Cici, with a hand firmly on her back, moved her out of the kitchen. Paul murmured sadly, "I was really starting to like the country." And Derrick, urging him through the swinging door, whispered, "Don't look back."

Ida Mae called after them, "And another thing! Why ain't you in church, anyway?"

No one dared reply.

Ida Mae, with a nod of satisfaction, opened the refrigerator and started to rebuild her angel food cake.

Paul and Derrick returned to the B&B in a glum mood. They barely even noticed the dive-bombing hummingbirds as they got out of their car, thunking the car doors closed and locking them with a *bleep.* Of course, Cici had wanted them to stay for Sunday dinner, but they preferred to be alone with their misery.

Paul said, as they trudged toward the steps, "Do you think Ida Mae could be right about us? Not really wanting to build the house in the first place?"

Derrick admitted uncomfortably, "We *did* make things a lot more complicated than they needed to be. And the truth is, I'm still not sure how I feel about retirement."

Paul looked at him thoughtfully. "Me, either."

"Good thing, I suppose," said Derrick with a sigh. "Because now we can't afford to retire."

Paul frowned a little. "I thought the house was what we wanted, but maybe . . ." He cheered marginally. "It was just what we thought we wanted."

Derrick considered this. "That makes the loss a little easier to take," he admitted. "But we're still homeless."

Paul's shoulders slumped. "That's true."

They opened the door and were greeted by a note propped up on the bowlegged little entry table. Derrick picked it up.

> Dear boys,
> I'm so sorry—another emergency! My daughter broke her ankle and someone has to take care of those precious babies! Can you fend for yourselves tonight? The Hendersons checked out this morning and no more guests are expected until

Wednesday. I'll be back Monday after-
noon to check on you.
Love,
Amelia

They glanced at each other, shrugged silently,
and went into the kitchen for coffee. They took a
tray out onto the back terrace and set it on the
wooden table that was arranged between the two
comfortable Adirondack chairs that overlooked
the wildflower garden. They sat in silence for a
while, watching the hummingbirds dart back and
forth amidst the yellow daisies and purple
coneflower, pink foxglove, and cobalt delphinium.
One of the folk-art painted bird feeders had
attracted a family of blue jays, and their antics
were amusing as they fluttered and hovered and
hopped between the feeder and the branch of a
nearby poplar. They began to smile without even
realizing it.

"I suppose," Paul said, "we could stay here the
rest of the summer."

"We could," agreed Derrick. "And then
what?"

Paul glanced at him hesitantly. "Do you want to
try to rebuild the house? On a smaller scale, of
course," he added quickly.

But Derrick was wincing before he even
finished. "I don't think my heart could take it, old
man."

"Mine either," admitted Paul.

They sipped their coffee in silence for a time, watching the birds.

"There's always Baltimore," Derrick offered in a moment, though without much enthusiasm. "Or D.C. We probably have enough money left for a condo."

"I suppose." Paul did not sound happy. "It's just that I was really starting to like the country."

Derrick sighed. "Me, too."

A black-and-white chickadee tried to join the jays at the feeder and was promptly chased away. From nowhere, a big red cardinal swooped down and chased the jays away. Paul chuckled out loud and so did Derrick.

Then Derrick sat up straight, struck by a sudden thought. "Wait a minute," he said, looking puzzled. "Isn't this Sunday?"

"A Sunday that will live in infamy," Paul agreed, his mirth fading.

Derrick looked at him. "Do you think Amelia forgot about the Sunday brunch?"

Paul drew in a breath for a reply and let it out wordlessly, since there really was nothing to say. The facts were irrefutable. It was Sunday. Amelia had fifteen reservations for brunch. Frowning a little, they both sat back, considering what to do.

And that was when they heard the first car pull up.

Sundays after dinner were peaceful, lazy times at Ladybug Farm. Dominic and Lindsay had gone riding, or perhaps hiking, or perhaps neither one. Noah was off with friends. Ida Mae was napping and Bridget was happily browsing through cooking magazines, making notes on recipes she intended to adapt for The Tasting Table. Cici sat on the front porch, her chair pulled up close to the rail and her feet propped up on it, with the *History of Blackwell Farms* open in her lap. She hadn't turned a page in some time, but simply sat gazing at the black-and-white photo of the stately brick mansion in its heyday. Tall columns, glistening white. Elegant windows framed by lace curtains. The formal gardens curving out on either side. The artistic pattern of the tiled roof.

The screen door slammed and made Cici flinch, drawing her out of her reverie. She looked up to see Lori, in tattered shorts and a Coldplay T-shirt, dragging another rocker up close to the rail. She sat and swung her feet on the railing beside her mother's. "I think Ida Mae hates me," she said.

"She doesn't hate you, sweetie," Cici said, turning back to the book. "No more than she hates everyone else, anyway."

"What does she care what I do with my time, anyway? I'm studying winemaking. Of course I'd take advantage of the opportunity to watch a young winery grow. Mark doesn't care. Why should she?"

"She has very old-fashioned ideas, honey. You have to be patient."

"She didn't sound very old-fashioned when she was telling you to get with the twenty-first century. What's gotten into her, anyway?"

Cici said, half to herself, "Over a hundred years old. No additions, no alterations. It still looks today the way it did when it was built. There should be something sacred about that."

Lori gave her mother a gentle, patient look. "Mom, I really don't think Judge Blackwell would mind if you got a new roof."

Cici smiled and closed the book. "I don't think he would either, honey. I'm the one who would mind. And I think what Ida Mae was trying to say is that it's stupid—and a little dangerous—to try to live someone else's dream."

Lori frowned a little and looked away. "Yeah. I guess so."

"I think that might be what happened to Derrick and Paul," Cici went on. "They just got so carried away with what they *thought* the perfect retirement house in the country should be like that they didn't give enough thought to what it really *was* like to build a house from scratch. Things go wrong, even with honest builders. They just weren't prepared."

"What do you think they're going to do now?"

"I don't know." Then she smiled a little ruefully. "But they usually land on their feet."

"I suppose so."

"So," Cici invited, "did you get to talk to Mark while I was gone this morning? How's the apartment-hunting going?"

"Oh, fine." But her tone was a little absent. "He emailed me some pictures of one place right on the Bay. It's nice."

"But?" Cici sensed the hesitation in her daughter's voice.

"Nothing." She shrugged. "It's just . . . I don't know. Not me."

"Well, when you're married, you'll find it helps to think less in terms of 'me' and more in terms of 'us'."

"I guess." She cheered a little. "Anyway, he's flying in next weekend for a few days."

"That'll be fun."

Lori said, without looking at her mother, "He wants me to come back out with him when he leaves."

"And? Will you?"

Again the uncomfortable shrug. "Maybe. Of course, there's not much for me to do out there while he's busy doing his thing. I don't know. Anyway, we still have a lot of wedding stuff to do here."

"We have *all* the wedding stuff to do," Cici reminded her.

"Well, things have been a little busy around here, what with all the fuss about Noah leaving, and Dominic really needs my help in the lab . . ." At her mother's look, she corrected herself with a frown. "Okay, maybe he doesn't *need* my help, but I shouldn't waste the opportunity to learn from him. That's why I wanted to spend the summer here, you know."

Cici said, "I know, honey, but summer will be gone before you know it and there are decisions that have to be made. Maybe," she suggested hopefully, "while Mark is here next week, we can all sit down together and make some of them."

"Sure." Lori returned a brief, absent smile. "Sounds great."

"In fact," pursued Cici, "you don't look particularly busy right now, so why don't I go get the list and we can get a head start? But first . . ." She looked down at the book in her hand as she stood, and the expression on her face was deeply regretful, almost apologetic. "I have to talk to a man about a roof."

Amelia Wriggly's plump chin quivered and her eyes grew bright with tears when Paul and Derrick told her what they had done.

"You . . ." Her voice was high and thin. "Did that . . . for *me?*"

She was a short, round woman with Miss Clairol champagne-blond hair, always perfectly curled and heavily sprayed, and a penchant for sweatshirts with pictures of cats on them. Today, she wore one with three sleeping kittens in a basket and the slogan *Puuur . . . fect,* along with a flowered cotton skirt and pearl earrings. She was sweet, and a good cook, but a fashion plate she would never be. Her usually immaculately powdered and rouged face was showing the wear of the day, and she stared at them in awed disbelief.

"Well, we couldn't turn all those people away," Paul explained. "There would've been a riot."

"And it really wasn't that difficult," Derrick added. "In fact . . ." He shared a look of modest triumph with his partner. "It was rather exhilarating, facing down a crisis and rising to the occasion like that. I made bellinis . . ."

"While I whipped together a frittata."

"There were all those breakfast steaks in the freezer . . ."

"Which I served with a champagne sauce I learned to make from the food editor at the *Post*," Paul said. "One-two-three, never fails."

"Then we mixed canned cherries with brandy to make cherries jubilee and served it over store-bought vanilla ice cream from the freezer," Derrick said. "Our friend Bridget taught us that. We served family style and everyone seemed to love it."

"Of course," Paul felt compelled to point out, "they had a quite a few bellinis by that time."

"I worked the front of the house and Paul worked the back," said Derrick with a self-satisfied nod. "We were a well-oiled machine."

"We were magnificent," agreed Paul, grinning at him.

Amelia Wriggly burst into tears.

Paul rushed to her while Derrick hurried to snatch a box of tissues from the storage closet. "Dear lady, we are cads, utter cads," exclaimed Paul. He put a solicitous arm around her shoulders and led her to the velvet sofa in the sitting room. "You must be exhausted, and here we are going on and on . . ."

"We did all the washing up," Derrick assured her, pressing a tissue into her hand as she sank down on the sofa. "The kitchen is spotless and all the receipts are safely locked away, so you don't have to worry about a thing. You just relax and rest. I can't imagine how stressful this has all been for you."

"It's not that," she sobbed into the tissue. "I mean it is, of course, the stress . . . It's just that you're so sweet . . ."

They sat, one on either side of her, and patted her hands. "It was our pleasure. You've made us feel so at home here, anything we can do for you only brings us joy."

She sobbed harder. Paul and Derrick looked at each other over her bowed head, puzzled and at a loss.

"And now . . ." She sniffed, blotted her eyes, and tried to compose herself. "You're just the sweetest things, and now that just makes what I have to tell you that much harder."

She straightened up, blew her nose, and seemed to strengthen her resolve. They waited in a mixture of dread and expectation.

"Boys," she said, "I'm so sorry, but I'm closing the B&B. My daughter and her husband have been begging me to move in with them for years," she went on hurriedly, as though speaking quickly would take away some of the sting of her announcement. "They even have an in-law suite all ready for me. I only opened this place to keep myself busy after my darling Andy passed, but now, with the triplets . . . Well, it's clear she can't manage by herself, and all this running back and forth is killing me. And forgetting about the brunch on Sunday—I declare, it never once crossed my mind!—well, that only goes to prove I can't keep up with both jobs. So." She took a deep breath. "I have to let it go. I'm putting the place on the market and closing down after this week's reservations check out."

Derrick sank back against the sofa cushions, heavy with disbelief. "We really *are* homeless."

"I'm so sorry," she said helplessly.

"It's all right." Paul sounded stunned. "As our young friend Noah would say, the Lord giveth and the Lord taketh away."

Derrick smiled wanly. "We've really grown fond of this place. I'll miss it."

Amelia gave an impatient wave of her hand. "I've been a terrible hostess. I'm surprised you stayed this long. You've done most of the work yourselves, cooking your own meals, doing your own laundry, even taking reservations when I wasn't here."

"That was half the fun," Paul assured her.

"We enjoyed helping out," Derrick agreed. "Who knew running a B&B could be so satisfying?"

"We definitely made a good team yesterday," Paul said, and then he looked at Derrick, the slow kernel of an idea forming in his eyes. "Didn't we?"

Derrick's expression grew cautious. "Are you thinking what I'm thinking?"

"Why not? It's not like we have anywhere else to go."

"And we can definitely use the extra income." The excitement in Derrick's eyes was growing.

"And I really *was* starting to like the country." Paul grinned.

"I would expand the gallery," Derrick said.

"And I'd knock out that back wall and put in a spa—"

"With a massage room!"

Amelia looked from one to the other of them in growing confusion. Over her head, Paul and Derrick beamed at each other.

"How much do you want for it?" they said as one.

Chapter Sixteen

Summer Wine

Noah came down the stairs with his duffel over his shoulder and paused on the landing, just for a minute, to look around the old place one last time. He didn't like the way that made him feel, so he quickly moved on.

The house was quiet, but it often was this time of day, and no one seemed to be around but Cici, who was absently leafing through a magazine on the front porch. He set down his duffel just inside the door and went out.

"Well," he said, shoving his hands into his pockets. "I guess I'm ready. My room's all cleaned out. I boxed up my stuff in the attic, in case you need the room for something."

She glanced up with a brief smile, turning a page. "That's nice, Noah. Thank you."

"I thought, you know, maybe the guys might be moving in here. You know, now that I'm going."

"Umm. I think they made other plans."

She seemed to be very absorbed in an article about composting toilets. Funnily enough, he couldn't remember ever seeing her just sitting around reading a magazine in the middle of the day before.

"Well," he said, clearing his throat a little. "I

don't have to be in Charlottesville until four. I guess I'll give the grass one last mowing."

"That'd be nice." She didn't look up.

"It's growing pretty fast now. You all are going to have to find somebody to take over for me pretty quick."

"I'm sure we won't have any trouble."

He waited for her to say something else, but she just kept reading. So he shrugged unhappily and started down the steps. "I'll get to it, then."

"Oh, Noah, I almost forgot." She closed the magazine then and stood up. "Lindsay wanted you to bring down some boxes from the loft in the dairy before you leave. Some old frames and things that she wants to get rid of. Do you mind doing that before you start the lawn? I'll show you which ones."

"Sure." He tried not to sound as low as he felt. "Might as well."

She walked with him across the yard to the dairy barn, now known as The Tasting Table, and he couldn't help but notice all the cars parked around it. "What are all those people doing here?"

"Oh, I think Dominic is doing something with the wine today," Cici replied vaguely. "I'm not sure what."

"He didn't forget he's supposed to drive me to Charlottesville, did he? I can't miss that bus."

"I'm sure he'll be finished in time."

He stopped just outside the door and turned to

look around: the freshly-painted barn that he had helped build himself, the new gravel road that encircled it, the rows of green vines stretching out beyond it—how many holes had he dug for those?—the chicken yard filled with clucking, fluffed-up, different-colored chickens, and the goat house he'd spent a good part of last spring building by hand. The vegetable garden he'd helped dig, now green with tomato vines and corn and beans climbing between the stalks. The dairy barn, where he used to sit and have his lessons, and afterwards, Lindsay would pull out the canvases and they would paint together. He had always loved the smell of it—oil paint and chalk dust. Now it was a restaurant, and the barn was a winery, and people were just driving up here and parking any time of the day. He gave a small shake of his head.

"Man, things sure have changed around here in four years," he said.

Cici smiled and touched his arm lightly. "Yes," she agreed, "they have."

Then she opened the door and stepped back to let him enter first. He crossed the threshold and an entire roomful of people burst into applause. He just stood there in astonishment.

There was a big red, white, and blue banner across the width of the room that read "Good Luck, Noah" and there were American flags all down the length of the long table, and red, white, and blue bunting on every vertical surface. Everyone was cheering and clapping and from a set of hidden speakers somewhere, The Marine Corps Hymn started playing. Amy was there, and Reverend and Mrs. Holland, and Farley, and lots of people from the church, and Jonesie and his wife from the hardware store where Noah worked for the past four years, and Paul and Derrick, and Dominic, of course, and Lori was bouncing up and down in the crowd, pumping her fist and giving him the Marine Corps *BooYah!* As he stood there in speechless amazement, Lindsay pushed forward from the back of the crowd, her eyes bright and her face stretched into a smile, and hugged him hard. "You didn't really think we'd let you get out of here without a going-away party, did you?"

Then Cici pushed her aside to hug his neck, laughing, and then Bridget, and then there was Amy, and he could hardly catch his breath for the people pounding him on the back and shaking his hand and making him feel like somebody special. It wasn't until he had a minute to look up from all the hugging and handshaking and people wishing him well that he saw Cici and Bridget and Lindsay, standing with their arms linked and smiling at him and looking so proud and excited and sad that he realized it was true: he was somebody special. And it wasn't hard to figure out why.

Lindsay said, pushing at her damp eyes with her fingertips, "I wish someone would turn off that damn music. It always makes me cry."

"I love the Marine Corps Hymn," Bridget objected, although her voice sounded a little wet. "Especially the last part, about getting to heaven and finding the streets are guarded by . . . United States . . . Marines." Her voice broke on the last and she turned away, blowing her nose hard.

Cici bravely dashed away tears with the back of her hand. "Kids grow up," she said. "If they don't, we haven't done our jobs." She gave a fierce, determined nod of her head, sniffing. "We did our job."

Dominic came up behind them and dropped one hand on Cici's shoulder, the other on Bridget's, leaving Lindsay in the center of the embrace. "Now then, my ladies," he said softly, "chins up. There's nothing a soldier hates worse than to see his mother cry. Happy thoughts, eh?"

At that moment, the stirring anthem came to an end and was replaced by an up-tempo and completely inappropriate selection from Katy Perry, and all three women managed to laugh. Lori was playing DJ.

There were speeches—mostly from the preacher—and sentimental well-wishes and funny stories from people who had known Noah since he was a ragged kid darting in and out of trouble all over the county. There was food and lots of it:

Bridget's tomato tarts and Ida Mae's meatballs, ribs soaked in red sauce, fluffy rolls stuffed with ham salad, deviled eggs and coleslaw, and a huge sheet cake decorated with a pretty fair replica of the eagle, globe, and anchor emblem of the United States Marine Corps.

"I looked it up online," Lori informed Noah, cutting herself a generous slice. "And did you know there's a company that will print any picture you want onto a slab of sugar? So that's what we did. Of course, I wouldn't actually eat it if I were you. It shipped all the way from Ohio, and who knows what they did to get those colors."

"Pretty cool," Noah said, digging into his own slice of cake. "Tastes like Ida Mae's cake."

"It is. She just put the sugar thing on top." She looked at him in assessment. "So. No offense or anything, but you know you're crazy, right? College is the best deal anybody ever came up with for kids. Four years of hanging out and living on your own while somebody else pays the bills, and really, all you have to do to stay ahead of the crowd is do what the professors tell you to do, because nobody else does. And for somebody like you, going to art school—on a scholarship no less—it's just crazy. Do you know how hot the art majors are? *I* couldn't even hang out with them; that's how hot." She gave a small sad shake of her head. "You turned down the chance of a lifetime, if you ask me. What got into you, anyway?"

He didn't even get mad, as he most certainly would have a year ago. "You just got to know where you fit, is all," he replied. "I'm not saying I won't ever go to college. The fact is, I'd like to, when I get out. But if I went right now, I'd spend the whole time wondering what else I was missing out on, and what good is that? If you're not where you're supposed to be, you're nowhere, right? Good cake," he added, setting down his plate as he spotted someone waving to him across the room. "Thanks for the sugar thing."

"Yeah," mumbled Lori as he left. "Sure." But she felt uneasy and confused, as though the eighteen-year-old kid she'd taken such pleasure in tormenting for the past four years had somehow outsmarted her. She was glad when Dominic caught her eye from behind the makeshift bar and waved her over. She left her cake behind.

"Do you know," she said when she arrived, "Aunt Bridget really needs to put a real bar in this corner, instead of a table covered with fabric. After all, it's a wine tasting restaurant, right? People should be able to sit at the bar and have a glass of wine."

"We're way ahead of you, sweetie," Lindsay said. "Your mom is going to start building it next week."

"Fortunately, this is a fairly temperate crowd," Dominic said, "because we're running low on the 'good stuff,' as you call it. Here, chérie, I want you to taste this." As he spoke, he poured a measure of red wine from a decanter into a tasting glass and handed it to her.

"What about me?" Lindsay objected.

He held up a finger, smiling. "Patience, love. First sip goes to the wine maker."

Lori's eyes went wide. "You did a thieving?" she accused. "Without me?"

"Thieving?" Lindsay repeated, looking alarmed.

"It's where we draw off a little wine from the barrels to taste," Dominic explained. "You can tell a lot about a wine in the laboratory, but the only way to really know what you have is to taste it. And so?" He nodded to Lori. "What do you taste?"

Lori inhaled the bouquet, considered it, and took a slow and thoughtful sip. "Vanilla," she said, surprised. "And bite of pepper."

Lindsay reached for the decanter. "Let me taste."

"Wait." Lori tasted again. "Is that apples?"

Dominic smiled at her, his eyes sparking with pride. "Excellent. I knew you'd spot it."

"A little sugary," she commented.

"That will fade with maturity."

"Kind of raw."

"It's summer wine. Unfinished."

Lindsay took a sip and looked at them both in surprise. "This is our wine? It's good." She tasted again. "I would pay money for this."

Dominic said, "Not yet, you won't. But give it some time and you could be paying a great deal of money for it."

Lori held the glass up to the light, examining it. "It's so much more complex than I expected. And it's still young." And she looked at him, puzzled. "It doesn't taste anything like Blackwell Farms wine."

"Of course not," Dominic said. "In my estimation, it has the potential to be even better."

Lindsay looked at him, surprised and delighted, and Lori frowned. "But I don't understand. The wine we sampled didn't have any of these flavors. We did everything just the way we were supposed to, and we should've gotten wine that tasted like I expected it to. How did this happen?"

Dominic said, "Wine is a living thing, chérie, and full of surprises. The oxygenation, the oak chips, the stirring and the pump-overs—all of these things change the chemistry, of course. But in the end it all comes down to alchemy. Which is, like so many of life's greatest gifts, a lovely mystery." As he spoke, his hand came to rest easily and naturally on Lindsay's waist, caressing it lightly, and she smiled into his eyes.

Lori, preoccupied with analyzing another sip of the wine, didn't notice.

"And so, my young vigneron," Dominic said to her, "what shall we do with your first vintage? Bottle it, or hold it in reserve?"

Lori's eyes flew wide with surprise. "*My* vintage? But you're the one who . . . All I did was . . ."

"You chose the crush," Dominic reminded her. "You chose the barrels. You tested for bacteria. You monitored the alcohol levels. You watched the temperature. You stirred down the CO2 . . . You made the wine."

"But . . ." She caught her breath on a note of wonder, and the protest faded from her eyes as she looked back at the glass of wine in her hand. She held it up to the light again and regarded it as though it held the elixir of magic. "I made this," she said. Her voice was soft with amazement and then bubbling with pride and excitement as she repeated, "I *made* this."

She turned back to Dominic, eyes bright and clear, and gave a decisive nod. "Bottle half of it," she said. "In three months it'll be completely drinkable, and we need the sales. Hold the rest in reserve until we get the first crush of Ladybug Farm grapes. I really want to see how this wine grows up." And she moved off, sipping her wine, looking extremely pleased with herself.

Dominic watched her go, chuckling softly. "So do I," he confessed and gave Lindsay's waist an affectionate squeeze.

Lindsay smiled into her glass. "This wine is good," she said. "But you're the one who's responsible for it, not Lori. That was nice of you."

He replied, "A winemaker never forgets his first

vintage, and she worked hard for this one. I wanted it to be special for her."

"And if it hadn't turned out so well, would you still have let her take credit?"

"Of course not."

She looked up at him, her eyes filled with gentle adoration. "You are the most extraordinary man," she said. "I really should marry you."

The corners of his eyes crinkled as he looked down at her. "Don't tease me, love. I just might say yes."

Lindsay was suddenly breathless. She said, slowly, just coming to the realization herself, "I don't think I'm teasing."

The humor left his eyes in stages and was replaced by a question, quick, hesitant, intensely searching. Her heart beat hard and fast. She watched his face. She didn't breathe.

He said softly, "Is that a proposal?"

She nodded, her throat so dry that she couldn't form the words.

The expression on his face was soft with amazement and cautious disbelief, still hesitant. "Are you sure?"

Again, she could only nod, although now her heartbeat began to slow with a quiet, gentle certainty, and a wonderful warmth spread throughout her veins. Better than wine. Sweeter than sunshine. She'd never been more sure of anything in her life.

There was wonder in his eyes and deep, quiet joy. "This is a little sudden."

"I know. Please say yes."

"Not something we should probably leap into."

"I know. Say yes anyway."

He lifted his hand and brushed her hair. He smiled. "Okay, then," he said huskily. "Yes."

"Look at them." Cici smiled indulgently at the couple in the corner near the door, standing close together but not too close, holding hands, heads bent urgently toward each other, gazing at each other as though they were the only two people in the room. "She's saying she'll love him forever."

"And he's begging her to wait for him," Bridget added, smiling.

"And she's saying until the end of the earth," said Derrick.

"And he's saying he'll never forget her, not ever," said Paul.

Cici sighed as Noah and Amy, arms around each other's waists, left the building. "In three months time, they won't even be writing to each other."

"By the time he gets back, she'll be engaged to someone else," said Bridget.

"And he will have forgotten her name," said Paul.

"Ah, young love." Derrick gave the departing couple a wistful salute with his wine glass. "As sweet as summer wine and just as mercurial."

"Thank heaven that's all behind us, huh?" said Cici, and they all smiled an agreement that was tinged with only the slightest bit of reminiscent regret.

"Nothing is certain but that everything changes," murmured Paul.

"Who said that?"

"Someone important, I'm sure."

Bridget said, "Speaking of which, big changes for you guys, huh? Do you know anything at all about running a B&B?"

"Of course not, darling," Derrick replied happily. "That's the adventure in it."

"Haven't you had enough adventure for one year?" Cici looked amused.

"Haven't you?" Paul returned, and she laughed.

"Just don't try to rebuild anything," she cautioned.

"And be sure to have the building inspector out *before* you close the deal," added Bridget.

"Not an issue," Derrick assured her with an airy wave of his hand. "We've learned our lesson."

"The real dilemma," said Paul, "is what color draperies to hang in the front room."

"I say no draperies at all," added Derrick, "but plantation shutters."

"That has possibilities," agreed Paul. "We're doing a complete repaint, inside and out," he added.

"Well, maybe not out," put in Derrick. "I've grown rather fond of the kitschy doors."

Paul grinned. "They are a showstopper, aren't they?"

"And we're renaming the place, of course. The sign just came in this morning."

"Oh?" Bridget said. "What are you—"

But just then the music stopped and someone tapped a spoon loudly on a glass. They all turned toward the sound.

"Ladies and gentlemen," the booming voice of Reverend Holland filled the room. "I've just been informed that our guest of honor will be departing to meet his destiny in less than fifteen minutes. Let's all go out and see him off, shall we?"

In fact, Noah had more than an hour before he had to leave, but Lindsay had known that it would take at least forty-five minutes for the party to wind down, and she was right. Amy was the last to leave, and Noah spent a long time standing morosely in the drive looking after her before he went to collect his things.

Noah had refused to allow the ladies to accompany him to Charlottesville, and though they were hurt by this at first, it didn't take much thought to understand why he preferred to say good-bye in private. So when Dominic brought his truck around, the women all gathered in the front yard, even Ida Mae, to say good-bye. Noah looked embarrassed when he came down the steps with his duffel bag and saw them all, and he quickly ducked down to pet Rebel, who charged out from under the porch to bark and snarl and nip at his ankles.

"You good old dog," he said, scratching the border collie behind the ears. "You good old dog."

Rebel tolerated the affection for only a minute, then dashed off in search of something to chase. Noah let him go and stood up, dusting off his hands on his jeans. "Well," he said. "I guess this is it."

Cici smiled at him. "I guess it is."

His eyes flickered from one to the other of them: Cici, Bridget, Lori, Ida Mae, and finally Lindsay, but he couldn't look long at her because he could see how wet her eyes were, even though she was smiling.

He said, "I put the car up on blocks in the barn and covered it with a tarp. I don't think it'll be in your way."

"I'm sure it won't." It was Cici who said that.

"Thank y'all for the party." He cleared his throat. "What I mean is . . . well, thank you."

Cici stepped forward quickly and hugged him hard. "Noah," she said in a tight, strained voice "your fingerprints are on every inch of this place. It won't be the same without you. You know you'll always belong here, don't you?"

He managed to nod, but he couldn't say anything just then.

Bridget was next, hugging him tight and whispering, "You come back to us, you hear?"

He said, somehow, "Yes, ma'am."

He was surprised when Lori stepped forward and gave him a quick kiss on the cheek. "They have video chat for military families now," she told him. "You can call us."

"Yeah," he agreed, and that made him grin. "I can."

Ida Mae just looked at him with those fierce eyes of hers, and then she grabbed his shoulders and gave him a hearty slap on the back. "Your grandma would be real proud of you," she said simply and let him go.

And then there was nothing to do but to walk up to Lindsay. She just looked at him for a moment, smiling through those wet eyes. "We're coming to South Carolina for your graduation," she told him. "All of us."

"Good," he said. "That'll be good."

"You be sure to send us your graduation packet, because they said on the website that sometimes recruits forget."

"I won't forget," he promised her.

"And write," she said, "or email. Because we'll be checking every day."

"I will," he said, "whenever I can get to a computer."

He glanced around, not knowing what else to say and feeling a little uncomfortable. "I never did get to that grass."

Her eyes were brimming now. "Don't worry about it."

He stepped forward and hugged her, and what he wanted to do was thank her for everything she'd done, but somehow that didn't seem like enough. It didn't seem like anything he could say would be enough, so in the end all he could whisper was, "I love you, Mom."

It turned out that was enough, after all.

Dominic took his duffel and stowed it in the back of the cab. Noah didn't trust himself to look back at the ladies, so he said instead to Dominic, in a quiet voice, "You're going to be around, right? To kind of keep an eye on things?"

Dominic replied, "That's my plan."

"That's good. Because all these women . . . they need a man around, you know?"

Dominic nodded soberly. "I couldn't agree more."

He took a breath and paused for a minute to survey his surroundings, to take it in one more time, to memorize it. The house had a new metal roof on the porch now. The barn had a fresh coat of paint. The goat was standing on top of its house, bleating. The sheep looked like puffs of cloud in the meadow, with that black-and-white dog crouched down in the grass watching them. He'd have to remember that and paint the picture someday.

Dominic said beside him, "Regrets, son?"

Noah looked at him, and straightened his shoulders. "No, sir," he said. "I want to be a

Marine." And in a moment he added, because he had seen them do it on TV, *"Sir."*

Dominic smiled and clapped him on the shoulder. "Okay, soldier, let's hit the road."

Noah got into the truck with everybody calling good-bye to him, and even when the truck was halfway down the driveway, he looked in the mirror and they were still there, waving.

Bridget, seeing the dejected look on Lindsay's face as she watched her two men drive away, suggested they clean up the party mess tomorrow, but Ida Mae was having none of it. "Idle hands are the devil's workshop," she declared predictably and handed everyone a trash bag.

"She's right, you know," said Lori, plucking sticky paper plates and frosting-coated plastic utensils off the tables and dropping them into her trash bag. "Physical activity increases endorphins, and when endorphin levels get high enough, it's impossible for the mind to focus on being sad. That's how the whole thing about women getting together to clean house after somebody dies got started."

"Ain't got nothing to do with it," Ida Mae declared with a grunt, placing plastic wrap over a tray of leftovers. "You clean house after a death to get rid of the bad spirits; everybody knows that."

Bridget suggested tactfully, "Perhaps the less said about people dying at the moment?"

Lori looked guiltily at Lindsay, who was determinedly placing glasses in the plastic dish tub and pretending to pay no attention to the conversation. "Really, Aunt Lindsay, I wouldn't worry if I were you. The president is pulling another 50,000 troops out of Afghanistan this year alone and hey," she added, on a sudden thought, "who knows? Noah might not even graduate basic! I hear it's really hard."

"Thank you, Miss Sunshine," her mother murmured and swatted her behind with a roll of bunting as she passed.

Lori looked offended, but Lindsay smiled at her. The smile was probably meant to be reassuring, but it looked a little wan. Just a little. "That's okay, honey. I'm not really sad. It's just that everywhere I look, I see him." Now she was gazing at the mural and at his signature in the bottom right corner beside hers. "The place won't be the same without him."

"Well, it looks like I just missed the party," said a male voice from the doorway, and everyone turned.

"Mark!" exclaimed Cici in surprise. "We didn't expect you until the weekend!"

"I got away early," he answered with a grin. His eyes were on Lori but broke away for an instant to sweep across the remains of the feast. "But not early enough, from the looks of it."

Lori recovered from her shock and cried, "Mark!"

She dropped the trash bag and launched herself into his arms. He caught her and whirled her around, laughing.

"Mark! Oh, Mark!" He set her on her feet and she caught his face between her hands and kissed him hard. "I love you so much!"

Then, still holding his face like a precious work of art, she leaned back and gazed up at him, her face filled with adoration and regret and longing. "I love you so much," she repeated, her voice quavering a bit. "And . . . I can't marry you."

She burst into tears and pushed away from him, running toward the house.

Mark stood there for one stunned moment, staring after her. Then called, "Lori!" and followed, stumbling a little, in her wake.

For a moment, no one spoke. Then Ida Mae slammed down the dish she was wrapping, placed her hands firmly on her hips, and looked from one to the other of them. "Now you tell me," she demanded, with only the slightest note of grim satisfaction in her tone, "who didn't see *that* coming?"

Chapter Seventeen

The Angel of Ladybug Farm

Dear Mom,

I'm so sorry I disappointed you, and everyone, and especially Mark. Please don't think I don't know how badly I've screwed up. I thought I could do it. I really did. I thought it was what I wanted. But in the end, you were right—you can't live someone else's dream. If I had gone through with the wedding, I would've spent the rest of my life wondering what I'd missed out on. And I guess, in the end, I'm just not the marrying kind of girl.

I'm sorry I left so abruptly, but I just couldn't talk about it. I still can't. I'll call you when I'm able, but right now, I just need to be alone for a while to think about things. Please don't worry about me. You know I'll always come home to Ladybug Farm.

Love,
Lori

Cici let the screen door squeak closed behind her as she came out onto the porch. The two women looked up at her from their rocking chairs, a mixture of anxiety and reassurance on their faces. Silently, Cici passed the printed email to Bridget, who read it and passed it to Lindsay. Lindsay read it and looked across at Cici. "Are you okay?"

Cici nodded and sank into her chair. "It just hurts to see your child in pain."

It had all happened so fast and mostly in silence. Mark left without speaking to, or even looking at, any of them. A few minutes later, Lori came downstairs with her rolling suitcase in hand, her eyes swollen from crying, and no ring on her finger. When Cici tried to talk to her, she just shook her head, choked out a few mostly incoherent words of reassurance—"I'm okay. It's fine. Don't worry"—and got into her car. She hadn't answered her phone for the past four hours, so getting the email had been an enormous relief.

Bridget said, "I read a story one time about how, when the gods finished creating woman, they stood back and looked at what they'd done. They had given her a body strong enough to run a marathon, a mind fast enough to do six things at once, a heart big enough to love even while it was breaking, hands that could paint a masterpiece or feed a family or write a symphony. And they were afraid, because they saw that what they had made was stronger than they were. They knew they had to create a secret weapon, one thing they could use to destroy her. So they gave her children."

The silence that embraced them was sweet and melancholy, and no one spoke for a time. Then Cici glanced at Lindsay. "How are you holding up?" she inquired gently.

Lindsay said, "I'm okay. To tell the truth, all the drama with Lori kind of took my mind off missing Noah. Who knew the poor kid was going through all that?"

"I knew she was a little ambivalent about the wedding," Bridget confessed, "but I never expected her to call it off completely."

Cici sighed. "Well, the good news is that she found out what she wanted before it was too late. The bad news is . . ." She glanced at the other two ruefully. "Jonathon and Diane are not going to be my in-laws."

The other two nodded regretfully, appreciating this.

Late afternoon had come and gone and the shadows on the lawn lay dark and still. A pale sky outlined the silvery mountains, and starlings looked like silhouette cutouts as they darted between the house and the barn. The chickens had gone in to roost. The sheep were huddled in the far pasture, awaiting the night, and Rebel, with his job done for the day, had gone in search of evening recreation. It seemed odd not to see a deer picking his way across the lawn, helping himself to the hydrangeas that nodded in the evening breeze, but no one said so.

Bridget absently flipped through the *History of Blackwell Farms* book, pausing now and then to read a paragraph or look at a picture, but mostly sipping wine and gazing out over the quiet scene. Lindsay munched on cookies left over from the party and rocked.

"It's so quiet," Cici said as she wearily stretched out her legs and leaned back her head. "I'd forgotten how quiet it can be here."

"The house feels empty," agreed Lindsay. "Almost haunted."

Bridget said after a moment, "It's funny isn't it? Here we are again, just the three of us. Just like we were when we started out."

"Well, not entirely," Lindsay said, and the ghost of a smile touched her lips as she glanced at the empty chair next to hers.

They sat and rocked in silence for a while, too physically exhausted and emotionally drained to even talk. Bridget absently turned a page of the book, barely glancing at it.

"Remember when all I was planning to do this year was read that book?" Cici murmured. "I never even got past the first chapter."

"Well, the year isn't over yet," Bridget said encouragingly, and Cici smothered a weary chuckle.

Lindsay helped herself to another cookie, and Cici raised an eyebrow. "The all-cookie diet?"

Lindsay shook her head and bit into the cookie defiantly. "I'm done with dieting. I'll never be a size six again, and who wants to be, anyway? I'd rather be happy. And . . ." She took another bite of cookie. "Since I stopped dieting, I've lost four pounds."

Cici kept her expression perfectly innocent. "That's probably just because you're getting more exercise."

Lindsay didn't bother to hide her smugness as she agreed. "Probably."

Cici reached for the decanter of wine on the table between them, then hesitated. "Is that the new wine? I need real wine."

"It is real wine," Lindsay insisted, pouring her a glass. "It's just not finished."

Cici took the glass and tasted. "Not bad," she admitted. "A little sweet."

"Dominic says that's the good thing about summer wine," said Lindsay. "It's like an unfinished story. The best is yet to come."

Cici smiled a little and took another sip. "I like that," she said. "An unfinished story."

They were quiet for a time, rocking, sipping wine, gazing out over the fading day. Then Lindsay said, "I'm going to marry Dominic."

Bridget looked at her. So did Cici. Neither woman said anything for so long that an uneasy anxiety crept into Lindsay's eyes. Then Cici grinned.

"Now I ask you," she declared, lifting her glass, "who didn't see *that* coming?"

Bridget sprang from her chair, letting the book tumble to the floor, and hugged Lindsay, laughing. So did Cici.

"Oh, Lindsay, I'm so happy for you!"

"Congratulations, sweetie, you know we're crazy about him!"

"This is the best news ever, the best!"

And Cici added, "If I don't get to have Diane and Jonathon for in-laws, at least I get to have Dominic for a brother." She thought about that for a moment and added, "More or less." And Lindsay laughed.

But when they were all settled again, and glasses were refilled to replace the wine that had spilled, Bridget looked at Lindsay with a mixture of affection and resigned regret and said, "Oh, Lindsay—does that mean you're leaving us?"

Lindsay smiled contentedly and leaned back in her chair. "Nope."

Her friends didn't attempt to disguise their relief. "Then Dominic will be moving in here?" Cici said, and her expression was a mixture of delight and uncertainty.

Lindsay sipped her wine thoughtfully. "I don't see how that can work," she said. "He has a house of his own, and a garden and two horses and a golden retriever."

"Horses?" Bridget's eyes lit up. "That's right! Dominic has horses."

"Golden retriever?" Cici looked worried. "I don't know how Rebel would like that."

Lindsay shrugged. "We'll work something out."

"Lindsay," said Cici, sounding both amused and curious, "don't you think that's kind of important?"

Lindsay just smiled. "Nope." She took a sip of wine and added, "I'm wearing the Vera Wang. I can let it out."

The three of them sat in happy contemplation for a while, plans and dreams dancing through their heads, the taste of summer wine playing on their tongues.

Bridget leaned forward to retrieve the book that had fallen open on the floor. She started to close it and then paused. "Well, will you look at that?" she observed. "It's a picture of Ida Mae, right here on the last page. I wonder if she saw it."

Lindsay and Cici glanced over at her. "Let me see," Lindsay said, reaching for the book.

Bridget held up a hand, her eyes fixed upon the book and growing wide. "Oh my goodness," she breathed. "Girls—girls, listen to this! 'The breach between Emily Blackwell and her son Andrew was never resolved . . .'"

"Breach?" interrupted Lindsay.

"What breach?" added Cici.

Bridget waved them silent impatiently and read on, "'. . . And when Emily Blackwell died in 1982, Judge Andrew Blackwell's inheritance was

347

limited to the house in which he was born, its furnishings, and surrounding acreage. The remainder of the Blackwell family fortune, valued at the time in excess of 1.5 million dollars, was left in trust to Emily Blackwell's longtime friend and housekeeper, *Ida Mae Simpson . . .*'"

The rest of her words were drowned out by exclamations of *"What?"* and "Are you kidding me?"

Bridget repeated, her eyes dancing with incredulity and excitement. "Ida Mae Simpson!"

Lindsay snatched the book from her. "Let me see that!"

Cici got up to read over her shoulder. When she had finished, she gave an exclamation of disbelief and collapsed back into her chair. "Ida Mae?"

"Don't you remember when we bought the place there were no living relatives and that's why the estate was so anxious to sell?" Lindsay said. "We just assumed that Judge Blackwell died broke."

"Well, he did, I guess," Bridget pointed out, "since Ida Mae had all the money."

"And remember when Ida Mae first came to live here and we offered to pay her a salary?" Cici reminded them. "She said she had a pension and didn't need our money."

"One point five million," Lindsay repeated, awed. "That is some pension."

"Our housekeeper is a millionaire," Bridget

said, shaking her head in disbelief. "I guess I'll have to be a lot nicer to her from now on."

"I wonder what the breach was between Judge Blackwell and his mother," Cici murmured speculatively. "Is it in the book?"

"Not that I've seen," Bridget admitted. "But I haven't read much of it."

"We could always ask Ida Mae," Lindsay suggested, and both Cici and Bridget shook their heads.

"Not for 1.5 million dollars," Bridget declared.

And Cici agreed. "More than my life is worth."

"I'll bet the lawyer, Frank Adams, would know," offered Lindsay. "After all, his firm is the only one in town and they must have handled the will . . ."

All of a sudden, all three women looked at each other, and understanding dawned. "Oh, my goodness," breathed Bridget. "Our secret investor."

"It has to be," Cici agreed, her voice stunned. "She was right there the whole time, and all she had to do was make a phone call to her lawyer . . ."

"Who happened to be the agent for Ladybug Farm Winery."

"Which she apparently wanted to see succeed more than she let on," said Cici.

"Probably for her fruitcakes," Bridget speculated.

"Ida Mae Simpson is our angel," Lindsay said, her eyes big with wonder.

And then they couldn't help it; they burst into

laughter. They laughed until they spilled their wine. They laughed until they couldn't see. And then they laughed some more.

Six miles down the road, Derrick gave Paul the thumbs up, and Paul climbed off the stepladder and came to stand beside him. Together they admired the sign that was perfectly centered over the red-doored entrance to the B&B: *Welcome to The Hummingbird House.*

At the international departure gate of Dulles Airport, Lori wiped a final tear, stowed her electronic tablet, and grasped the handle of her carry-on bag, moving into the boarding line for her overnight flight to Rome, Italy.

Several hundred miles away, Noah got in line behind twenty-seven other recruits and marched determinedly forward.

And on Ladybug Farm, all was well.

About The Author . . .

Donna Ball is the author of over a hundred novels under several different pseudonyms in a variety of genres that include romance, mystery, suspense, paranormal, western adventure, historical and women's fiction. Recent popular series include the Ladybug Farm series by Berkley Books and the Raine Stockton Dog Mystery series. She lives in a restored Victorian barn in the heart of the Blue Ridge Mountains with a variety of four-footed companions. You can contact her at http://www.donnaball.net.